The Chameleon

By David Farrell

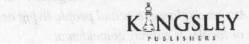

KANGSLEY
PUBLISHERS

First published in South Africa by Kingsley Publishers, 2022
Copyright © David Farrell, 2022

The right of David Farrell to be identified as author of
this work has been asserted.

Kingsley Publishers
Pretoria, South Africa
www.kingsleypublishers.com

A catalogue copy of this book will be available from the
National Library of South Africa
Paperback ISBN: 978-0-620-99313-5
eBook ISBN: 978-0-620-99314-2

Dedication

I dedicate this book to my life partner and soul mate, Jeanne Mendonca.

And to the courage of immigrants worldwide.

We are all exceptions to a rule that shouldn't exist.

There are no norms.

Prologue

My name is Rorke Wilde. Most call me Rory. I have no other names and my parents offer no explanation why. My sister Cara Evelyn Wilde does, but, that I am told is because Mum and Dad couldn't make up their minds.

We are of Irish descent, but I'm not sure what that means. The family is from Belfast, the capital of Northern Ireland. That's all I know, apart from history lessons and the briefest time when we lived there in 1972, but I digress. I will return to that later.

I was born in Gatooma. A pastoral town swathed in gold dust from nearby mines and the swirling lint of the cotton plantations. Small enough for everybody to know your business, but of a size they could turn a blind eye to if they so choose. It mirrored many of the settlements in the colony of Southern Rhodesia three years before the unilateral declaration of independence from the United Kingdom. My father became an officer in the British South Africa Police and my Welsh mother worked at the tax office in their dream of life in a far-off land.

This is my story of how history touched me. It's not about clichéd heroes who triumph over wrong in a predictable plot, but of a reality of life at the end of colonialism in Southern Africa.

I don't have many friends. I am a follower of nature, happier with animals and the sanctity of Mother Earth.

Why, you ask?

Animals are without deceit or greed. History books depict the author's sway. Memoirs affords a perspective whilst historical fiction covers a commercial need. The truth lies elsewhere.

Many elect not to listen, adopting a rendition that suits our bias, for which I make no excuse. I have yet to meet anyone lacking an opinion or an agenda.

I spend my life watching from the corner of a room, or

similar such places. I devote this story to those who do the same, for there lies the testimony. I am not the champion, villain, or warrior, just someone who was there. This is my version and how I dealt with it, be it right or wrong. That is for you to decide.

Chapter One

I pressed my scrawny ten-year-old frame against the granite; the embedded lichen filled my senses. Veins of quartz and the glint of fool's gold brought the rock formations to life. With my airgun in hand, I peered over the ridge and selected a lead pellet from beneath my tongue. I was ready for my prey, a large rock lizard, to make a move.

I had forgotten to change after school with the thrill of the chase. Besides, the khaki camouflaged me here on the edges of the Kalahari.

Mum will be furious, but this is more important.

The heat burnt my lungs as sweat oozed from my *Worzel Gummidge* straw hair onto my brow and ran along the back of my neck.

That talking scarecrow looks nothing like me.

I flicked the flies from my eyes and spat out the bugs through chapped lips, cursing the unkind comments of the kids at school. The hunt had ended without success, so I sought shelter beneath the tree. I enjoyed the chase but not the kill. Guilt added to my self-loathing with every pursuit. It sounded glamorous in the cocktail lounge of the country club where my sister Cara and I messed around in the plush grounds while Mum and Dad attended soirees. Father, in his austere police uniform, oblivious to the kids pinching swigs of beer from the tables. More concerned with his waxed moustache as he twirled it between his fingers and patted the sleek blue-black hair. His efforts of a smouldering rock-and-roll stare was stranger than it was striking, without the complementary chin or impressive jawline. Mum always uneasy in a sleeveless floral dress preferring the freedom and functionality of slacks. On such evenings she puffed up her hair until it defied gravity, applied copious amounts of makeup and wore contact lenses, which turned her cobalt eyes red as the evening progressed.

In the valley below, I could see my home among a belt of

steel roofs and terraced gardens. The granite contrasted with the yellow soil, whilst the collieries in the distance spewed coal dust into the Zambezi valley air. In the opposite direction was my Eden — the Wankie National Park.

Nowhere was I more secure than here in the arms of this leafless giant tree, fantasising about her bygone visitors. The San bushmen sharing tales around the fire and the pith-helmeted colonials with their enslaved porters. Reliving stories of today's guerrillas and freedom fighters in an escalating civil war.

'Hello, my old friend.' I hugged the soft bark of her trunk so shiny I could make out my reflection. I brushed the twigs and withered leaves from my favoured place amongst her voluptuous embraces.

With hands behind my head, I lay in the dappled light as I savoured the aroma of the sweet-spicy fruit of the Baobab protected beneath the hard shell of a green velvet husk. The dry pulp inside had a citrus flavour when chewed or added to drinking water, known as cream of tartar or monkey bread. Fabled to give strength and protection from the ever-prevalent Nile crocodile.

I hoped there was time to catch up with Bow. I combed through the bush on my approach into the valley, careful to look beyond the camouflage of nature's veil.

'Bow, where the hell are you? Don't fool around, man.' I clambered into a thicket, mindful of the thorns.

'There you are. You little shit.'

He co-ordinated his eyes, then edged towards me.

'I've brought food.' I offered a black and red beetle from between my fingers. 'Your favourite.'

With a flick of his foot-long tongue, the insect disappeared. Bow stood ten centimetres tall and forty centimetres from tip to tail.

'At least you're in a better mood. What happened?' I looked him in the face. 'The jacket you wore yesterday just didn't suit you.'

He focussed one eye on me, the other rotated back and forth in search of danger. Today he dined in a mustard suit to match the parched savannah.

'I guess something must have upset you. I can't stay mad

4

at you, buddy. Watch out for the snakes and those nasty birds.'

Bow's back arched as I stroked him, and I swear he gave a wry smile.

'I'll see you tomorrow; it's getting dark.'

Twilight lasted but minutes. I kicked at stones and rustled the surrounding vegetation to secure my friend's safety, then slipped away into the blackening basin.

The last ray dipped beneath the horizon, bringing up a burnt-orange hue. The earth cooled. A symphony rejoiced at the close of day. Christmas beetles joined the sonata, as it surged to a crescendo of clicks and chirps. The double bass of the bullfrog entered the fray.

I paused on the slope, admiring my *kopje* against the kaleidoscopic blue and black of the night sky and the dying orangeness of the sun.

The smell from the kitchen confirmed dinner was ready. I muttered a hello to Themba, the family's domestic worker. A tall man of proud *AmaNdebele* heritage with thickset shoulders and muscular limbs. The kindest of faces that could frighten the bravest enemy if the occasion warranted. A wide forehead beneath his short-cropped hair sported a shaved parting that moved in sync with his emotions. His high cheekbones stressed the whites of his eyes and a nose which changed shape with his enormous grin. A Zambian from the north, disillusioned with politics, unfulfilled promises, corruption, and unemployment in his country of birth, he sought a better life in Rhodesia.

Themba Dube ran our home, from the cooking and cleaning to the laundry. In a house void of modern conveniences, he wax polished the wooden parquet floors on his knees, hand-washed the clothes in the bathtub and later dry-ironed them.

'Hi, Themba,' I said as he flashed me a toothy grin. 'I cooked your favourite food.'

'Sausage and mash? Wow, thanks, Themba.'

'Yes, and without gravy.' He waved a frying pan aloft and danced a jig.

'Dad will catch you again if you're not careful.'

Themba dished up dinner as he whistled.

Mum's old yellow Renault 12 sat in the driveway. Her sewing machine echoed through the walls of a house built of corrugated iron, louvre windows and an asbestos roof. Cut into the bedroom walls were air conditioners, which shook the foundations when turned on at the same time. Without them, the place became a giant convection oven and instead of tranquil African nights; we slept to their incessant drone. Our home, at the end of a row of identical houses, perched on the side of the largest *kopje* on the outskirts of Wankie town, confirmed our status as civil servants. It was temporary accommodation built for government workers before Rhodesia's Unilateral Declaration of Independence in 1969.

Dad arrived home early. Sometimes he never showed. If he wasn't in a criminal case, the political unrest kept him busy.

I fought the urge to rush to his police truck and hug him.

'Hi, Dad.'

'Hello.' His voice was monotone and without a glance, he headed for the bedroom.

I opened my closet and changed into a pair of shorts and tucked in a white T-shirt with an elephant waving a *Rhodesia Is Super* banner on the front. The skinny little boy glaring back at me in disgust caused me to stop for a moment.

When am I going to grow like the rest of my friends?

Knobbly knees, angular elbows dominated the image in front of me. The pudding bowl haircut of straight blonde hair covered the eyes and the sloping shoulders didn't portray what I saw in myself. The young lad in the mirror flashed two fingers and disappeared.

One day is one day. I'll get there, you'll see.

At 18:00 sharp, we sat at the wooden pot-marked dinner table in rickety chairs with threadbare cushions sagging through the frayed leather supports. The dining room a mere space between kitchen, the lounge, and the hallway leading to the three bedrooms.

Themba served as he and I pulled faces while my parents chatted. Meals were dour affairs with the minimal of tableware. On occasions there were salt and pepper shakers. For special celebrations, a jar of English mustard caked in dried mustard adorned the centrepiece.

'May I have a drink, please?' I asked.

'Your father doesn't allow it, dear,' Mum replied.

'Yes Rory, don't you know that?' Cara, my six-year-old sister, tutted at me. Her dishevelled golden tassels irritated me as it invaded every part of her delicate round face, doleful brown eyes, and dainty ears. In fact, her good looks annoyed me to no end.

It's just not fair.

"What are you looking at, creep?" She added with a devilish look.

'But it's hot and I'm thirsty.' I ignored her.

'You heard your mother, no water. Now finish what's on your plate.'

'Yes, Dad.' I avoided eye contact with Themba.

After the meal, we retired to the lounge, where Dad changed the radio to his favourite evening talk show. Mum settled into her chair with a romantic blockbuster in hand.

Why does she read those silly books? They're all the same, full of daft grown-ups, dressed up — fainting and kissing — ugh.

Bored and in no mood for adult company, I traipsed along the passage to my sister's room. Through the crack in the door, I watched Cara bossing her dolls around for wrongdoings. A look she often used on me after one of our spats.

'What are you doing?' I asked.

'Nothing, stupid, what do you want?'

'Nothing, stupid,' I replied and retreated, not keen for one of our battles.

She flicked her long, messy hair and resumed her make-believe. The dolls bore the brunt. It was time for bed.

The sweet tunes of wild birds woke me. I flipped off the air conditioner, pulled back the curtains, and took a deep breath to shake off the airless night. I sat and watched as morn ascended the horizon and lit the scorched lawn into a pasture of diamonds. It replaced the monochrome blanket of night by the orange of the sun, exposing a spectrum of blues from ultramarine to the azure of the African sky. Creatures quenched their thirst to prepare for the day's tussle with the elements.

Dad tended to his uniform, a splendid colonial outfit — pompous and impractical. Meticulous long socks turned at the knee, khaki shorts, a grey-cotton shirt, and polished belts crisscrossed his chest. Medals adorned his breast. A peaked cap and the three bars of inspector sat on his shoulders. Being the member in charge's son filled me with pride. I respected the position and what it commanded, despite the lack of financial reward.

'Rory, open for me,' Dad said.

I ran and opened the cast-iron gates. He reversed out of the driveway, too busy on the police radio to return my goodbye.

The walk to school took me through the arid *veld* with its centre parting of olive foliage that grew along the banks of the *spruit*. The alternative was a laborious, mine-sponsored bus through town. On foot, I crossed the town's revered, if not sacred, golf course. A weird place guarded by even stranger people. The greenkeeper and his henchmen patrolled the fairways, looking for any breach of their beloved turf by non-members, infidels, or rebellious children. I was never brave enough to cross on my own.

My best friend Alan waited on the corner of the street next to the golf club. His thick mop of curls wafted in the breeze. He was a heavy-set lad, with flawless olive skin, better suited to the climate than my freckled infested lilywhite hide.

We chose a dusty path that led into the bush and would bypass the clubhouse.

'Take it easy. One false step and it's over,' I said.

Alan nodded and scuffed through the gravel. 'I know, don't want to get near those thorns either.'

At the bottom, we peered through the undergrowth. To our left, a tractor offered no immediate threat; to the right, two golfers were teeing off.

Alan whooped and bolted like a warthog.

'Bloody hell,' I added as I followed.

Halfway and with little grace, we swallow dived into a sandy bunker to catch our breath. The thud of a golf ball landing nearby set us off in another wave of panic as we headed towards the far side of the fairway. Hysterical, we gasped a lungful of air.

8

'How cool. Bloody close though, hey?' Alan said.

'For sure. Check. I got their golf ball.'

'Shit!' Alan shouted. 'What are you doing with that?'

I shrugged. 'Don't know. Seemed a good idea.'

'Get rid of it, *now*.' Horror etched across Alan's face.

'But we can get fifty cents at the caddy shack.'

'Bugger the money, check out those golfers.'

Over my shoulder, a man dressed in plus fours, followed by a caddy, strode towards us. I lobbed the ball back and slithered into the scrub. Capture was beyond comprehension. Punishment meant washing the dishes in the cafe or cleaning the pool. Worse still was being sent to retrieve golf balls on the driving range.

Closer to school, we crossed a barren piece of land once earmarked for sports fields. Despite the attempts of the ground's staff, it remained a wasteland. This mystical land oozed, like puss from a boil, from which a pungent smell of boiled eggs rose from its shell — the by-product of ancient forests fossilised into rich deposits of coal and gas.

'Catch,' I said as I tossed Alan a box of matches.

'Thanks, hope it works.'

We scratched the surface and collected the powder.

'That'll do,' I said as I added the sulphur to the matches.

'Quick, before school starts.'

'Okay, okay.'

'Are you ready?' We slid a lit match in with the others and ducked to safety.

'It won't work,' Alan said.

'Maybe not.'

The cocktail burst into a ball of fire with flames shooting in every direction.

'Did you see that, man?' Alan danced and gripped me around the neck.

'You'll strangle me, dumbass.'

'Sorry.'

We lumbered into the school grounds.

The buildings were of military design with red-face brick, white-steel windows, and the usual asbestos roof. Our town was too small for a secondary school, so the townspeople sent their pre-teens to boarding schools, the closest being hundreds of kilometres away.

Shrill laughter stemmed from the classroom. Inside, a blackboard with a numerical black and white clock perched above covered the front wall. Chalk dust spattered the wooden floor, showing the teacher's imprints as she wrote on the board. Dusters littered the bottom shelf complemented by a disarray of coloured chalk.

'Settle down and take your places, children.' The schoolteacher handed out forms, her jersey covered in the same powder. 'Give these to your parents to fill in and make sure you return them tomorrow; any delays will reduce your chance of being given the school of your choice. Make a list of where you want to go to in order of preference, please.' She paused, then pointed to the boys. 'You lot get an extra sheet to register for national service.' She looked at us with slanted eyes from the tight bun of hair tied on top of her head. Her coloured cheek bones a curious red vied with the dollop of lipstick on her wafer lips.

My stomach turned at the prospect of military duty.

'Who cut the cheese?' a voice said and reduced the class to wails of laughter.

'Let's not go there today class.' The teacher crossed her arms.

A change in wind direction bore the odour of the sulphuric fields. This time, the aroma eased the nervous tension, much to the student's relief.

On my way home, I studied a dust devil's lethargic effort to cross the road.

Should I go into the hills or visit Themba?

I headed for his shed at the rear of our garden.

'Hi, Mr Rory. Do you want lunch?' Themba asked me.

'Nah.'

'Tough day at school, huh?'

'Why can't things stay the way they are?' I asked.

'Change is life, my young friend.'

'I have to leave for boarding school soon, and I also have to choose which regiment I want to enlist with.'

Themba blew hard. 'How can they ask the innocent to fight their wars?' It was a rhetorical double-edged question that I didn't understand.

'Never mind. Come, join us for lunch,' Themba said, changing the subject.

'Thanks, but what about Mum?'

'Don't worry, she's out shopping, and then she'll be staying late at the library.'

'Great.' I perched on one of the tree stumps the family used to sit around the fire while Themba disappeared into the house in search of his wife.

Their home comprised a fireplace between two whitewashed rooms discoloured by years of soot. Tin doors and exposed light globes hung from rafters without ceilings. One a bedroom, the other ablutions with a shower and a hole in the floor for a toilet, flushed by a rusty chain dangling from the roof.

While maize-meal was cooking over a wood fire, the acrid aroma of carbolic soap wafted from laundry hanging on a makeshift clothesline. The bare earth shone from the relentless brush of a straw broom.

Themba re-emerged wearing slacks and a T-shirt.

'Come, Mr Rory, let's rest and talk awhile. My wife and daughter will prepare us food.' He chose the largest of the sawn-off trees. 'A man's life is tough.'

Uncertain what he meant, I nodded, noticing a gaunt teenager wearing tatty shorts and a stretched t-shirt, approaching.

'What are you doing here?' he asked me with a scowl and pursed lips.

'Your dad invited me. Why?'

'Thought your parents didn't want you here.' He stamped the ground with giant feet.

'They're not me, are they?'

'Sit beside me and let us enjoy each other's company,' Temba said.

Sipho glared at me, in two minds. 'Okay Father, but only because you ask.'

Themba manipulated the conversation to avoid delicate topics, aware of Sipho's demeanour of late, while his wife, Precious, a stunning woman with an ample bust and wide hips, brought mugs of sweet tea with the youngest of their children strapped to her back.

'Hi Rory, how you?' she asked me.

'Fine. How's the baby?'

'We're good thanks.' She gave one of her infectious smiles that lit her oval face. Her chocolate brown eyes emphasised by pencil thin, mesmerising eyebrows.

Custom dictated that she served Themba first, the guests next, then the children and the woman last.

'When you're finished, wash up for lunch,' Precious said.

'Quiet wife, the men are busy.'

Precious chuckled and said, 'What fools' men are.'

Themba gave an impish grin. 'If we brothers don't stick together, women will run the world.'

We changed the subject rather than go down that road.

I snuck out of the house and joined Themba's family for supper whenever my parents went out for an evening. Tonight, was no different. A hearty affair with a three-legged, cast-iron *potjie* brimming with cornmeal and flame-grilled brisket. Exotic spices, influenced by the spice trade, wafted up from enamel bowls. We rolled the porridge in our right hands and dipped the food into the thick peri-peri sauce — a seasoning made from ground bird's-eye chillies introduced by early Portuguese settlers.

Idle gossip wound down the meal before Themba's side-splitting belch, accompanied by an appreciative rub of his belly, declared an end to proceedings.

His wife and daughter cleared the dishes and brewed mugs of tea for everyone except Themba. Instead, he accepted the first carton of traditional beer, an opaque brew fermented from sorghum and corn, with regal poise. The letters *SHAKE, SHAKE* printed on the side, advised drinkers how to avoid a mouthful of sour gruel at the bottom. He threw back his head and swallowed with gusto. The low-slung canopy of stars etched his form against the night sky.

'Much better,' he said as he wiped away his cream moustache with the back of his hand and launched into ancestral fables and myths, each one more outlandish than the last.

'That's not a fire…' He grabbed a pile of logs by his side and tossed them onto the coals. The flames created the backdrop while the empty cartons of beer strewn across the ground were the props to the spectacle. With each show, the alcohol brought the final curtain, followed by silence, but for the spit of the embers.

Trying not to break the trance, I peered from under my fringe at the whites of Sipho's eyes as he stared at me.

'Time to go home. Your mother will be here soon,' Precious said as she shook me by the shoulder.

With the evening over, we washed and packed up before I hurried home in time for my parent's arrival.

'Hi, Mum,' I said, wishing she had stayed out longer.

'Hi Rory, how was school, my boy? Please help Themba get the stuff out of the car.'

Themba arrived as Sipho vanished into the darkness.

Days later, I summoned the courage to approach my father, choosing a quiet evening without the usual family dramas.

'Here Dad,' I said. 'You must fill in these for tomorrow.'

At first, he didn't respond.

'Dad?'

'What is it, boy?'

'I've got the forms I need for high school and my national service.'

'Well, have you decided yet?'

I shrugged.

'Typical. This boy of yours is so indecisive,' he said to Mum, who was across the living room.

'He's your son too,' she replied with disregard.

'Fine, get me a pen and let's settle this.' He snatched the forms from my hands and scowled over the top of his reading glasses. 'For starters, consider the police, not the half-baked conscripts' regiment.'

'How does the S.A.S. sound?' I asked and watched the disbelief cross his face.

'You were... you do? Not an awful choice. What do you say, Mother?'

'That's nice, dears.'

'What do you mean, *that's nice*? Our son has chosen the most elite armed force, the Special Air Service, and all you got to say is *that's nice*?' Dad turned back to me. 'Well, it's your decision, my boy. Who are we to stand in your way?'

'I tried for Plumtree School, too.'

His eyebrows rose further. 'Are you sure? Plumtree is a

long way away?'

'Yes, but it's the best school in the country.'

'Splendid boy, perhaps you are a chip off the old block after all.' He leant forward to punch my arm but couldn't reach. 'This country needs every man to do his bit. We must stop the communist-backed infiltrators terrorising… ah! I want to listen to the end of this programme.' He turned to the radio station.

'Thanks, Dad. See you in the morning.'

'Bloody idiot has no clue what he's talking about,' he said as he threw his arms in the air at the words spoken by the voice on the wireless and knocked me aside.

'Goodnight, Dad. Goodnight, Mum.' Neither responded.

I lay awake contemplating my future, boarding school, national service, Sipho and the imminent civil war. It was all so far removed from the warmth of Themba, Bow and the safety of my baobab on the *kopje*. My mind raced, unable to grasp the magnitude of the impending fear. Sleep brought relief.

Chapter Two

The last days of junior school involved goodbyes and preparing for higher education.

'Rory, it's your turn to see the principal, but you can't go in looking like that,' my teacher said and clicked her tongue. 'Come here so I can fix you. Better buck up your ideas at Plumtree School.' She tucked in my shirt and pulled up my socks. 'Just look at the state of those shoes.'

I lifted each foot and buffed them on my socks and took off for the headmaster's office.

'Enter,' the principal called out in a gruff English accent.

I peeked through the doorway.

'Ah! Rorke, it is you. Time for you to leave us, is it?' The circles beneath his eyes were darker than ever, his pink jowls hung lower, the frosting of his hair snowier, even on his eyebrows and ears.

'Afternoon, sir.'

'Sit, young man and let's discuss your future.' He spoke of ambition and expectation, and I of dread and anxiety.

'A last piece of advice, my dear boy. Always do your best, keep your head down and mind your own business.' In Churchillian fashion, he rose from his desk, grasped the lapels of his jacket, and gazed out of the window. 'Be a chameleon, lad.' He stood in silence before continuing. 'Be a chameleon. Blend in with your surroundings until you are ready to stand up for what you believe.'

I edged towards the door, which broke his wistfulness. He gave a forlorn smile and waved me out. 'Good luck, God knows you will all need it.'

A week later, on my twelve birthday, a brown envelope marked *On Government Service* arrived. I sat on the edge of my bed and pondered the postmark, unsure whether to open it. My indecision, cut short by the shrill ring of the telephone, startled me.

'Hello?'

'Did you get your letter? Mine came today. Guess where I'm going?' Alan said before the line went dead. I replaced the receiver and dialled him back.

'Have you gone crazy? You didn't give me or yourself a chance to speak,' I said.

'Sorry man, just can't believe they accepted me at Plumtree. How about you?'

'Haven't looked at it.'

'You say I'm mad? Hold on, I'll be over in five.'

The phone buzzed in my ear.

Alan arrived windswept from riding his three-speed bicycle. 'Hey! Have you opened it yet?'

'Nah, I stuck around for you.' I waved the envelope at him.

'Well, come on then. Get on with it.'

'Maybe I should wait for the folks?'

'Bullshit.' Alan snatched the letter and tore it open.

'What's it say?'

Alan's eyes grew wider, then grinned. 'Same as me, buddy. Plumtree School.'

That afternoon we spoke of boarding school and leaving home, of joining the army, and if there was life thereafter — excited yet frightened eleven-year-old boys.

My family set off on a four-hundred-kilometre road trip to Bulawayo for Christmas shopping and provisions. It was a torturous seven-hour journey on roads with a strip of tar for each wheel, between which and either side was loose gravel. Vehicles flashed by at breakneck speeds, leaving clouds of dust in their wake.

This was Matabeleland anglicised from *AmaNdebele*, the land of the Northern Ndebele — *Men of the long shields*.

I imagined the conflicts and hardships back in the 1830s when Mzilikazi, one of Shaka's generals, fled north after a disagreement onto seventy-five thousand square kilometres of inhospitable terrain — for those who didn't respect it. The infertile soils of the Kalahari sands and low rainfall excluded commercial farmers who were changing the landscape of my Africa. Nature's miracle providing a refuge for the most majestic wildlife on the planet. Where elephant roamed in herds of up to a hundred, who walked up the streets of Wankie village drinking water from swimming pools. They were gentle giants with a wicked sense of humour as they kicked items around and turned on our garden taps to quench their thirst. Leopard, lion, cheetah, giraffe, rhinoceroses, and hippopotamus made up part of the hundred different mammals and bird life. Humans were in the minority, and I prayed to the distant hills out the window they would stay that way.

The only respite was a hotel on the Gwayi River.

'Okay guys let's take a break. A quick drink, and then we must set off again,' Dad said as he pulled into the old colonial building — the car ashen from the silt. Weather-beaten and faded, the *Halfway House* sign welcomed us, along with the head waiter at the front door.

'Good morning, sir, madam. Can I interest you for lunch? A refreshment to begin?' His once-white uniform resembled clotted cream, while his fez was threadbare and missing tassels.

'Thank you, we'll have drinks by the deck,' Mum replied.

'Excellent decision, madam.' He summoned a line of waiters across the way.

'Thinks she's bloody Lady Muck on toast,' Dad muttered.

Mum ignored the insult. 'Thank you, my good man.' The steward showed us to a chipped wrought-iron garden table and rusty chairs.

'Drop the phony attitude,' Dad said to Mum.

'Oh, shut up, why don't you? Try to enjoy the trip.' Her reply blunt.

I waited for the retaliation, but Dad let it slide.

'Let's go for a swim, dumbass.' Cara shouted as she grabbed her towel and darted for the changing rooms.

'Okay, last one is a dung beetle,' I replied as I chased after my baby sister.

Trees formed a canopy over the murky water of the reservoir. Leaves and twigs were life rafts to hapless insects that littered the surface. We shared the water with schools of tadpoles and a choir of frogs. A covert water scorpion glided every which way as it sought its next victim. The boys dived for strange forms lurking in the slime at the bottom; the girls braved quick dips

17

before losing their nerve.

'Lunch! Come and get it,' Mum shouted as she waved at us from beneath her straw hat.

Two Cokes, an enormous pot of tea and four rounds of sandwiches with limp lettuce waited for our return.

'Is this Rory's going away party?' Cara asked.

'Don't be silly, dear, just a family treat,' Mum replied.

I ate without saying a word as the icy grip of loneliness tightened.

My dread grew as we neared the outskirts of the capital of Matabeleland province. 'Bulawayo means the *Place of Slaughter*,' I said.

'Really, dear?' Mum in the front passenger seat peered at me through the rear-view mirror on her sun visor.

'Yup, Mzilikazi's *kraal*. His son, Lobengula, ruled from there for thirty years.'

'I'm not sure about that, my boy. It's the country's second largest city with three hundred thousand people,' Mum responded.

'What's with the traffic today?' Dad asked.

'Don't know, dear,' Mum answered, then turned to me. 'Be quiet for a minute. Your father needs to concentrate on where we are going.'

I leant my forehead against the window and studied the ostentatious colonial buildings that contrasted with their commercial counterparts in streets built to accommodate the turning berth of ox wagons from the earlier century.

'Christmas lights. Can we see them tonight, Dad, please?' Cara asked.

'We can, my sweetheart.' Dad grinned in the mirror at Cara.

Later we strolled along the high street window shopping the expensive boutiques, jewellers and bistros whilst avoiding the beggars on the corners. We ambled in the park for the Yuletide pageant with twinkling Christmas lights, the sounds of the carol singers and the curious one-man shows together with the sniff of candy floss, popcorn, and hotdogs, all mixed with the laughs from the crowds.

Exhausted, we retired to the rented apartment for the

evening.

The next day we picked up my school trunk and lugged the black chest with white stencilled letters onto the roof of the car and headed home.

Rorke Wilde
Gaul House
Plumtree School

'When will I find the time to stitch the name tags into your uniforms?' Mother said, flushed with emotion as she turned to me in the back seat and squeezed my knee through the gap between the seats.

The days raced by and before long, Christmas was upon us.

Themba served up a turkey dinner before he organised his own. As tradition dictated, they dressed in their best outfits and waited at the back door. Precious wore a vibrant dress of red, blue, yellow with the beaded headdress of the *AmaNdebele*. Sipho was in grey shorts, a light blue shirt, with polished black shoes, but still wearing his sour demeanour.

Precious curtsied and offered Mum a crocheted bedspread of the finest cotton. My sister Cara received less intricate doilies for her bedside cabinet from Beauty, Temba's fourth child, visiting from the tribal lands. Sipho made me a slingshot from the fork of a tree. On earlier occasions, he fashioned me cars and bicycles shaped from wire, each to scale. Dad accepted pipe tobacco from Themba and a tin of snuff, though he never used it.

In return, we gave them presents from the Far East, which were received with immense joy. Precious danced as she held her summer frock in front of her. Themba enthused over a pair of leather boots and an imitation Swiss army knife. The children drooled at the cheap-plastic toys and sweets. Dad gifted the grown-ups the traditional box of fresh meat, coffee, jams, biscuits, butter, and such luxuries. Themba broke into song, joined by his household, who swayed to an inner rhythm as tears streamed down his face. They sang of compassion and thanks and the occasion ended with a carol from their church.

Why do such scenes leave me so empty? I wondered with a sense of guilt. Shouldn't we always do this? Not just at Christmas.

The day before boarding school started, I dawdled into the hills to find Bow, where we sat together in silence. One last time, I lived in my paradise, as tears smudged the view, my nerves were ripe with fear.

'I'm not sure what will happen, but take care, my friend. I'll be back soon,' I said as I caressed my pet chameleon. The lump in my throat so large my chest tightened.

Themba waited as I descended my hill after my goodbyes to Bow.

'Hi, I see you have paid your respects. Time to move on,' he said as he put his arm around my shoulders. 'Do not mourn the past. It lives forever in your soul. Face the future and pursue your path. You may not know where it will take you, but follow it without worry.' Then he clutched me tighter. *'Lihambe kuhle, jaha. Lisale kuhle,'* he whispered in my ear.

'But I'm not a chameleon?' I replied.

'You are not, but you can be. It means goodbye, young man, go well. *Lihambe kuhle* is also used to describe the chameleon because of their cautious step.'

The dreaded trek to Plumtree School meant a stopover in Bulawayo at the police-training depot where chalets were available at fees well below hotel rates. Dad and I offloaded the trunk from the roof rack while the girls unpacked.

I was hoping for downtime to relax before we left the next day.

Perhaps take in a film at the posh movie houses or a treat of fish and chips for dinner. Alas, it turned out to be a fretful ordeal of waiting for time to pass. Enjoyment couldn't have been further away.

My eyes opened to the dawn call of the doves, and I crawled out of bed to find mother cooking bacon and eggs. 'Mum, let's leave early for high school,' I said, greeting her.

'Morning. What? Are you sure…? Wouldn't you prefer to

relax by the pool or something?' she replied.

'Let's pack up and get going, please Mum.'

The thought of goodbyes was more painful than the unknown. The adrenalin and Themba's advice to *face your future* played on my mind.

'Let's ride. Rory wants to make an early start,' Mum said to Dad.

'That's my boy. Can't wait to see your new school, hey?' Dad poked his head from behind the bathroom door and winked. 'Find your sister and let's make a move.'

I left my parents to pack, perturbed at their willingness to leave earlier, and went in search of Cara. I found her hunched over by the pool.

'Come on. We're leaving for Plumtree.' She didn't respond. 'Hey, stupid, are you deaf? We must get ready because we are going soon.' Her hair remained draped over her face. 'Are you okay?' Concern replaced my annoyance. 'What's wrong?' I dropped to one knee beside her. Tears rolled down her cheeks and splattered into the luminescent pool. She was squinting because of the glare and the sting of salt. 'What happened?' I asked and hugged my sister.

'Nothing.'

'Then why are you crying, dummy?'

She threw me a short-lived smile. 'I don't want you going to that stupid school.'

'Me neither, but I have no choice.'

'Dad could change his job and move to the city.' Cara's eyes grew wide at the prospect.

'Yeah, right?'

'Yeah, right?' she mimicked. 'I heard what goes on there, with bullying and stuff.'

'It's just idiots trying to scare you, I promise. Come on, before Dad sees.'

She held onto me for a while longer.

'Okay, is everybody ready? Jump in and let's go,' Dad said.

'We're fixed up. Just need a shot of Rory in his new outfit. You know he won't let us take them at the school,' Mum said as she scrambled to find the instamatic camera.

Dad shook his head. 'Hurry, your mother wants a photo,' he

said as he climbed behind the steering wheel where he waited out another of Mum's torturous photography sessions.

I skulked out of the bedroom, a cardboard cut-out because of the starch in my oversized uniform. My skinny arms and legs emphasised by my knobbly knees and elbows.

Dad hid a smile.

'They're a wee bit big, but space for you to grow. The others will be in the same boat,' Mum said as she brushed my new clothes.

The baobabs thinned out as we progressed into Bulilimamangwe District on the border of Botswana. The native flat-topped mopani tree, which thrived in the shallow river soil deposits and arid climate replaced them. Land perfect for livestock. Most of the ranchers hailed from the great treks by early Dutch colonisers in the late 1800s. Because of a vexed history, they co-existed with the wildlife and locals.

I sat upright for a glimpse of my new home as a signpost flashed by.

Border Post 10 km, Plumtree 3 km — population 1,284.

I licked the perspiration from my upper lip.

'Well, look at that. It's smaller than home, isn't it?' Mum said.

'A real one-horse town.' Dad grinned at Mum's gaping mouth.

The main road split the township, residential on one side and commercial on the other. Tiny houses with red-corrugated roofs, dry gardens, rusted fences, and bored pets on porches. Across the street, a post office, a liquor store, a butcher, and a bakery were in similar disrepair.

'Is that the school?' I pointed to a huge double-storey building.

'Let's see, shall we? See how it shimmers in the haze,' my father said as he raised his sunglasses and squinted. We laughed.

We read the words **Plumtree Hotel** painted in gold against the silver walls.

'A sight for sore eyes. We'll stop for petrol and ask for directions.' Dad broke the silence and pulled up at a single pump outside the front of the bottle store.

22

A lad dressed in oil-stained overalls approached. 'What you want?' he asked in pidgin English.

'Fill up,' Dad mimicked and glanced at us in the mirror.

Cara held her nose, determined not to laugh.

'Sure thing.' The attendant wasn't paying any attention or chose not to. He placed the nozzle into the petrol tank, then ambled back to pick up a steel bar and attached it to the syphon before pushing the lever back and forth. The manual digits on the pump flipped over. We chuckled behind our hands at the relic.

The assistant raised a thumb to show that the vehicle was full. Dad tore out the petrol coupons from his ration book and tipped the boy — more from guilt than generosity.

'Can you tell us the way to the high school?' Dad asked.

The lad dropped on to his haunches and sketched a map in the sand. Dad thanked him and we headed for Plumtree School.

Around the bend, we found the school in all its glory. A vista of lush grounds and noble buildings. The words **Plumtree School** arched across ornate gates. On one pillar stood the embossed school crest, while on the other, a polished brass disc.

Dad brought the car to a halt. 'Take a peek, shall we?' he said as he strolled over to read the shield. 'Come and see, guys.'

'What's it say?' Mum asked.

'It's a commemorative plate devoted to the memory of the boys who died in the Second World War.'

I remained in the Renault. The rusty marks running down the wall from the plaque reminded me of tears.

We continued along the dirt road to a Spanish-American style chapel. Guarded by a wizened fig tree with a sweet perfume that attracted an abundance of fruit flies; birds were dining to their heart's content. A dozen marbled steps led to pious oak doors.

'We must investigate. Isn't it too amazing? Look, there's more plaques,' Mum said as she led the way.

Pursued by Cara, I tagged along before bounding up the steps of the church.

His Majesty King George VI dedicated this multidenominational shrine in the year of our Lord 1947.

'They don't mess around here, do they? I don't think you'll have any problems here, my boy.'

'No, Dad,' I replied. To him, royalty was sacrosanct, and woe betide anyone who didn't approve.

Inside, a serene calmness prevailed. The smell of aged books intermingled with the acridity of candle wax. Pews stretched down either side. The aisle led past the choir's station to the altar. Lustrous stained-glass filled arched windows and battle-scarred flags hung from protruding brass poles.

I couldn't breathe and I held my hand over my mouth as I tiptoed for a closer peek. The Lady's Chapel nestled to one side of the congregation, and instead of a shrine, there was a font. On the balcony above a further row of pews. Teak boards with carvings in gold leaf lined the walls. It was a roll of honour, of war, past and present. The number of recently killed in action (K.I.A), letters from the current civil war, troubled me.

'What a belfry. You can see the history and tradition,' Dad added with his hands on his hips. 'It's in the air. We made the right choice here.' His theatrics continued. I smiled; happy to please him yet perplexed by his use of the royal *we*.

We drove further along the road and stopped at a large double storey building with wide archways and polished verandas.

'Those are the boarding houses,' Mother said as she patted my back.

'How many boarders are there?' I asked.

'Oh, four hundred boys, most are resident. Now jump in, Dad's waiting,' she replied.

'Ah, here we are,' Dad said as she pointed to a sign with the words **Gaul House 1941** burnt into the wood.

'At last.' Mum heaved a sigh of relief.

Families milled around the car park. Parents fussed over their sons.

The stink of victims' past haunted me. With unstable knees, I climbed from the car and scrutinised my new home; my mouth was as dry as the surrounding Kalahari.

'Help me lift the trunk out of the boot,' Dad said.

'Wait, we must introduce ourselves first,' Mum said. 'Why are you always in such a rush?' Mum threw her bag over her shoulder and marched over to the largest of the groups.

'There she goes again.' Dad shot dagger eyes at Mum's back.

'Get your stuff,' he said. 'No doubt your mum will find your housemaster.'

'Rory, over here quickly. Mr Winker wants to meet you.' Mum hustled me towards the group.

'Don't, Mum. I'm fine. Don't embarrass me in front of everyone,' I said.

She ignored me and thrust me through a gap in the gathering. 'Mr Winker, my son Rorke.' Mum waited for approval.

The man ignored her. Instead, he peered at me.

'Welcome, Master Rorke Wilde. Are you ready to join the most illustrious school in the country?' He didn't wait for me to answer. 'I can't hear you, *boy*. If you don't speak up for yourself, who shall?' He bent over and looked me in the eye.

'Yes, sir.'

'That's better. These young men will show you where you're staying. Then bid farewell to your parents and find me back here. Jump to it, laddie.' Mr Winker spun on his heel, tucked his papers under his arm and strode away.

Bewildered, I walked back to my father.

'What's wrong with your mother now?' Dad asked.

I shrugged my shoulders and perched on the edge of the grass.

'I don't appreciate that man's tone. Nor do I understand his temperament. They're just boys,' Mum said.

'Don't fuss, he's been doing this for years. He wants to show them who is boss. Imagine, four hundred teenage boys in the middle of the bush. Rather him than me.'

'I expect you're right,' Mum said.

We said our uneasy goodbyes, conscious of boys peering out from the windows and others loitering in the car park. Relieved, yet heavy with uncertainty, I waved until the yellow Renault disappeared around the corner.

What a strange place with its grand buildings and mud huts and talk of religion and war.

I mustered the strength and headed into the dormitory.

Chapter Three

Two boys carried my baggage to a dormitory on the ground floor, where I stopped in the doorway leading from the polished veranda and counted twenty beds. The rows of mosquito net dangling above the cots reminded me of hangman's nooses, each complete with a casket in the shape of a wooden footlocker. The bearers pressed on.

'Come on, choose one without clothes on it,' one of them said.

The pine floorboards creaked as I hunted for a vacant bunk, and it was then that Alan waved — he had reserved a bed for me.

There was no time to settle in before the housemaster to where we were to do our homework beckoned us — the prep room. Bookshelves lined the sides, a television older than the scholars and the size of a sea chest stood in one corner. Burnt-orange curtains covered arch windows overlooking flawless gardens.

'Gentlemen, I trust you have accustomed yourselves to the layout of the house.' Mr Winker eyed us up, his balding head covered by a few strands of hair. 'Over the next couple of days, familiarise yourselves with school timetables and amenities. I will give you a heads-up on how best get along without drawing attention. I advise you to pay attention because when the rest of the pupils arrive, you'll have to fend for yourselves.' He paused for dramatic effect, his mouth on the brink of a patronising smirk. 'Are there questions?'

We shook our heads.

As he droned on about rules and regulations, I studied the photographs hanging on the prep-room walls. Each frame showed a year of students who had excelled in their field. The annals began in 1941. Unfocussed pictures of lads with puffed-out chests, long shorts, and centre partings contrasted with the slimmer-fitting clothing and more modern hairstyles of 1974.

Their faces donned similar expressions.

'My apologies for boring you, Rorke Wilde. For the sake of everyone else here, will you indulge us?' the housemaster said.

Alarmed at being called out, all I managed was a nod.

'You're so kind.' A scar on Mr Winker's left cheek smouldered.

'Nice one dip shit,' Alan said and nudged me in the ribs. 'What's that on his face?'

I ignored Alan, not wishing to attract Mr Winker's wrath again.

'At the risk of the rest of you losing focus,' Mr Winker concluded. 'If there are no further questions, gentlemen, I will bid thee farewell, we will meet you here for prayers after supper.' Mr Winker exited the room.

An uneasy hush fell upon the room, except for the hum of the fluorescent lights. I repaid Alan's dig with interest.

'Ow, you bastard,' he said as he chased me around the desks. The clatter of chairs and leather-soled shoes on the floorboards caused Mr Winker reappearance.

'Enough, gentlemen, desist from such raucous behaviour.' His facial blotch belied his restraint. 'Wilde. You again? I suggest you reconsider your behaviour before I am forced to,' he threatened, then spun on his heels and left the room.

That evening, we hustled for a turn in the communal showers with their six rusty shower heads set into chipped ceramic tiles. Washbasins and tin lockers lined the walls that made up the junior washrooms.

Water soon covered the waxed-red floors, and two of the rowdier lads took running dives and slid on their bare backsides. I watched the antics from the corner with a school-issue white towel, embellished with the letters *OHMS*, wrapped around my midriff.

My thoughts turned to my family causing the lump in my throat to reappear. In the first available shower, I buried my head beneath the cascade of lukewarm water to hide my tears. For the first time, I prayed for myself.

Mr Winker ushered us to the dining hall, a cavernous room filled with rows of tables and benches, sitting ten boys at each. One side of the room swing doors led to the kitchens and a massive scullery to wash the dishes where the left-over food was sent to the pigsty. Further along the same wall was a hatch where they served the food from cauldrons, whereupon we met the other lads from the hostels.

Alan and I stuck close as we acknowledged friends from home. On entering the hall, we joined the queue at the service hatch that billowed like a steam engine. Three bored assistants ladled what we assumed was food but resembled a regurgitated hairball onto the trays, unconcerned whether the savoury ran with the sweet.

'Reminds me of the prisoners my dad gets to work in our garden back at home,' I said to Alan.

'Yeah, like the movie we saw?' Alan suggested.

'Which one?'

'You know, Steve McQueen with the tattoo,' Alan said, rubbing his forearm.

'Oh yes, *Papillon*, what a brilliant film.'

'Hope the grub's good.' Alan held his stomach.

The jugs of milk, albeit reconstituted milk powder, went down a treat. The stew had cabbage in it and the odd hunk of indistinguishable gristle. Boiled potatoes crumbled into dry lumps and, of course, there was no debauchery such as butter or cream.

'Can you imagine how it tastes?' Alan asked.

'I suppose this is what they mean by TV dinners.'

'What are you talking about?' Alan looked perplexed.

'Those meals on television are also black and white.'

We returned to our table with our meals and muscled some space on the pew when Alan held up his hand, 'What the hell?' He presented a finger of unrecognisable gunk from beneath the tabletop.

We searched under our benches to see if we might find more.

I helped myself to a slice of bread and mixed-fruit jam. The bread tasted of maize rather than wheat, but at least it was fresh. I was not that hungry, so I spent the time watching. While several pupils chattered like excited monkeys, others sat to one side and were quiet.

When the hammering of a gavel called for attention, a sheepish master waited for silence. 'All boys will now return to their respective houses and meet with your housemasters in the prep-room' he said as his face turned to the colour of beetroot. 'Please stand for grace.' He bowed his head and stuttered an unassured prayer. 'For all these many mercies may the Lord's holy name be praised.' He stepped from the podium dressed in a safari suit, the shorts many sizes too small and glided on tiptoes to the exit. 'Tidy your tables before you leave. Right, off you go. Have a good night.' He smiled, relieved the ordeal was over, his face flushed with anxiety — ashamed.

The din of scraping chairs and the clatter of utensils heralded the end of mealtime. Each boy headed for their respective hostel in time for prayers.

The prep-room fell quiet with Mr Winker's entrance. 'Good evening, I hope you've eaten your fill. A reminder about no food in the dormitory. Keep your tuck parcels from Mummy in the washroom lockers.' He paused, daring any of us to protest.

'Light's out is at eight p.m. and not a minute later. That gives you an hour of free time. Use it well. Any untoward behaviour and you will answer to me and my little friends in the office.' He made eye contact with me.

I gave Alan a puzzled glance. He shrugged.

'We shall wake you at six a.m. Roll call is at the front of the house half an hour after that. Are there questions?' Mr Winker added.

Silence ensued but for an embarrassed cough, bowed heads and shuffling feet. The man then mutated from evil monster to pastor as he opened a pocket-size book. 'Let us pray,' he said with reverence as he inspected his flock.

A muted Amen ended the proceedings.

'Come on. Let's get out of here,' Alan said as he slapped me.

'No, wait until after the rush.' I pulled up a chair with my foot.

Alan sat next to me and rocked back.

'What a day, what a bloody day,' I said as I whistled through my teeth.

'You can say that again. And so much praying.'

'Yup, not surprised, though. They need all the help they can get.'

29

We sat as athletes psyching ourselves before a major tournament, gathering our wits for what lay ahead.

Before a master switched off the lights, I turned down my counterpane and exposed a threadbare blanket. The same words that were on my towel, *On Her Majesty's Service,* imprinted on the worn sheets.

But the unilateral declaration of independence (UDI) was ten years ago?

A breeze wafted through the entrance of the dormitory. Contemplation replaced delinquency as the group reflected on the day. Some huddled in groups, others in pairs, while the majority sought seclusion.

As I sat crossed-legged on the coir mattress, the steel-lattice base pressed into me. I reached for the crumpled envelope beneath my pillow and read the scrawl. Themba had run after the car and stuffed it into my hands as he clapped and danced farewell. I opened the note.

To Mr Rory

Howzit Mr Rory, I am fine to thank God.

We wish you luck on your journey. Please God, you come home safe.

You will be back soon.

I cannot miss you. You are always in my heart.

Did you see my joyous goodbye to you?

May the Spirits bless you, jaha?

Themba

I replaced the letter and smiled at how our customs differed. My traditions viewed elated farewell as disrespectful, while Themba believed loved ones returned quicker with a heart-warming goodbye. He reserved sad departures for those he didn't wish to meet again soon.

What a day it had been.

I thought of Themba, and his family preparing their evening meal around the fire and wished I were there. Then there was the sight of my sister waving through the rear window as

30

they left me at school — that hurt — mother in an incoherent pantomime and father ranting at the radio about politics.

'Better get your mozzie net before Mr Winker gets here,' Alan said as he tucked his into the mattress which brought a sense of security behind the net.

'Evening gentlemen, I trust we have tended to ablutions.' Mr Winker's voice carried from the far end of the dormitory.

No-one responded.

'Good, so how was your first day?' he asked, again not waiting for a reply. 'It will get worse before it gets better, gentlemen. The rest of the school arrives tomorrow. Let us see how many of you will endure.' With one hand on the light switch, his eyes turned to slits. 'We have a war to fight. Sleep tight boys.' He plunged the room into darkness.

'The bastard's a psycho,' I said to Alan.

'You're not wrong. We must watch out for that one. Night Rory.'

'Good night, china.'

A cocktail of fear, trepidation, and a slice of anticipation permeated the dorm. I held my breath and turned in. A deafening silence engulfed us all.

From nowhere, an eruption ripped through the dorm causing raucous laughter, followed by repeats and further hilarity. Apart from the immediate respite, it cemented the bonds of a camaraderie that would last a lifetime.

The night was full of horrors involving my mother, who had Mr Winker's face; of being swallowed by crud in the dining hall and chasing dozens of canary yellow Renaults. I woke every hour breathless, preferring the onset of dehydration rather than brave a trip to the washrooms. The eerie silhouettes of the nets pirouetted to the soundless tune of an evening zephyr, while mice moshed to the same beat beneath the floorboards. I recalled how the ravages of malaria made me hallucinate the same way years earlier.

The false dawn's deception teased until the sun broke the horizon with white rays cutting into the purple darkness. A noise startled me. I lifted my head and listened. More footsteps.

Thank heavens for that.

I climbed from behind the netting. The rest of the pupils were in varying stages of consciousness.

That morning Richard, a good-looking lad with an athletic body, wavy brown hair, a fiery look in his eyes and a square chin, who had an older brother at the school, led our recce through the hostel. 'There are more toilets outside, guys. We can't all use this one,' he said. It hadn't occurred to me that one inside urinal would not suffice. With Richard's counsel, we shuffled barefoot to the backdoor. Outside stood a narrow-whitewashed building with a flat-zinc roof. There were no windows, just four toilets on either side of a wide urinal. The cubicles reminded me of public latrines with locks that never worked, where the door only covered the centre, exposing legs in various poses. The stench cleared any lingering effects of sleep deprivation. An all-consuming need to go outweighed the obnoxious odour.

By now, the sun had risen into the pale blue, the silvery heat from the sun promising another scorcher. I passed Alan in the hallway on his way to the washrooms.

'Hurry,' he said. 'Before the rest use up the hot water.' He flicked me on the backside with a towel.

'Bastard, I'll get you for that,' I said as I rubbed the sting and scampered after him, thankful the night was over.

The time was ours to explore before the official start of the term the following day. I sat with my five buddies.

'Okay guys let's go over the plan again,' Richard, who formed part of the posse because he'd been head boy at our village primary, said. Alan was in awe of Richard, whereas I found him aloof and a snob, who was now a small fish in a big pond.

'What did you say about fish?' Richard asked.

'Sorry guys, I was just thinking.' I hadn't realised I'd spoken aloud.

'No time to be dreaming of food, Rory,' Alan said and pulled a face.

'Yeah, but he's got a point. We don't want to sneak around on an empty stomach.' Vinny, the stout crew cut blonde replied as he headed for the hostel in search of food. The rest of us sat back and waited for four-thirty p.m., half an hour before the train's arrival.

The fifth boy was Jannie. Of Afrikaans descent, his half-hooded eyes and vacant expression didn't endear him to the teachers. He and Vinny came to Plumtree without knowing a soul. Their purpose was to fill their father's shoes as per the family tradition.

With plans in place, we passed the time by throwing a ball around on the lawns out the front of the hostel, careful to avoid the needles of the ornamental palm trees. Richard snatched the ball out of the air and grubber kicked it along the ground to Jannie, who was a natural with an oval ball, and scooped it up with ease.

'How long have you been playing?' Richard asked as he clasped the back of his head.

'Since I was five, my pa bought me my first ball,' Jannie replied, his Dutch heritage reflected in his throaty accent. 'What about you, *ouens?*'

'Nah, we played football,' Alan said before anyone got a chance.

'*Ja.* I wonder why the day scholars play soccer whiles the boarders play rugby. Maybe because we're tougher?' Jannie threw dummy passes and dived at our feet with fake touchdowns. 'One day I will be a Springbok.' He kissed the ball and kicked it into the air. Was he imagining eighty thousand fans watching him? He was not the awkward skin and bone he appeared to be.

Why did Jannie dream of becoming a Springbok rather than playing for his homeland, Rhodesia?

Vinny returned with a concealed satchel filled with biscuits, fruit, and water. We had a mission, and that was to get a closer look at the seniors by crossing to the other side of the playing fields undetected. The two rugby fields offered little shelter apart from the wishbone goal posts.

Butterflies fluttered about in my stomach. Alan fidgeted and kicked his heels against the wall, while Richard and Jannie stopped playing but continued to discuss sport. Vinny lay on his back, watching the clouds. I regarded the anxious group with an eye on the setting sun, tinting the candyfloss pink clouds against a blackening horizon.

'Come on, guys, let's move out,' I said as I considered barking like Donald Sutherland in *Kelly's Heroes*, but resisted the urge. The mob splintered and regrouped at the garden edge under the shelter of the palms.

'Now remember, if anyone gets caught, he takes the rap alone. No ratting, okay?' Richard said, as he rallied the group.

Because of the bush war, the rail tracks that passed through the grounds were a no-go zone — green light to youngsters without supervision. Plus, it was an opportunity to show the military prowess we had picked up from movies and the burgeoning junta within the country. We crept on all fours — commando style. Our khaki uniforms blended with the patchy straw-coloured grass and gravel sprinkled with ferocious devil's thorn. The vicious-looking seeds of this ground creeper stick to anything and everything and the plant can live where few others can.

'Ouch, fucking thorns, how are we meant to play rugby on this?' Jannie stood up; his chest studded with barbs. He picked them off with his fingertips while we agreed to continue our journey, doubled over to avoid both disclosure and the spikes.

We waited for the seniors to arrive. Propped against tree stumps, rocks, and termite mounds, the bush provided us with ample cover. The rumours and myths told by older boys terrified us, not that any of us admitted it. Curiosity demanded we investigate our adversaries. In the distant haze, Gaul House peeked from behind her green apron and beckoned to us with menace.

We tried the biscuits, but they were stale and tasteless. 'Feels like something shat in my mouth,' Vinny said as he passed around the bottle to wash down the dry biscuits.

The ground vibrated long before it came into view. Birds took flight. Apprehension grew with the approaching black plume blemishing a flawless sky. We scrambled to our vantage points, craning our necks.

'Whatever you do, don't let them see you, or they'll kick our arse,' Alan said as he peaked from behind a two-metre-high anthill. 'And don't forget your backs.'

The angry face of the locomotive hissed jets of steam. A whistle blast startled Alan and almost knocked him onto his backside.

'Shit, here it comes,' I said under my breath. The demon snaked ever closer.

'Keep your bloody heads down. If the seniors see us...' Alan said once he'd recovered before another blast drowned him out.

I withdrew into the shade of a *wag-n-bietjie* bush to hide any reflection from my pale face. The engine slowed and spewed cinders like tobacco into a spittoon. Heads peered from the windows and bodies hung from the doors; all were wearing the unmistakable bottle-green blazers of Plumtree School.

'There are hundreds of them,' Jannie said as anxiety covered his face. *'Dit is nie mooi nie, ons sal kak vandag.'*

'What did you say?' I asked, and nudged him.

One of Jannie's incisors that was capped in gold glinted when he grimaced at me. 'Not great. We are in for shit,' he replied and flicked his head towards the tracks.

'Best we get back before they do,' Richard said as a halo caused by the setting sun formed around his crown. Late afternoon turned to evening, with the sky blackening the earth. We raced back to the hostel, safer under the imminent dusk. Alan and I skulked behind the toilets before sauntering into the house with the glare of the fluorescents blinding us. We stripped in the showers with no one the wiser.

Before we left for dinner, Mr Winker stuck his head through the dormitory doors. 'Gentlemen. We'll have a roll call after supper with the rest of the house. Tidy up if you want to impress.'

I tied my shoelaces, then rubbed the scuff marks of my shoes with a wet finger. 'How long before they arrive?' I asked Alan.

'Won't be long.' Alan pointed at two boys running towards us. 'Action stations guys, the shit is hitting the fan.' We converged at the doors leading onto the red-polished veranda.

'What's that noise?' a voice asked. A rustle at first, until it intensified into a deluge of stampeding wildebeest.

'Shit, they're on their way and in a fucking hurry.' Unsure what to do, we withdrew and waited. The noise of running footsteps accompanied by yelling and laughing came from everywhere. Deep voices called to one another.

'Hurry.'

'Book me a bed too, but not near the doors.'

'No problem.'

'Don't want stinky anywhere near us this year.'

Riotous laughter followed by chants.

'Stinky. Stinky. Stinky.'

The voices were deep and alarming, but I couldn't make out their faces for fear of revealing our position.

The clamour of tin trunks being unpacked and raised voices echoed through the building as allies got reacquainted and caught up with their holiday antics. The house buzzed.

Richard peaked through the curtains. 'Oh, boy,' he whispered.

I glanced at Alan, then at Vinny. They both nodded and we moved to the windows.

'Wait for me, man,' Jannie said as he leapt to his feet.

'Is that more coming? Vinny pointed further down the road, where a handful of green blazers materialised out of the dark.

'Maybe, but they're not worried about where they sleep,' Richard said as he shook his head without taking his eyes off the approaching group.

'That's because they're prefects. Look. White shirts, not khaki,' I said and wrinkled my nose at the smell of cologne as they swaggered past. Nervous about leaving our protective shell, we lingered until the house left for dinner.

Chapter Four

We stood outside the dining hall in age groups. The first years being the furthest away. When prefects called us in according to our ages, we were last to enter the building.

'Take it easy china, whatever happens, don't show you're afraid,' I said.

'Easier said than done,' Alan answered.

'It's in the mind. It won't last forever.'

'We heard of this shit, but it's mental, man. Don't you worry about me, just take care of yourself.' Alan went on.

We entered the hall and split into our designated tables. I reached mine, and unsure of the protocol, I scanned the table from beneath my fringe, not wanting to draw attention to myself. My heart skipped when the head of table beckoned me with his index finger.

The tables were so close together that it was difficult to pass between them. I didn't want to brush against his chair, so I lifted my hands and eased past and stopped silently beside him.

'Hey, shithead, what's my name?' he asked.

'I don't know,' I replied.

'And his?'

'No, sorry.'

'Him?' He pointed at a third boy.

'Before the next meal, you'll learn our names. Do you understand me, arsehole?'

'What's your name?' the smaller third senior asked in a warm voice.

'Rorke.'

'We're not interested in the name Mummy gave you,' said the mean boy at the head of the table.

'Wilde, sir.'

The seniors burst into laughter.

'Where are you from, arse wipe?'

'Wankie.'

'Sounds right. I hear the boys from Wankie are wankers. Is that right?'

I stood in silence.

The head grabbed my shirt collar and pulled me to his pock-marked face. 'If we are to get along Wilde, you will show respect by knowing our names.' He lifted my feet off the ground with ease. 'Do you hear me, prick?'

'Yes, sir.'

'And stop the fuck calling me, sir. Do I look like a teacher, arsehole?'

My chest constricted. Tears welled.

'Leave him, Ant, it's his first day.' The smaller senior intervened.

The bully shoved me away and sent me sprawling. I picked myself up and stood to attention.

'Get back to your seat and know our names at breakfast,' said the bully.

On the short walk to my chair, I dashed away a tear and pulled myself together. I sat and gave a fleeting smile. It was the best I could do. The rest of the table were third-year students who chatted among themselves, who chose or pretended not to have seen a thing.

The new boys waited at the tables at every meal. Their job was to collect steel bowls of food from the hatch and deliver them to the seniors at the head of each table. The older boys helped themselves and then passed on the bowls.

By the time the meal reached the end of the table, only dregs remained. A few tablespoons of thin colourless gravy, leftover mash, or a crust here or there. On the breadboard were mere crumbs, and the milk jug was empty.

I forced down the cold fatty slop, being careful not to look at anyone. My knees shook beneath the table despite the sub-tropical heat.

The strike of a wooden hammer declared the end of dinner. Hundreds of chairs scraped the floor as the students stood for prayers of thanks for the food. 'For all these many mercies may the Lord's holy name be praised.'

The entire school sat for the announcements from the duty master, who ate with the prefects at a raised table in the centre of the room.

After everyone had gone, I stared at the mess in front of me. I fixed my eyes on the empty fruit bowl. It was time to clean the table. Just then, cleaners dressed in dirty white aprons appeared and removed the bins full of trays and half-eaten food. One stopped at my table and put a palm on my shoulder. 'Be strong, *mnumzane,* you are not alone.' He slipped an orange into my hands and left.

Who the hell was that? What is happening? This must be hell. What have I done to deserve this? No wonder everybody is praying.

I had finished wiping the table when I saw Alan at the far end of the hall. I snuck up to him and grabbed him by the scruff of his neck.

'What's my name, arsehole?' I screamed into his ear.

Alan jumped. 'You scared the shit out of me. Don't do that.'

'Just joking. How did you go?'

'What is wrong with these bastards?' Alan's glazed eyes filled with tears.

I shrugged. 'Don't know. Maybe they'll get tired and leave us alone.'

'Yeah, and hell might freeze over.'

'Damn right. Let's get out of here.'

'You got it,' Alan said and threw the washrag on the table and headed for the exit.

We assembled in the prep-room, juniors to the front, sixth formers to the rear before Mr Winker entered, accompanied by a prefect. 'Evening, gentlemen. For the benefit of the new boys and those with short memories.' The seniors coughed and spluttered. 'Let me introduce this year's head of house, Philip Hart.'

The response from the older boys was one of sarcasm as they broke into polite applause.

'Settle gentlemen.' Mr Winker's facial blemish throbbed. 'Okay, Phil, let's get this on the road,' he added.

The head prefect pulled a card from his pocket and began calling surnames and pausing for a reply.

'Adams?'

'Adsum.'

'Aspen?'

39

'Adsum.'

'Wilde?'

After an eternity, I squeezed out a high-pitched response, not knowing the Latin, for *I am present. 'Adsum.'* I wiped the sweat from my hands.

Post roll call, the heads discussed absenteeism between themselves before Mr Winker faced us.

'Right, gentlemen, welcome back to another year at Plumtree School and Gaul House. This year we had better win the athletics again, so I expect one hundred percent commitment from each one of you, no matter your ability or lack thereof.' His eyes settled on a chubby freshman with glasses, who turned crimson at the innuendo and the subsequent mocking laughter. His head bobbed, and he joined in on the cruel mirth, as if to conceal the pain of ridicule.

'All right, quiet,' Hart called out.

'Thank you, gentlemen, you get my gist. I expect you to give the house and the school your all and remember, no matter where you are, you represent Plumtree School,' Winker said as he scrutinised the boys, and yet again dared anyone to challenge him. 'There will be no homework, after prayers. Finish settling in and be ready for school tomorrow.' He opened his little red book and prayed.

Now he's praying. What the hell?

Then he warned us against unruly behaviour and promised to return for lights out.

When Hart dismissed the assembly, the first-year students scrambled for the relative security of the dorm room. I longed for the sanctuary of bed and the darkness.

Mr Winker entered our dormitory at eight thirty p.m. on the dot with another boy. 'Gentlemen, let me introduce you to Happer, your house prefect. He will oversee you and the dorm.'

Happer smiled and waited for the housemaster to leave. 'It's very simple, guys. Don't give me a tough time, and I won't reciprocate,' he said, his shoulders hunched like a bird of prey with a protruding mouth for a beak. Dusty John Denver glasses hid his blue eyes, adding to his scavenger form akin to the characters in Rudyard Kipling's *The Jungle Book*. 'You must be on time and keep everything tidy. Any buggering around and you'll be in for it.' Happer tried to confirm his words with a long, serious stare. Unsuccessful, he thrust his hands into his pockets and splayed his legs, emphasising his concave chest and bowed knees. 'Well, you know what I mean.' He gave us a coy grin.

Just then, the doors flew open, and two boys entered, carrying a bed. 'Perfect, thanks guys, put it over there,' he said, flicked his wrist and left, promising to return later.

Vinny, unable to resist, slipped out from underneath his net. 'Jannie, keep watch,' he said.

As if we were criminals with pantyhose over our heads, the rest of us pressed our faces against our mosquito nets. Vinny sank into Happer's bed. 'Shit, it's got springs and everything. Plus, a decent mattress.' He pointed under the bed. 'Lucky bastard.'

'Chips! Chips!' Jannie sounded the alarm. 'He's coming back. *Hy kom terug.*' He reverted to Afrikaans. Jannie scampered to his bed and collided with Vinny on the way.

'Idiot, watch where you're going,' Vinny said.

'Who are you calling an idiot?' Jannie asked.

'Get yourselves into bed.' Alan forced them apart. 'You can sort this out later.'

They broke off the staring match and dived for cover.

Happer opened the door and digested the atmosphere. 'You see. We can get along,' he said. 'Good night, guys and no talking.' He flicked the light switch.

Darkness brought relief and although some whispered, most of us slept. I plumped my pillow and doubled it over for comfort, even so my efforts at bed-making proved unsuccessful. The bottom sheet pulled away from the mattress and grains of sand filled the bed because I hadn't wiped my feet. The discomfort added to my homesickness. I dozed, dreaming of the home amenities I took for granted. Bed-making, clearing the table, cleaning my shoes were new to me.

'Don't worry, Mr Rory. We will fix everything and make your bed,' Themba said with a generous grin.

'Thanks, Themba, I'm glad you came.'

'When I'm done, I'll do bacon and eggs. Yes?'

'You bet. Smells great. Wake me when it's ready.'

'Sure thing, whatever you say, boss.'

My eyes flew open to find mother and Bow grinning at me. 'What are you doing here, Mum? What's going on?'

'Who do you think you're talking to in that manner, boy?' Mr Winker asked as hymnals popped from his mouth like a Pez candy dispenser.

'None of you are real.' I forced myself awake to ward off the nightmares. The promise of breakfast still in my nostrils.

'Quick, Mr Rory, over here.'

'Themba, is that you? Where are you?'

'Over here in the laundry.'

'What the hell you are doing in the wash box?' I hunted for him beneath the dirty uniforms.

'The others mustn't find me; they don't want me to tell you.' Themba held a finger to his lips.

'What are you talking about? Doesn't it stink in among that soiled underwear?' I paused. 'Hang on a minute, you're not here. I'm dreaming, aren't I?'

Themba stood up out of the wash box and placed a hand on my head. 'Yes, *indodana,* you are, but do not ignore them. It is how the soul talks.' Themba hesitated at the moronic laughter from upstairs, the whites of his eyes luminous in the dark. 'This is a place of significant danger. Trust no one, Mr Rory. Count on nothing.'

I wrestled myself back to reality and sat upright, swearing under my breath. I lay back, listening to the night. Intermingled were the sporadic whimpers of boys and their terrors. To shun the torment of further sleep, I controlled my breathing and forced my mind towards happier times. I thought not only of Plumtree School, but of the country, deducing there were two options available. To continue or get out.

That's it. I'll run away. Back to Bow. We'll sleep under our baobab.

The image of everybody searching and the uproar that would cause appealed. Success was imperative. The risk of getting lost in hundreds of square kilometres of African bush a probability. Early capture meant endless ridicule. The chances of running into a terrorist gang were probable. A road and a single railway line led through the village. The city, with its wide streets and fancy buildings, lay in one direction, the

Botswana border in the other.

That's the answer. It is time to run away.

A cabaret lauded the breaking dawn. The birds were happier. The prospects of escaping via the border lifted my spirits. Train the quickest but limited to the places to hide. Ten kilometres from Plumtree stood Botswana, unsympathetic because of politics. The track ran through Botswana to South Africa, a place I'd heard was paradise.

Unable to contain myself, I snuck out of bed and went outside so as not to wake the others. The cool dawn breeze brought goosebumps, the dew on the Kikuyu grass soaked my feet. A secluded spot at the end of the gardens was a perfect location. I loitered in my shorts as I scratched my crotch and yawned aloud.

'What the hell should I do?' I called out to the heavens. The faint rustle of palm leaves was the only reply.

'Morning, Wilde. Watch, you don't catch your death of cold sitting there half-naked.'

'Morning, sir,' I spluttered at Mr Winker's presence.

He waved and continued jogging.

I half lifted a hand and returned to the hostel, still groggy from a tough night.

Time for school. Here's hoping the seniors had forgotten their threats if I didn't know their names.

Outside the dining hall, I discovered peers in a similar quandary. Jannie sat on the curb, scowling. 'This is crazy, man,' he said as he scrunched up his face and clicked his tongue. 'We can't let this happen. *Boetie,* you must help me, man.'

Still annoyed with Jannie for the collision the previous evening, Vinny lifted his hands. 'What's the Dutchman saying now?'

'You guys must help, and Vinny, ease up on the insults. Jannie won't put up with them,' Alan said as he jumped to Jannie's defence.

Vinny glanced at Jannie's thunderous expression and shut up.

'What are you thinking, Jan?' I asked as I punched his shoulder.

'I will hook that *soutie.* '

'He isn't worth it. Just leave him,' I said with an uncertain smile. 'What's a *soutie?'*

Jannie collected himself. *'Soutie* is short for *soutpiel,* an Afrikaans word we use for the English.' Jannie hesitated at my puzzled expression. Alan and Richard waited for the punch line. *'Sout* means salt and *piel* is a penis. Put it together and you have a salt penis.' Jannie collapsed into another fit of hilarity and walloped my back.

'I don't get it,' I said with a grimace as I rubbed at the pain.

Vinny listened from behind Jannie as he played to his audience and wiped away his tears of laughter.

'Sorry man. Okay, I'll tell you. We refer to the English in South Africa as *soutpiel* because they have one foot in Africa and the other in England, having left their dicks dangling in the ocean,' Jannie added as he stood with his legs apart to enhance the image. He laughed so hard he had to hold his stomach. The glint from Jannie's gold tooth reminded me of *Elmer Fudd* in the *Bugs Bunny* cartoon.

The others grinned and shook their heads, mindful that they could fall into that category. Vinny, who was indignant, ignored them. The call to enter the dining hall ended the foray.

I took my place at the end of the dinner table, avoiding eye contact. When grace was over, I darted to the food hatch. Thankful of time away from the table.

The seniors appeared to have forgotten. They were deep in conversation, or at least too busy to bother with me. A single fried egg swimming in oil slid from the large stainless-steel platter onto my plate. I eyed the bread in the centre of the table but decided against it in case it invited their attention. Cold and with no salt and pepper, I ate the egg; it tasted like rubber. Every minute was hell.

As usual, the gavel sounded, and an announcement called for the new boys to assemble in the school hall. The head of table left without a word — reprieve until lunch.

I cut myself a doorstop and scraped the jam jar clean. I didn't mind the sour tang of stale bread or the lack of butter. Instead, I cut another and another.

Alan joined me, clutching a white container. 'Got any jam or butter left over?' he asked.

'Fat chance, why do you ask?'

44

'Well, I've been emptying jam from the pots into this jar at the end of every meal,' Alan said as he opened the plastic tub and revealed recycled jam, sprinkled with blobs of butter and breadcrumbs. 'What do you say?' he asked as he puffed out his chest. 'Want to help? We can do the same with sugar?'

'Sure, why not?'

'We'd better go. School is in ten minutes.'

I nodded and hid the piebald sugar beneath the table.

On our way out, I caught sight of someone waving to catch my attention. It was the cleaner who gave me the orange last night. He pointed at his watch and held up a single finger.

'He wants to see you at one o'clock,' Alan guessed. 'After lunch.'

I showed a thumbs up.

'You must come; we'll talk to him together,' I half asked, half instructed.

Alan remained quiet.

As we headed for our hostel, I deliberated how I could ask my friend walking alongside me to join me in escaping.

Chapter Five

The walk to the classrooms led us past the grand buildings of the other hostels: **Milner House 1911, Lloyd House 1924, Grey House 1926.**

We also passed two swimming pools, one full-sized and sparkling, the other pea soup and narrow. Next to the baths, a thatched cottage split the dirt road. One street led to the rest of the hostel, the other to the classrooms. An impenetrable hedge, two metres tall, hemmed in the cottage which had the tiniest entrance. We doubled our pace. The prefect's common room was not a place even the masters ventured.

'That's where the prefects hang out,' Richard said, enjoying the influence that came with an older brother. 'Whatever happens, don't get called in because…'

'Ag, we've got no business there. Why would they call us?' Jannie said.

'Use your brain.' Richard tapped himself on the skull. 'They want us to serve tea and run errands.'

'What's wrong with that?' Jannie asked.

'Shit. You just don't get it. They then interrogate you on names and sports teams. A new boy went in once and never returned,' Richard replied.

I rolled my eyes at Richard; I didn't believe it.

'Bullshit, man,' Jannie said, and punched Richard's arm.

'I'm not shitting you,' Richard lifted his palms in defence.

I felt sure we each made a mental note to steer well away from the prefect's lair. I took Alan by the elbow until out of earshot. 'We need to talk.'

'What's up?'

'Hurry,' Vinny called as he waited for the two of us.

'I'll tell you later,' I said to Alan.

'Nothing crazy, please,' Alan said before responding to Vinny. 'We're coming. Hold your horses.' Alan put his arms around our shoulders and swung his feet into the air.

The hall overlooked the school's main sporting facilities.

'Look at that, guys.' I swept my arm across the panorama as we stood on the edge of a ceremonial garden of rose bushes and miniature-sculptured hedges. Insects buzzed back and forth; impertinent wasps darted among lumbering bumblebees. Spider webs glistened in the morning aphid rush hour, waiting for clumsy drivers.

'Wow, that's so cool,' Alan said.

'*Magtig,*' Jannie said with astonishment in his soft guttural 'g'. 'Check out all the sports.' Jannie couldn't believe it. In the forefront, two rugby fields converted into a cricket ground, dependent on the season. Beneath the blue gums stood a pavilion for the hierarchal spectator to partake in cream teas. Benches lined the field for the plebs.

'There are squash courts and that there is an all-weather hockey field.' Jannie swung to the opposite side of the vista, overbalancing on the verge of the vantage point.

'It's a long way down, man. Be careful,' Alan said as he caught Jannie by his shirt.

'*Ek weet boetie,* but check the tennis courts there must be at least six.'

While they marvelled, I turned back to the school hall, which was supported by contoured pillars. Oval lead windows filled the walls. Birds nested in the eaves. Imprinted above the teak doors was the lettering, **Established 1930**.

We milled around as we waited for instruction. Bored, the anglers among us inspected the fountain for any sign of fish. Some played the fool, others sat eager for proceedings to start. One boy lost his shorts in the horseplay. His clothes, two sizes too large, underscored his diminutive frame. Purple with rage, the lad pulled them up and chased the offender, stopping every so often to fix his pants.

'Hey shorty, lost your knickers?' A thickset boy baited him; others kicked him in the rear as he passed. I resisted the temptation to intervene, holding fast to Themba's advice to be a chameleon.

This is bullshit. I'm out of here. With or without Alan.

A teacher called us to order. 'The name is Stenk, Mr Stenk to you lot, I am your form master.' He spoke with a faint lyrical vernacular. 'I teach English literature and coach under fifteens at rugby and water polo. One day I hope to produce a Gareth Edwards or Willie John McBride.' Stenk's green eyes danced through thick lenses as he caressed his hands in glee.

We moved nearer, and Jannie lifted his hand.

'Yes, boyo. What words of inspiration do you have to delight us?' Mr Stenk lilted, as he opened his arms to the group.

'Well, if it's all the same to you, sir. I will play for the Springboks and not the Welsh,' Jannie replied. The gathering roared with their approval. The closer ones patting Jannie on the back.

Stenk raised his hands for silence. He stopped smiling and faced Jannie. 'That's what I want to hear, boyo. Tenacity,' Stenk said, and his eyes flashed. 'It was a figure of speech, boys. There are no intentions of poaching you for the Welsh rugby side, but I intend to produce the best players possible.' He rubbed the top of Jannie's head with a mischievous glint in his eye. 'Besides, the South African's need every bit of help they can get if they hope to beat the Welsh.' He cringed at the booing and steered us into the Beit Hall.

We followed our new *Pied Piper*.

It took a couple of seconds to grow accustomed to the dingy, dank interior of the school hall. The smell of oil paintings and fusty fabric hung in the air. Portraits of former dignitaries and the velour curtains of the theatre reached from ceiling to floor. Boards of honour lined the pretentious walls; each depicting captains of sport or boasts of academic excellence. Chorus lines of padded chairs faced a flamboyant stage. Ornate ceilings, complete with gargoyles, contrasted the teak-lined walls. The balcony looked down its judicial nose at the proceedings.

We assembled in the front rows, daunted by the magnificent building. Stenk clapped and rubbed his hands. 'Right, shall we kick off?' His voice carried in the cavernous room. 'By now, they will have introduced you to the boarding aspects of the school. Let me present you with another. One of Academia.' His tone turned sombre. 'Look around.' He opened his arms as if he was an evangelical preacher. 'You are among the privileged few to attend the country's most elite scholastic establishment.' His Welsh inflexion became more pronounced with his histrionics. 'Which boyos avails you to one of the finest educations on the planet. The English public-school system envied the world over.' He peered over heavy-framed spectacles, clearly pleased by his own rhetoric.

'Bloody hell, he can't half lay it on thick. He should stand on that thing.' I pointed at the podium, which flaunted an embossed gold cross on a green-velvet background.

'And he can stick his pompous English school right up his…'

'Okay, don't get crude, my good man.' I stuck my tongue in my cheek and imitated a stylish English accent.

'What you boys do is up to you. Very few chances of this magnitude are likely to avail themselves of you again.' Mr Stenk clapped once more and reverted to his jovial self. 'Questions? Let me have them if you do.'

'Ask him about the hall,' I said to Alan.

'What about it?' Alan asked.

'Don't sit whispering, boys. Stand up, Laddie. Tell us your name and let's have your question.' Stenk looked at me.

'Rorke Wilde, sir.'

'Ah, music to my ears. Rorke meaning *famous king. A* solid Gaelic name, if I'm not mistaken. Complimented with the old English surname Wilde — to *lead others*, hey? A fine name, son. Now, where do you seek clarity?' Stenk held out a cleansing hand.

'I'm wondering why the hall has the same name as the bridge at the South African border, sir,' I said and sank back into my seat.

'Simple, young Rorke, an English civil engineer named Alfred Beit, constructed the bridge spanning the Limpopo River. He built many structures, which made him very wealthy, so he founded a trust to fund educational buildings, to give something back to the country, so to speak.'

My thoughts flicked to the fireside suppers at Themba's two-room home, and I recalled the hostility of his son, Sipho. Then they moved on to conversations with my father and his awe at the roll of honour boards that depicted fresh fatalities in gold lettering. A familiar sense of dread washed over me.

It was to be a day of academic assessment as they graded students into streams. Rows of scholars sat in various degrees of distraction as they answered multiple-choice tests.

To my relief, we didn't adjourn to the dining hall for lunch. Instead we had trays of peanut butter sandwiches and an urn of milk brought to us. We used our tea break to find out the names of the heads of our tables. A lad from the next table knew the three seniors on mine.

Stenk stood at the front of the hall and clapped. 'Okay boys, thanks for your efforts. It's been a long day. Tomorrow we'll grade the papers. Meet here same time in the morning. *Iechyd Da.*' He bid farewell in Welsh and gave me a wink.

We left, shielding our eyes from the brightness of the late afternoon sun.

Alan and I stuck with the rest of the gang and broke into a gallop past the prefect's common room, laughing at the slower runners. Vinny brought up the rear, his nostrils flaring as if he was being chased by *Regan* from *The Exorcist.*

'Chips behind you, Vinny,' Alan said.

We spurred him on until he reached the hostel gardens where he sprawled on his back, gulping for air.

'You're a mad fool,' Alan gave Vinny a playful kick.

'I didn't want to go in alone,' Vinny replied.

'There wasn't anyone in there. It's something to five,' Alan pointed to his watch.

The others pounced onto Vinny, thumping him, sufficient to hurt, yet soft enough for him to realise they were playing. 'Piss off, you bastards,' he rolled around in agony. Vinny flipped on to his stomach and pressed himself to his knees, instigating us to flee in every direction. 'Bloody shits,' shouted a dishevelled Vinnie as he followed us into the dorm. He had accepted his punishment for his earlier mischief towards Jannie and was thankful for the reprieve and reacceptance into the faction. Being alone was not a choice anyone relished.

I took my position at the end of the table, confident this time. I forced down the mince on toast, then asked for a slice of bread. The third years tossed me a slice without incident. I considered the margarine but changed my mind, all the time trying to catch the head's attention.

I know your names, dumbasses.

After grace, the dining hall emptied, but the heads of my table continued to chat over a cup of tea. I took the initiative and sidled up to them, pretending to wipe the table.

'Excuse me, Campbell,' I swabbed around his cup.

'Excuse me, Turner,' I continued, as he eyed me with a wry smile.

'Don't get smart, we realise you have learnt our names.' He turned his face to hide his amusement.

Campbell grabbed me by the scruff. His greasy skin shone, and his breath stank of cigarettes. Silver fillings decorated his tartar mottled teeth. 'You're a cocky little shit; no doubt we'll get along.' The brute released me and continued his tête-à-tête with his friend.

Back in my seat, I reached under the table for my jar of sugar and transferred it into a plastic container. Sugar was only available at breakfast, so I offered it to Campbell and Turner.

'You learn quick sprog, not too shabby,' Campbell said as he sweetened his tea and went on with his conversation. Their approval gave me the freedom to collect the contraband under the guise that it was for them. I would use their names to protect our spoils from those of lesser seniority.

I slept well, or at least better. The morning choir didn't disturb me, and it wasn't until a plough disc struck by a piece of steel suspended from a tree sounded the alarm that I woke. I vaulted from my bed and headed for the showers. Ready to take on the world, I was fitting in, fading into obscurity as Themba advised.

Should I run away? Or can I see this through?

My thoughts turned to Bow, whose colours changed to suit his environment. I missed his naughty, revolving eyes.

The class returned to the school hall to await results. In the meantime, Richard handed out slips of paper. 'I must have these signed by lunchtime if we are to go on exeat this Sunday. Stenk needs them.'

'What a hassle. Just to go for a few hours,' Vinny said.

'Thanks for that, but they have to keep track of where everyone is. With the terrorists and all that,' Richard replied.

'Yes, but it will be great, fishing, swimming, hunting? No seniors, no teachers,' Alan said, clicking his tongue. 'How are we meant to hunt, fish, without rods or weapons?'

'Don't worry, I have a plan,' Jannie winked at Alan.

I listened to the banter as the gang relaxed beneath the trees. It would be nice to return to my much-loved nature and leave behind the mayhem. Even if for a moment. The familiar aroma of freedom floated on the faintest breeze.

'I wonder how long this will take?' Alan asked. No-one answered.

Although each day became more tolerable, I needed to complete my escape plan. I squinted at Alan, who fought off a persistent fly.

We ducked through a rusting wire fence and marched towards the scrublands on our first Sunday exeat. The teachers considered it free time for us to enjoy the bush with friends, away from the pressures of boarding school. The dress code didn't apply, khaki shorts, unbuttoned shirts, and bush shoes were fine. Richard wore a pair of Nike sneakers. World imposed sanctions on the minority government post unilateral declaration of independence (UDI) put an end to international brands, and only those who holidayed abroad returned with licenced merchandise.

'What's in the bag, Jannie?' Alan asked, unable to keep his curiosity in check.

'Things to help us out, *boet.*' Jannie held onto the contents until he was ready.

I led the expedition in search of the dam. Uncertain of its location, except for vague directions we gleaned from others, I waited under the sparse shade of an infamous thorn bush for the stragglers. The city boys, Richard and Vinny, less sure-footed, battled over the terrain. I plucked a blade of grass and held it in the side of my mouth. 'City slickers, we want to get there before the fish stop biting.'

'Hold your bloody horses. We can't all be *Tarzan,*' Richard said as he arrived out of breath and perspiring.

A little after nine o'clock, the heat kicked in. We swigged from our water bottles, careful not to consume too much, because it must last the day.

'How far?' Alan asked me as he wiped his mouth.

I frowned at the horizon. 'Shouldn't be too far. We'll be there now, now — soon.' The lie of the land and the change in vegetation guided us to a dam built to service the school and the village.

'At bloody last,' Alan said as he careered over the embankment in full flight. We followed, whooping at the top of our voices, clothes, and all, into the murky water.

'Man, this is good.' I lay floating on my back, looking at my toes.

'Sure is, man,' Jannie yanked me under the water. Moments later, he grabbed a handful of black sludge from the floor of the lake and plopped it on his head and crossed his eyes.

'You are a lunatic,' I pointed at Jannie, who stripped off his clothes and headed into the undergrowth yelling, *'Kaalgat kleilat.'*

Within seconds, we were cutting bendy sticks ready for the battle of attaching balls of clay to the end and flicking them at an opponent — every boy for himself. Clay whistled through the air as we chased one another naked through the *veld* and muddied water. It was a miracle no one lost an eye, or worse. Leaden from exertion, we rinsed off and replaced our shorts.

'Let's set up camp over by that tree overhanging the water,' I said, and the boys followed my suggestion by clearing the land and securing our belongings. I folded my shirt and put it on a stone next to which I placed my shoes.

Jannie opened his backpack and chucked a small parcel wrapped in waxed paper to each of us. 'Catch. This is our packed lunch from the dining hall.'

I stuffed the package into my shoes for safekeeping. 'Come on. Let's see what we can find.'

'You're on, I need a piss first.' Alan gripped the front of his pants and disappeared behind the bushes nearby.

Richard and Vinny lay flat on their backs with their shirts over their faces while Jannie sat on a log unpacking his bag.

'This is more like it,' Alan peed behind a shrub.

'And how?' I said, climbing the tree.

'Can you spot anything?' Alan asked.

I scanned the horizon from the top of the enormous tree. 'No, but I see smoke over there.'

'Who do you figure it could be?'

'Don't know, let's find out.' I jumped from my perch.

'Okay, but be careful. You never know who's there,' Alan said and fell in behind as I headed for the spiral of smoke. We moved downwind until the stench of the fire hit our nostrils. 'Take care, could be poachers or even terrs.'

'Doubt it. They can't be so stupid as to attract attention with a fire.'

'Well, I hope you're right, for our sakes.'

I shushed Alan and gestured for him to crouch lower. We leopard crawled the remaining metres, copying the soldiers we admired on adverts, inviting us to sign up for national service. The mixed herb odours of foliage and dust prickled our senses and made me want to sneeze. 'Don't move or make a sound,' I said.

Alan nodded and lay his head on his arms, their personal effects strewn across the clearing.

'It's another bunch of new boys,' I said to Alan, who lifted his face and peered through the thicket.

'Are you sure? Who do you think it could be?'

'Don't know. Let's tell the others… we don't want to alert them,' I said.

'Sounds great to me.'

I surveyed the site and made mental notes of the fire's location, as I determined that there were five or six in the group.

Once we were out of range, we bolted through the bush, dodging trees and thorns, until we burst back into our campsite.

'Where the hell have you been?' Jannie said, feigning interest as he attended to his fishing line and squatted on a rock with his baseball cap pulled over his eyes.

'Is that line and hooks?' I asked.

'*Jy sien, ek is nie dom nie. Ek is a Boer,'* Jannie smiled with pride.

'I never said you were dumb, farmer boy,' I replied in jest.

'Do you want to join me?' Jannie asked. 'Cut a branch and fetch a piece of bark for the float. The rest I've got right here.' Jannie tapped the pocket on his shorts.

'Sounds great. What are you using for bait?' Alan asked.

'Ooh, God.' The soft 'g' reverberated in his throat. 'That's the best part. Look here.' Jannie unravelled the wax paper from his packed lunch and showed us a cold, stale burger.

'The fish bloody love it. At least we'll eat better now. Rather than this shit, hey?'

'Sounds good to me,' I replied.

Fed up with the lack of bites from the fish, Jannie stretched and pulled in his line. 'I'm moving around to those reeds. Nothing's happening here.'

'Watch out for that campsite. We're not sure if they're seniors or not,' Alan pointed to ant-sized figures splashing in the distance.

'Not serious. I'll check them out when I'm over that side,' Jannie said and headed out. 'You guys coming?'

'Nah. we'll stay put. Check you later.' I shook my head.

'I'm fine here, not much shade over there,' Alan said.

We sat in silence, enjoying the quiet, apart from the faint shouts of the group across the water. 'So, what do you think so far?' I said, as I seized the opportunity to quiz Alan.

'About what?'

'Plumtree School.'

'I know where I'd rather be than here.'

I waited for Alan to finish.

'It's a nightmare, isn't it? I mean, why do they find it necessary to make our lives hell for tradition's sake? They're bastards. It doesn't turn us into men,' he continued. Alan's tirade ended with him shaking his head and casting a line of fresh bait.

'We don't have to, you know?' I spoke.

'What do you mean? Yes, we do. Our folks won't let us out, they believe this place is wonderful.' Alan tried to mimic Stenk's Welsh accent, but he sounded more Indian. 'The land's most prestigious scholastic institution.'

'Shut up, you'll scare the fish,' I replied.

'What fish? All we've caught are bloody platannas.' Instead of fish, we'd caught an abundance of the prolific slimy-black African clawed frog.

It was time to tell Alan the plan.

But he hadn't finished. 'There's not much we can do?' he said and studied me, fishing for a response. 'Is there?'

'Maybe.'

'Well, are you going to tell me?'

'It's not for the faint-hearted, buddy.'

'It's one of your hair-brained schemes, isn't it?' Alan's eyes widened.

'What do you mean *hair-brained?*'

Alan raised his eyebrows at me.

'Yeah, well, this time it'll work.'

'So, tell me then.'

'Maybe I will. Maybe I won't.'

Will he go for it? What he doesn't know won't hurt him. It will piss him off if I don't tell him, though.

'Okay, but you're not to breathe a word to anyone.' As I shared my idea with Alan, he stared out across the dam.

Well, he knows now. He just needs time.

I attached a fresh piece of burger to my fishing line, waiting for Alan.

'Just the two of us?' Alan said aloud. 'To South Africa, through Botswana, the sworn enemy?'

He reminded me of Buddha resting on a rock, looking at the elements for guidance.

'You don't have to come.'

'You can't do it alone,' he said.

'I could always ask Jannie.'

'Yeah, right, can you imagine? No, I must go with you.'

'Good man, now you're talking.'

'But we must plan it to the last detail. It's too dangerous otherwise.' Alan disappeared into his own thoughts as he sat upon his rock.

'What are you guys talking about?' Vinny asked as he and Richard joined in on the fishing.

'Are you two rested?' I said, as I changed the subject.

'Yeah, but it's bloody hot. Let's go for a spoof,' Vinny said.

We agreed and waded into the lake up to our necks. The odour of the water reeked from the raw sewerage pumped from the school, but the relief from the heat overrode that discomfort. We floated on our backs for hours, using our arms to guide us around the dam, and competed at diving under water to see who could hold their breath the longest.

'They look like prunes,' Vinny said as he put his hands in front of his face.

'Never mind that, check your legs,' I said as I bent over and discovered the same problem on my own.

'Don't pull them off, they're leeches. You need to burn them off,' Jannie said.

Vinny was by far the worst off, with twelve of the

bloodsuckers attached to his skin. 'Thank goodness we kept on our shorts,' he said as he pulled the material tight against his skin.

'What's going on?' Jannie stood on the embankment puzzled by the commotion.

'Leaches, china, they're everywhere,' Richard replied as he slapped a bloodsucker on his chest.

'No shit, man. I'll build a fire for the barbecue.' Jannie held up a cache of fish, one on each finger, as he grinned with pride.

'By the time you stop bragging, I'll be a flat tyre,' Vinny said.

'*Stil*, man Richard,' Jannie said to shut him up. 'I'll make a fire now, so we can burn the bastards.' He dropped his catch to collect firewood, muttering about the lack of appreciation of his fishing skills.

We cremated the predatory worms with a fiery stick. 'Be careful.' I held the tail end of a leech attached to my thigh.

'Don't be such a baby,' Vinny said as he approached the creature with a smouldering scalpel. I clenched my teeth at the heat and tugged at the vampire worm until it let go.

'Perfect, three more to go. At least you got less on you than him,' Vinny said as he pointed at Alan, who was sitting on a rock waiting his turn with half a dozen squirming on his legs.

Blood poured out of our wounds because of the anticoagulation injected by the leeches, but it clotted after a brief time.

Meanwhile, Jannie gutted the fish, rubbed them with margarine from the burger buns and placed them on a flat stone in the embers. 'Come and get it.' He dished the charcoaled fish on to large banana leaves from a random tree he had found in the bush.

'Tastes great,' I said, being mindful not to get a mouthful of bones from the six-inch fish. The rest nodded, engrossed in picking every morsel from the carcasses.

I fetched the canteens of water from the dam, where we kept them cool. 'Who wants pudding? Give me a sec.' I disappeared into the undergrowth and returned with a hat full of Marula — a round plum-like fruit the size of a golf ball.

'That's gross, man.' Vinny curled his lip in disgust.

'You're such a wimp. Try it first, then decide,' I replied as

I washed the Marula and put them in the middle between us.

'How are you meant to eat them?' Richard asked.

I chose one from the pile and bit into the leathery skin, tearing it away from the sweet flesh. Its mucky juice oozed down my face. 'Now that's good.'

'What's it taste like?' Vinny asked.

Alan grabbed a couple. 'Feels like a lychee but tastes like a mix of granadilla and pear.'

'A leech?' Jannie threw up in his mouth a little at the idea of eating the worms we had just burnt from our bodies.

'Lychee Jannie. Not leeches.' Alan corrected.

'Thanks, guru chef,' Vinny said, unconvinced.

The troop dug in.

When the sun toned from white-hot brilliance to a warm-terracotta glow and a stiff breeze blew in swabs of haloed lilac clouds, I knew change was coming. 'Rain is on its way,' I said.

'Yup. We better make a move, hey?' Alan said.

Behind us, the world darkened with the impending storm.

Alan caught up and placed a hand on my back. 'Been thinking more about what you said. Reckon we can make it. If today's anything to go by.'

'What do you mean?'

'Surviving in the bush on our own. If we can manage it here, we can do it anywhere.'

'Good to hear, Alan, my china.' The spring in my step returned, fed by the joys of nature and the bond of noble friends.

The promise of rain lifted our spirits. We were invincible. I clipped the back of Vinny's head and sprinted past the guys, causing a chain reaction of ear slapping and rugby tackles. Burnt, blistered, and bloodied, we bantered our way back to the boarding house. Our existence was changing. Our freedom in the bush and in life is under threat. An uncertain future on so many levels.

Chapter Six

In the weeks ahead, we familiarised ourselves with the hindrances of tradition. The execution of conformity and the peer pressure of boarding school. We learnt about the Rhodes scholar winners into Oxford University. The prestige of national sports players and the bullies who preyed on the timid because of birthdates, looks or ability.

I peered at the list posted on the house noticeboard. Alan stood on tiptoes.

'Can you see who you're skivvying for?' he asked.

'You've got Mason.'

'That's cool. He'll be okay, and you?' Alan asked.

'I've picked up the games room.'

'What do you mean?'

'That's what the paper says. I'm skivvying for a building.'

We laughed at having a structure to do chores for and how one might pander to its every whim. Then we headed to the dorm room to tease those who were unfortunate enough to land the more unpleasant prefects.

'That's nothing guys, Rory does the games area.'

'Serious?' a voice broke the silence.

'You got to be kidding?' another said.

'Lucky bastard,' the first boy continued.

A wave of faces turned my way. They grabbed my hands and legs and swung me like a skipping rope. The lights swirled in unison with the raucous laughter of the pranksters. I crashed into the floorboards and cracked my head on a footlocker.

'You, okay?' Vinny leapt to my side.

'Course he is. He's not as soft as you,' Jannie said as he lifted me, his fallen comrade.

I rubbed the bump on the rear of my cranium. 'Bloody lunatics.'

'At least they like you. It could have been far worse?' Alan inspected the injury with morbid curiosity.

Happer slouched in fifteen minutes later. 'Hi, guys, who knows what skivvying is?' He took our silence as a nope. 'Good, then let me explain,' he added as he checked he had everyone's attention. 'School prefects get allocated three skivvies because house prefects have two. You collect the prefect's books from the common room and bring them to his study.' Happer waited for the group to digest the information. 'Other chores involve polishing shoes, making beds, tidying their rooms and making coffee after prep. Plus any other reasonable ask.' He headed towards the door. 'A word of advice. Get on the prefect's good side because they can be protective of their skivvies.' He winked and bumped off the lights.

Thank goodness I don't have to skivvy for a bully. They must know people aren't my favourite. Wonder who told them?

I tried to get comfortable, then fell asleep.

With no homework the next day, I played pencil cricket in prep time. The numbers one to six etched on the flat sides represented runs. Another pencil marked the dismissals — catch, bowled out, stumped, runout and leg before wicket.

'Skivvies may go,' the prefect on duty called from his elevated desk at eight p.m. 'Quiet, morons. We're still working.'

I wished Alan luck before heading to the games room at the end of the grounds. Palm leaves rustled in the dark and the glass door squeaked open, silencing the crickets. A lone frog croaked beneath the trickling fountain. I groped for the light switch, trying not to panic.

This is bloody nuts, man. Better not be any terrorists hiding in here or ghosts.

The fluorescents flickered before lighting the partitioned room. To one side was a turntable, accessorised by a faded lounge suite with threadbare armrests. A frayed paisley carpet covered uneven parquet flooring and clashed with the same House orange curtains. The other section contained a torn pool table, a warped dartboard, and a rickety table-tennis table. Both rooms were in disarray, with cues, bats, darts, magazines, and newspapers strewn everywhere. I set to cleaning and rearranging, in no rush to return to the hostel in case they gave me other chores. I didn't mind tidying, but not skivvying for a person. To waste time, I refolded the papers and came across the front page of *The Rhodesian Herald.*

Bush War Intensifies, said the headline. I held my breath, confused by the fighting. One side identified as freedom fighters, the other a bastion against communism. Our prime minister, a World War II fighter pilot in the Royal Airforce, warned us against British complicity and the dangers of majority rule.

What's a communist, anyway? Who is in the right? This finger pointing was driving me crazy.

The wind howled with the threat of an impending thunderstorm.

Bloody rainy season.

I wiped the stereo off, switching it on by mistake. A voice played through the speakers, distorted by the click of the needle on vinyl. *Oh, very young, what will you leave us this time. You're only dancing on this earth for a short while.* I turned over the album cover and read aloud the singer's name. Cat Stevens.

This was nothing like my Gary Glitter singles or Father's Shirley Bassey records.

I continued to tune in to the words and enjoy the music, keeping a lookout through the curtains should anyone approach.

Before long, I lost my nerve, switched off the stereo and replaced the record, while I browsed the rest of the albums, Pink Floyd, Bob Dylan, and Jethro Tull. 'I'll listen to a different one every time I tidy,' I said, the echo of my voice startling me. I hit the light switch and jack-rabbited back to the dorm room.

'Howzit. How did it go?' Richard asked as he lay sprawled on his bed in sleeping shorts.

'Not too shabby, and you?'

'Okay, I was lucky to get Happer. At least he knows me.'

'True. The others should be here soon. Lights out in ten minutes. Hope it was okay for the guys.'

'Me too.' Concern crossed Richard's face.

I pulled back the bedclothes and wiped the underside of my feet.

All but one of us had returned by the time Happer arrived. 'Where's Vinny?' he asked.

'Not back yet. He's still with Minnaar,' Richard said.

Happer disappeared, shaking his head.

'Is he mad at Vinny or Minnaar?' Alan asked.

'Minnaar. He knows we have to be back, but anything is possible.'

A few minutes later, Vinny barged through the doors, flushed, and trailed by our sullen dorm prefect.

'Get yourself changed, then wipe your face,' Happer said as he escorted Vinny with paternal regard.

Without acknowledging us, Vinny strode to the washrooms, trying to mask his puffy eyes. Happer tailed him, avoiding eye contact.

Murmurs swept through the room. 'What the *vok's* going on, man?' Jannie blurted out.

'Do not start your shit. We don't understand the problem yet,' Alan said from across the aisle.

Before Jannie could respond, the door re-opened and Vinny darted to his bed, slipping beneath the sanctuary of his mosquito net, his bottom lip trembling.

Without a word. Happer turned off the lights and left.

'Hey, buddy, are you okay?' Jannie asked.

'Yeah, thanks.' Vinny's voice quavered.

'What the hell happened, china?'

'Come on, Vinny, split — tell us,' Alan asked.

'There isn't much,' Vinny said as he sat up to share his ordeal.

'Hold on, we can't hear a thing,' I said as the lads clamoured to the base of Vinny's bed, despite the threat of detection and painful splinters from the wooden floor. 'Okay, we're ready,'

Vinny faced his audience. 'Well, I found my way up to Minnaar's study, introduced myself and asked what he wanted me to do.' Vinny cleared his throat and drew a big breath. 'Guess he took an instant dislike to me. He didn't like my face or something, or it upset him having me as a skivvy. Not sure.' He wiped his eyes before reliving the incident.

'So, you're the petty arsehole,' Minnaar scowled at me.

All I could do was nod; he was so scary.

'Answer me when I talk to you, prick.'

'Sorry, Minnaar,' I replied, shaking as I stood to attention.

'I'll be back in five minutes. Make sure my study is tidy and a cup of coffee is waiting.' He slammed the door after him.

Unsure, I looked around the room. An old wooden desk and writer's lamp sat against one wall opposite a pine chest of drawers. Farrah Fawcett pin-ups, red Ferrari's and the sweaty pictures of Led Zeppelin covered the walls. I heard voices pass by the study, which got me started with the tidying.

Vinny hesitated in front of his audience in the darkened dormitory, gathering the savvy to continue.

'Take it easy, man,' Alan said. 'We are here for you.'

'Yes, my friend, *moenie* worry *nie.*' Jannie consoled his friend.

'Thanks, guys,' Vinny replied and continued relating his ordeal.

I turned on the kettle that was balancing atop the school files because of its short electrical cord. I mixed coffee granules with milk powder and added three sugars into the cup, then tried to pour the boiling water. Problem was, it caused the mug of coffee to tip over my skivvy master's files.

Before I had time to clean up, he returned.

'What the...' Minnaar didn't or couldn't finish his sentence. Instead, he lashed out, catching me here. Vinny pointed to his solar plexuses. *It sent me reeling against the wall.*

'You, dumb shit, get up off the floor.' He was oblivious to my distress or just didn't care. 'Get up before I get you up,' Minnaar's eyes flashed at me with such anger.

Weakened by the body-blow, I pulled myself up, doing my best not to show any pain.

'Put your fucking hands by your sides.' Minnaar's face centimetres from mine.

Terrified at another assault, I stood sideways to him but without warning, the six-foot senior hit me in the chest once more. I dropped to the floor.

The dormitory sat in silence.

Grateful, it was not them, though mindful of their classmate's predicament.

Vinny continued with his story, growing stronger.

'What are you doing there, shithead?' Minnaar kicked at me. 'Get the hell off my floor.' Tears forced their way through, not just from pain but the humiliation. I got to my feet and tried to smile.

'You're an ugly rat. Has anyone told you that?'

I nodded.

'What teams do I represent?'

'What position do I play?'

Minnaar asked me question after question, trying to catch me out, but I had done my homework on him before reporting for skivvy duty. The stroking of his ego calmed him. Well, at least to where he didn't hit me again.

After a knock, Happer entered. 'What's happening?' I knew he was aware, but I don't think he wanted to risk making matters worse. 'Juniors must be in bed by eight-thirty, otherwise Winker goes ape-shit.' Happer said, shrugging, as if to say it was more than his job was worth.

Minnaar glanced at me and pointed to the study door. 'Get out of my sight.'

'He didn't have to tell me again.' Vinny gave a weak smile under the darkness. 'The rest is history.'

Jannie shook his head. 'I am ashamed. His family name, Minnaar, is Afrikaans, meaning *Lover.* It's just not good enough. He is a shame to our *volk.*'

'Thanks, Jannie.' Vinny crumpled onto the bed in exhaustion.

Anger replaced fear as the conversation in the dorm went to retribution and revenge, then to humour, with each plan becoming more and more outlandish. We headed back to our beds where my concerns turned to the morrow. I listened to the stifled tears of our friend; homesickness was his bed-fellow tonight.

What gives him the right? Where are the adults? Were my

last thoughts before Cat Stevens serenaded me in and out of consciousness.

Although Vinny recovered from the ordeal, it remained on everyone's mind. After lunch, we mooched to the hostel. 'Come on guys, our rest-time is starting soon,' I suggested as I squinted through the heat haze and wiped the perspiration from my face.

'Yup, we've got two minutes. Let's make a move.' Alan checked his watch.

We were the last to remove our shoes before Happer's arrival.

I lay with my head on my hands waiting for the dormitory prefect to work his way over the creaking floorboards, as he flung letters to the fortunate. I held my breath, hoping, praying. He paused at the end of my bed.

'Wilde,' Happer said as he looked up from the stash of mail. 'The first one, hey?' He grinned. 'Glad I don't get to pass your ugly mug without a letter again.'

I snatched the note out of the air and fell back on to my mattress, disappointment gripping me as I recognised Mother's handwriting.

Who else is going to send a letter, you idiot?

Enclosed were two pages, one that matched the envelope, the other a page torn from an A4 examination pad. I savoured the moment, glancing across at my mates. Vinny was on his stomach, using a pillow for a desk. Alan's nose was deep in another of his mother's epic letters that reflected the household's day-to-day activities. Jannie flashed a smile and displayed a white post-office slip showing he'd received the long-expected parcel. Richard looked down his nose at Jannie and turned over. He was drifting from the group as he did at junior school.

What a snob.

I returned to my prize.

Dear Rorke.

Life has very much carried on as normal since you left for high school, although everyone is missing you, more so Themba. He mopes around, complaining that you shouldn't be away from home, mumbling mumbo jumbo about evil spirits and prophesying impending doom. The poor man doesn't understand the idea of a top education, but I suppose he means well.

I grimaced at the passing slur and needless undertone.

Cara misses you, asking often when you will return. She puts on tea parties with her dolls in your honour, insisting that you are present, encouraged by Themba, who tells her you are always with us. She has grown in your absence even though it has been just six weeks.

The postmark read 27.03.75, showing the letter took a week to arrive. I went on reading the letter.

Your father has been busy, what with the unrest with the natives. Not to mention the liberals' complicating matters. Though he doesn't say so, I know he misses you on the rare occasions he is home. Other than that, everything is the same. Except, the house is quieter and much cleaner. You are halfway through the term. So not long before you are home. I will try to enclose money with the next letter.

Love, Mum.

Annoyed at the gist of mother's remarks, I unfolded the second letter. A sense of peace engulfed me as I recognised Themba's scrawl.

Howzit, Mr Rory, I am fine to thank the Gods.

It was the same start to the note he'd stuffed into my hands that fateful day. The thought of Themba dancing and running behind the car warmed my heart.

The home is quiet without you.

I am sure a tokoloshe has taken your place and haunts the house.

Everyone is too busy to see the truth.

I cannot mourn you when I sit by the fire because you are ever with me in my soul, but I miss our talks.

Terrible things are coming, my friend.

The country does not talk.

People are not praying.

That is why they sent you away, to learn to fight.

I hung on his every word. The impending conflict he referred to was on everybody's lips, all over the television, in the newspapers, and folk spoke of it nonstop. A tremor ran through my body as I continued reading Themba's letter.

My son, Sipho, wants justice, as do his comrades, and I can't stop the boy's ideas.

How I wish we could enjoy God's world sitting around a fire worshipping the world and its people.

The spirits are not happy.

But you and me, with God's help, will sit again soon to sort this madness out.

Our ancestors say it must be so.

Themba blended Christianity and tribal culture with such ease, sorrowing with the world in one sentence, bouncing back in the next. I recalled Sipho's icy reception and his hostile suspicion of me. I read the farewell over and over, drawing strength from his words.

Kumele ngihambe khathesi — I must go now.

Size sibonane njalo — Until we meet again.

Lihambe kuhle jaha — Go well, son.

Themba.

The remarks reminded me of my buddy, Bow.

Will Themba help me? He's from thereabouts, but that would mean putting him in danger. They wouldn't put up with a black man and a young white boy being friends. Let alone helping one escape.

I chose not to involve my ally, careful to hide his letter from prying eyes.

Life was hard enough without me adding to Themba's problems.

The metal simbi hitting the plough disc announced the end of the rest period. To ease the dreary homework session, I spent the time writing about the day in a textbook, a pastime that became not just a habit but a need. After which we returned to the dormitory, to change for the afternoon activities.

Alan changed into white shorts and orange running vest. 'What's the aim of cross-country?' he asked, scrunching up his face.

'Don't worry,' Jannie showed his abs. 'It gets easier the fitter you get.'

'Doubt it. Ask Rory. I was hopeless at junior school,' Alan replied.

I shrugged, not wishing to get involved.

'Badenhurst, your parcel is here.' A second-year boy held up a package as he stopped at the entrance to the dorm. He wore the bottle-green blazer over khakis complete with a green and red striped tie. It was the second-year's task to collect mail from the post-office in the village after lunch.

Jannie opened the package on the bed. 'Check,' he said. 'It's from my uncle in South Africa.' He poured the contents out for everyone to see. A horde of goodies in vibrant wrappings beckoned. Chocolate bars, bubble-gum, and toffees. Our mouths drooled. Some recognised the tuck from holidays to South Africa; others recalled them in glossy magazines that were no longer available in Rhodesia. World sanctions isolating us from the outside world. Petrol was short, and new cars were impossible to buy. Local business rose to the challenge, but the treats made here didn't taste the same.

No shortage of money for army trucks rumbling along our streets or weapons, though?

Jannie opened a packet of sweets. 'Here guys have one.'
A flood of appreciation erupted, followed by the clamouring
of outstretched hands. Jannie dispensed the sweets, vigilant
not to succumb to the determined sleight-of-hand efforts. Such
bounty elevated Jannie within the collective, albeit while they
lasted. I popped a gum into my mouth. A burst of spearmint
brought tears to my eyes.

'Wow, that's much better than the local stuff, hey?' I slurped,
taking the sweet from my cheek and showing Alan.

'Too bloody right,' Alan said, grinning. 'At least I won't get
a dry mouth running today. Are you wearing shoes?'

'Nah, they hurt and are slippery anyway,' I said as I kicked
my white canvas *tekkies* under the bed.

'Chips guys, Stenk's waiting for us on the lawn,' Vinny
hailed from the doorway. We hurried outside, pulling on our
attire.

'Hello, boys. I see you are in fine fettle.' Stenk's eyes glinted
with sarcasm, complemented by his sing-song accent.

'But sir,' Alan said. 'What's the point of running through
the bush when we have a track and fields?'

'An excellent question, young man.' Stenk raised an
index finger and scrutinised our faces. 'Simple. It promotes
endurance and strength. Useful in every sport.' Vacant looks
brought a smile to Stenk's face. 'Put it this way, lads. The ones
who excel will do athletics. While those bringing up the rear
will belong to me. That's right, boyos. You'll be mine to shape
into endearing rugby players.' He glanced at his watch. 'We
digress, gentlemen. We'll start with warm-ups and then be on
our way.' Stenk wore an Adidas crimson sweater with three
feathers and the initials WRU.

Did Stenk play for rugby for Wales, or is he just an avid
supporter?

I changed my focus to Richard's group, all of whom strutted
around in their branded footwear.

'What the fuck? Check out the *laanies,*' Jannie shouted.
'What a bunch of pretty boys.' The rest of us bayed and taunted
the elitist group, who came back with bravado and feigned
aggression, like small dogs behind a large fence, threatening
harm to passers-by.

'All right, that's enough, keep your energy for the run

boyos and follow me.' Stenk broke into an unconvincing jog and headed for the school's perimeter, pursued by a waddle of orange and white ducklings.

The heavens opened, soaking us before we reached the edge of the school grounds. A trail of discarded vests lay scattered across the playing fields. I was in my element, running barefoot through the bush, with the rain on my back. Not the quickest or the slowest. Alan and Vinny dropped behind. The ambitious boys, Richard and Jannie, forced the pace. I battled with the competitiveness, just for the sake of it. I lifted my face skyward, like *Chariots of Fire,* opening my mouth to drink the cool-fresh rain. The mud squelched between my toes and splattered on the backs of my legs; water streamed over my body. Branches stung and tugged at my limbs, and thorns tore at the soles of my feet as I negotiated the uneven ground.

This is what Themba meant by enjoying nature and life. The two are one.

The trail took us past *kraals,* inhabited by the school's employees and their families. A huddle of kids sitting beneath a thatched mud hut watched us jog by. Their large doleful-brown eyes intrigued by our behaviour. Bedraggled goats stood in the downpour, continuing their attack on the diminished ground cover. A skinny mongrel loped after the joggers. The smallest child shivered, dressed only in a ragged T-shirt as twin lines of snot hung from his nose. I waved, unsure what else to do. The children lit up and cheered. The elder ones ran behind and imitated my gait to rapturous applause. I weaved and bobbed my way in and out of the huts. Not wishing to fall too far behind, I noticed a squad of soldiers searching through the undergrowth. I bid them farewell and caught up with the slower runners, finishing in the middle of the pack. Again, adhering to Themba and my tactic not to draw attention to myself.

Meanwhile, an army truck filled with security fencing edged its way through the terrain to erect a safe zone for these impoverished families.

'Safe for who?' I wondered.

Chapter Seven

I finished my homework halfway through Friday evening's prep session, wrote a couple of pages into my journal, then turned my attention to the approaching half-term break.

Seems another lifetime. Will anyone remember who I am? What of Bow? Themba and his family, at least, will welcome me home. If others don't, then too bad for them.

The break was an age away. I doodled, too worked up even to play pencil cricket. Instead, I perused the room. The malign buzzing of the lights and the occasional subdued cough betrayed the dull atmosphere.

'*Wilde*, telephone.' Mr Winker yelled through the door. I leapt to my feet.

'Hurry, boy, phone calls cost money.' He tapped me on the temple.

'Yes, sir.' I excused myself from the prefect on duty and left for the housemaster's study.

'Come in, Wilde. The phone is over there,' said the housemaster as he pointed to a large black instrument with a round dial. The earpiece rested on the table next to it.

'Thank you, sir.' I lifted the weighty handset.

Mr Winker sat behind an oak desk bedecked with two empty wire baskets, *IN* and *OUT*. A fountain pen lay beside a bottle of black Parker Quink. The dim yellow light of a writer's lamp illuminated his face.

Count Dracula himself.

I turned my back, cradling the earpiece in the crook of my neck. The stink of past callers lingered. 'Hello?'

'Hello, my dear. It's Mum here,' her familiar voice crackled.

'Hi, Mum,' I said in a monotone, not wishing to show emotion in front of my housemaster.

'What's happening?' she asked. 'You sound distant. Is someone with you?'

'It's nice to hear from you too, Mum.'

'Can't a mother and son have a private conversation? What's wrong with those people? 'Mum asked.

'Never mind, Mum, it doesn't matter.' I glanced over my shoulder. Mr Winker sat in his chair with his bamboo cane in his hand, feigning interest in an ageing world map on the wall.

'I have to go,' I said.

'What do you mean, go? We've just started. Ignore whoever is there. It'll be okay. There'll be hell to pay if not. You'll see.'

I never experienced such outrage from my mother. 'Don't stress, Mum. How's everybody?' We discussed the long weekend, the bus trip, and the car giving problems.

More like father is too busy, or they don't have enough petrol coupons.

'That's fine, I don't mind. Most will be on the coach. I miss you too. Say hi to everyone. Yes, I'll see you soon. Don't worry, okay bye.' I replaced the earpiece.

'Splendid news from home, I trust, boy?'

'Yes, sir. Thank you, sir.' I managed a feeble grin and made a beeline for the door.

'Rorke Wilde?'

I stopped in my tracks. 'Yes, sir.'

'No need to return to prep.'

'Thank you, good night, sir.' I pranced up the veranda, heading for the games room to make a start.

I selected an album from the record cabinet and placed it on the turntable. An eerie noise filled the den before the vocals began. I listened to the deep lyrics but couldn't find the band on the black album cover with a rainbow shining through a prism. Except for the words — *Dark Side of The Moon*.

On completing my skivvy duties, I re-joined the boys preparing for the night.

'Hi, who was on the call? Your Mum?' Alan asked the minute I walked in.

'Yup. We spoke about half-term.'

'It's always great to hear from the family, hey?'

'Who's travelling by bus?' I asked.

'Everyone. The petrol shortage is kicking in.'

'I guess so.'

Alan moved closer. 'Jannie's staying here for the break.'

'What do you mean?'

72

'He's not going home. So, he must spend the weekend here.'

I snuck a glance across at Jannie, who was tucking in his mosquito net. 'How come?'

'His folks are emigrating to South Africa and have their hands full. Poor bastard.' Alan shook his head.

'What did he say?' I asked.

'He keeps it bottled in.'

'Who doesn't in this place?'

'That's not what we need, Rory. You're getting pissed off within spitting distance of the long weekend,' Alan said, tapping my shoulder.

I ignored him.

'Hey, what's this about you not going home?' I asked Jannie from across the room.

'*Ja*, my folks are moving south, so there's nowhere to go. Just bad timing.'

'I can ask if you could come to my place.'

'You would do that for me?'

'Sure, why not? You can't stay here alone.' I stood up, uncomfortable with the closeness.

'Hey, *boetie*. I appreciate the offer, but a few of the guys are staying. So, it won't be so bad. It's only four days, anyway.'

'Okay, but the offer's there if you change your mind.'

'Cheers, Rory, you're an excellent mate. *Jy is my boet.*' Jannie rolled the word on the end of his tongue.

I accepted the honouree term of brother from my Afrikaner friend. 'Sweet, I'll see you in the morning.'

'Sweet, later, man.'

Alan pressed his face up against the net. 'So, how did it go? Is he all good?'

'Yeah, he's fine.'

Alan waited.

'But you know what pisses me off?'

'What now?' Alan showed the whites of his eyes.

'I bet those seniors didn't start out mean. This place bloody teaches them to behave that way. It's worse than *Lord of the Flies* around here.'

'You might be right,' Alan said. 'But what can we do not to be like those boys on that island?'

I huffed and climbed under the sheet. Humidity was high,

rain on its way. 'We have two options.'

Alan rested on his elbow. 'And what are they?'

'Fight or flight.'

Happer interrupted our conversation by switching off the lights.

'Alan?'

'Yes.'

'Are you with me?'

'As always, my friend. As always.'

The next day, before disappearing into the bush, we attended church, followed by the weekly house inspection. The first years lingered beneath the fig tree at the chapel entrance. I stuck my fingers between my throat and collar stretching my neck. My tie was constricting, and my oversized blazer added to the discomfort. Richard was across the road with his friends. 'Check out the over-dressed baboons,' he shouted just before he wolf-whistled.

'Ignore the *laanies*. They're just trying to get us back,' Jannie said.

'You're right. Bloody la-di-da fashion freaks,' Vinny replied and offered them a finger.

'Richard has a cheek. We were good enough in the beginning. Now look,' Alan said, pointing at the group.

'Don't even worry, he's not worth it,' I answered.

'It's not right.' Alan came back at me.

'They might have a point, though.' I suggested.

'What the hell are you on about?' Alan asked, unable to believe his ears.

'Vinny and Jannie, come and stand here alongside Alan,' I said and lined them up shoulder to shoulder. 'Now look at yourselves, boys. Not a pretty sight.' Confusion turned to grins, then to guffaws of hilarity.

'Shabby, my good man, shabby,' Alan said a high-class accent.

'You can say that again. Check this out,' I said as I showed the arms of my blazer covering my hands and how the blazer hung like a skirt because it was so long.

'That's nothing. Look here,' Jannie, whose jacket strained at the seams like an overfilled sausage, said.

Vinny's face, for the second time that morning, turned a host of red as he tried to button his collar and adjust his tie. 'Bugger this. No cruelty for beauty,' he said, and another bout of jovial backslapping followed his remark.

I marvelled at the class and grace with which the *laanies* donned their uniform of bottle-green blazers, white long-sleeved shirts, green and red striped ties, grey trousers, and black shoes. We wore best dress on visits to the city, to church, or a public event.

The chapel bells beckoned us. Self-conscious, I joined in the shuffle towards the doors. Once inside, the boys assembled in their respective houses, the more senior at the back. They reserved the front benches for staff, civilians, and the choir. The seniors did not consider the choral society macho enough, and those who enlisted suffered the consequences. I slid into the pew and pulled my hymnal from my breast pocket. 'Got yours?' I waved the green hardback at Alan.

'Yup, not going to leave that behind. If the prefects find you without one, it's an imposition.'

I contemplated the imposition scheme administered by the prefect body for breaking of the rules or a poor attitude. Alan knocked my knee with his own and pressed home the issue. 'To make matters worse, it's a school imposition,' he said.

I nodded, not wanting to attract attention. A school imposition meant reporting to the dreaded prefect's common room for an hour of gardening. I preferred the three-strike rule where the offender incurred two strokes of the cane and wiped the slate clean.

The congregation rose when the priest appeared at the altar. 'Let us pray,' he said. As everyone took their seats and bowed, an apologetic cough disrupted the expectant hush. Unable to keep my eyes shut, I peeped over the top of the pew. Several boys rested their heads on their hands against the bench in front of them. Few listened to the reverend, who droned on and on, akin to his infamous maths classes. 'Amen,' he said as he peered over half-rim glasses. His face had a strange pallor furrowed by years of chain-smoking. The audience echoed with a touch too much zeal. 'Please stand as we sing hymn number three hundred and twenty,' he said in his notorious drone.

I found the page and waited for the organ to introduce the

first line. The school belted it out in a fine baritone. *'There is a green hill far away outside a city wall...'* The enthusiasm belied the mindset of the boarders who treated the hymns as a mere sing-along. Yet the power of their voices raised gooseflesh on my forearms.

'Please be seated.' The reverend signalled with both hands before he cleared the phlegm from his throat and launched into a sermon from his pulpit. He lost his younger audience after the first couple of sentences and the rest a few moments later. Boys fidgeted and kicked one another under the pews, flicking whoever's ear in front of them. Anything to pass the time. Alan stifled a sneeze that emitted a peculiar noise and set the boys off in fits of suppressed giggles. Vinny gagged as he tried to conceal his amusement, and tears streamed down his face. Jannie doodled on the inside of his hymnal, adding to the full page of sporting sketches. Sensing someone was watching him, he raised his eyebrows and mouthed, 'Boring.' I gave a fleeting smile and turned to the preacher in phoney concentration, contemplating all before me. The setting was perfect. Sun shone through the stained glass and large candles burnt at the altar among the finery of the multidenominational church. History adorned the walls, depicting world wars via tattered flags and brass heads. Stunning cut flowers filled every crevice, and the pews were full. Yet something was missing. It didn't add up.

I don't go to church much. But this couldn't be right. Prayers and services on every occasion, but all words and no action. The same for the present war and sanctions.

After the final Amen, we waited for the teachers and civilians to leave before erupting with *joie de vivre*. The impending half-term break added to the sense of freedom.

We cut and ran back to the dormitory to make sure our areas were spic and span, not wanting to risk impositions or spoil our Sunday exeat. I straightened my counterpane for the umpteenth time, making sure I ironed out every wrinkle. I rechecked my foot and washroom lockers — clothes to toothbrush all lined up military style.

'How's my tie?' Alan asked.

'Fine, how's mine?'

'Cool.' I turned Alan around and brushed the fluff from his

back.

Just then, Happer slunk into the dormitory for a final check-up before shushing us. 'Okay, gents, Mr Winker is on his way. To your stations.'

We completed the last touches, then clamoured to the side of our beds and stood to attention. The head prefect, Hart, accompanied Mr Winker, who was wearing a tie. Happer fell in behind as they scrutinised each boy. I controlled my breathing; my stomach churning with a rivulet of sweat running down my spine. During the inspection, Mr Winker discovered a line of ants leading to a packet of mouldy cookies in the shoe closet. When no one owned up, he punished the entire dormitory by putting an end to our bush exeat.

'Whose food, was it?' I asked.

'Don't know, but I'll *klap* the bastard around the ear if I find out.' Jannie threatened.

'Wasn't one of us, that's for sure,' Alan said, shaking his head.

'No, *boet*, it's one of those *laanies,* I'm sure. They're the ones with the goodies.' Jannie added.

I raised an eyebrow. 'We don't want to start a witch hunt.' I suggested, then continued. 'It'll come out in the wash.'

'Our punishment is to work the gardens. But not to worry. By the time I'm finished with those who didn't own up, they'll wish they did the gardening,' Jannie added.

Alan and Vinny raked the gravel driveways while me and Jannie weeded. I squatted on the lush turf of the beds surrounding Gaul House and began removing weeds while the prefects gave the rest of the miscreants their chores.

The sun bore down on us as we worked, dressed only in shorts. We toiled in silence under the relentless heat, taking the occasional tepid swig from an outside tap. A prefect watched our every movement from the shade of the veranda. I wiped the sweat from my forehead, blinking from the sting of the salt. 'How are you doing?' I asked Jannie.

'*Ja, nee,* I'm all right. How much longer do you reckon?'

'Good question. Won't be soon, though.' We fell silent again and continued gardening despite blisters and painful fingers.

The thud of steel on earth, the smell of stale sweat, and

pungent wood smoke jolted my senses. I looked up at a man stripped to his waist, who was wielding a shovel. I was sure I recognised him from the kitchens. He struck another blow, humming to an inside rhythm. His ebony back glistened.

'Wilde, what the fuck are you staring at? Get to work,' Minnaar, the prefect in charge, yelled from the coolness of the red-polished stairs, his mean, arrogant jaw jutting out.

'Sorry.'

I never hated as I did today.

An exhausting emotion that gnawed at me took a deeper hold.

'Hello, my friend.'

Taken aback, I pretended not to hear.

'Come closer, *Ubhuti wami.*' The man chose the Zulu word for a brother. 'I have news for you.'

'What do you want? I'll report you if you keep bothering me,' I said.

'I doubt you will, *umfana,* Themba knows his man.'

I held my breath. The man had yellow in his eyes. 'How do you know Themba?' I asked with scorn that he dared use my sage's name.

'That is not important. What is crucial is you trust me.' His perfect yet stained teeth revealed the incessant smoking of dagga, the effects of Africa's marijuana etched upon his face.

'You're the one who gave me an orange in the dining hall, aren't you?'

'That was me. I have been trying to get hold of you.'

'Why are you working in the gardens?' I asked.

'The same reason you are, punishment is a means of cheap labour. They pacify their shame that we have only ourselves to blame.'

'Who do you mean by they?'

'The scourge of Africa,' he spat as his eyes flickered.

'You're English is good.'

'Not all of us are ignorant.' A flash of annoyance died the moment it arose. 'No one must see us talking, I will contact you again soon.'

'But what do you want?'

'Nothing, *Ubhuti wami.* They have instructed me to watch over you, that is all.'

'Do I need looking after?'

The man grinned and nodded. 'Themba is right, you have spirit. My name is Ticky. *Lihambe kuhle.*' Ticky threw his tools onto his shoulder and crossed to the other side of the lawn, where he resumed trimming the edges.

I checked if anyone had noticed our exchange. Jannie was returning from a visit to the ablution blocks, and Minnaar was busy bawling at the others. Although they were in the vicinity, I was sure they had heard nothing.

Was he a sympathiser or a terrorist? Why was Themba asking him to look after me? Am I in danger? The questions danced through my mind. Why did someone call themselves Ticky, a silver two-and-a-half cent piece that buys a bottle of cola?

I tried not to dwell on it and chatted to Jannie instead.

With our impots complete and after a late lunch, we disappeared into the bush without delay.

'I'm glad that's over,' Alan said and blew out his cheeks.

'Yeah, but the day has gone. We only have hours left,' Vinny added as he wiped away sweat.

'Better than nothing,' Alan said.

'I suppose so. Guess we can have a swim and chill out.' Vinny lifted himself out of the sulks.

The gang, minus Richard, found its favourite spot beneath the overhanging tree and cooled off in the refreshing water, careful not to stay long in case we suffered another attack by the leeches. Shattered from our morning labours, we relaxed. Alan opened a dog-eared copy of *When the Lion Feeds* by Wilbur Smith; Vinny lay on his back and covered his face with a hat while Jannie sat on the bank throwing stones into the dam. Still perturbed by the morning's incident, I joined Jannie.

'You look worried,' he said.

'Not at all.' We sat in silence, listening to the water lap at the banks.

'What's happening to this country?' I asked him.

'Hey, but that's a serious question for a Sunday afternoon, my friend.'

'Just wondering. It's in the papers every day when I tidy the games room.'

Jannie rubbed the bristles of his crew cut with both hands, then turned to me, his newfound brother. 'I'm not sure. The problems are those in South Africa. The locals want majority rule. One man, one vote. The colonials don't accept they are ready,' he said.

I nodded, trying to fathom out the politics. 'Is that their right to decide?'

'Whose?'

'Both.'

Jannie examined an insect in his hand. 'My father says we must return to save South Africa from the communists, who are using the locals as pawns. He says our ancestors defeated the British and the Zulus before and if necessary, we must do it again...' He stared into the water. 'But I don't want to leave. This is my home,' he added.

'Have you told your father?'

'I did. He said this country is all but finished and that South Africa is our last chance. Whatever that means.'

We fell into a contemplative silence before Jannie broke the interlude. 'Let's take a swim before heading back to school, shall we?'

'You're on, follow me.' I gave a sly grin, and slipped into the lake, and swam to the tree under which the other two rested. I held a finger to my lips. Jannie followed me up the tree and across a branch that extended over the dam. We launched ourselves into the air and bombed the water. 'Geronimo,' I shouted as I drenched Vinny and Alan. The thrill of the upcoming long weekend had lifted our spirits.

At last, the day arrived for us to leave for half-term. Public municipal buses puffed and wheezed into the grounds and queued outside the school hall. The tall fir trees waved their farewells in the light breeze. Scholars in best-dress milled about, waiting for orders.

The head boy strode through the expectant throng and bounded up the polished steps, followed by an entourage of studious prefects. 'Quiet,' he said as he pushed his fringe from his face. 'Listen, divide yourselves into your houses. A prefect will inform you which bus to take.' He whispered a few words to his henchman and disappeared, clutching sheets of paper.

'Gaul is over here,' Alan said to me as he slung his sports bag over his shoulder and shuffled towards familiar faces.

'I wish they'd get a move on. We could be on our way,' Vinny said as he sat astride his holdall.

'It's the usual story of hurry and wait,' Jannie replied.

I joined the others on the tarmac with my heart beating against my chest in a cocktail of excitement, dread, and apprehension. The sun mutated from a soft ginger dawn glow to an inferno of yellows. I was unwilling to risk taking a drink in case I got caught short on the ten-hour trek. 'It'll be another killer,' I called to Alan.

'Don't tell me. We must try to get a window seat. Here, have one of these.' Alan slipped me a piece of gum. 'Don't even ask,' he said as he held up his hand. 'They put me on a different bus.'

'Okay, I'll check you in Bulawayo.'

'Sure. Keep me a seat on the bus if you get there first.'

I gave him a thumbs-up.

'Leave your bags outside the bus, the driver will load them,' a prefect said, ticking off names as we embarked. The juniors waited for the seniors before climbing in themselves. The heat inside was claustrophobic. I picked my way past the senior boys. The only places left were aisle seats at the rear. I weighed up which one to choose. 'Excuse me, Christo, may I sit here?' I asked.

The hefty boy looked up from his book and nodded as he wiped the sweat that oozed from every pore and rivulets ran down his smooth, flushed cheeks.

'Thank you.' I eased onto the edge of the bench.

The bus burst into life, spewing clouds of exhaust fumes — the smell of diesel filled my sinuses. Relief flooded the coach as it shuddered, then jarred into action and joined the armed convoy of cars travelling en masse, protected by soldiers from ambush on their journey to the city.

Christo remained preoccupied with his paperback *My Family and Other Animals* by Gerald Durrell, and I heard the surreptitious rustle of sweet wrappers and covert movement of his mouth. I eased further onto the bench, between the rips in the upholstery where foam padding exuded. The floor had remnants of earlier excursions, and it tainted the windows with months of grime. Etchings of past travellers carved into the back of the seats depicted dubious humour.

I observed the world pass by through the grubby window. The occasional ox cart pulled over to see the procession and recoiled from the resultant dust squall. I relished the wind blowing in through the window, every kidney-numbing shudder of the coach taking me closer to home.

The drone of forty boys cooped up soothed me into a daze. The organic reek of cattle, the earthen aroma of the soil, and the sickly-sweet perfume of Christo next to me coaxed imagery in my mind's eye. Every now and again, a Bell helicopter buzzed overhead. On occasions they came so low, I made out the sunglasses on the machine gunner hanging from the door.

My anticipation grew as the fleet approached the outskirts of Bulawayo where the single lane tarred road widened, and pavements replaced eroded culverts. For many, we were home, while the rest were ready to starburst throughout the country.

The journey transformed seniors with each kilometre, until on arrival, they greeted their parents with gusto and treated the juniors with more respect, turning their attention instead to heckling kids from other schools and closing rank to show a united front. Despite the last two months, there was a sense of patriotism and camaraderie with these boys who had done nothing but insult and abuse us. Disquieted at the notion, and with my ears ringing from the cacophony, I disembarked and sought my luggage.

I searched for Alan in the deluge of coloured school uniforms at the vacant plot that doubled as a bus depot. Coaches roared in, dumped their cargo, and left again. Others idled, waiting to whisk their payload homeward. Organisers held aloft large destination boards in valiant attempts to attract children to the right coaches. Dust swirled among the horde of unresponsive participators, casting a red hue from the super trouper sun.

I wiped my mouth on my collar, which left a coral-lipstick stain before I dug the ochre grit from the corners of my squinting eyes. Unable to detect anyone, mild panic set in.

What if I get left behind or board the wrong bus?

'Hey Wilde, over here,' a voice from deep within the red

fog called out.

I twisted round to find a boy I recognised from junior school. 'Hey, Kev, howzit'

'Not bad, and you?'

'Can't complain, I guess.'

'Are you going to Wankie?' the boy asked.

'Yup, and you?'

'Nah, we've moved to Mazoe, so I'm taking the Salisbury bus. The Wankie buses are over here.' The lad pointed past me.

'Thanks, man, appreciate it. Check you around.' I saluted and made off.

A sense of loneliness filled my chest as I searched from bus to bus. My heart jumped every time I imagined I saw someone familiar. I slowed to a dawdle and kicked at a stone when a hand grasped the nape of my neck, causing me to freeze. Judging by its size and the presence behind me, it wasn't any of my friends.

Hope he doesn't want me to run to a cafe and buy a soda or something. I might miss the bus. Or what if he wants me to carry his baggage, or worse still, find cigarettes?

I remained rooted to the ground, waiting for the owner of the hand to make a move. It felt soft. A bouquet of perfume found its way through the stench.

I know that smell.

Behind me was my mother. 'Mum, what the hell are you doing here?'

'Language, Rorke. I hope that's not what they've been teaching you.' Her sharp tone lasted a millisecond.

I couldn't understand my eyes or ears; though my heartbeat slowed down with relief as I fought back tears and resisted crumbling. 'That's great, Mum,' I said, feigning disinterest, embarrassed by the attention.

'*That's great?* Is that all you've got to say? Come here and hug your mother.' She squeezed me.

'Mum, not here, the guys will tease me.'

'Oh, all right, macho man.' She lifted my bag. 'Follow me.'

The lightness in my step returned once more.

'Hey, Alan. Over here.'

'Hey Rory, where've you been? I've been looking for you.

Thought the seniors had thrown you overboard.'

'Nah, I'm fine. I'm more than fine, guess what?'

'I don't know. What?' Alan shrugged.

'We'll have the best trip home ever, check here,' I said as I lifted a shopping bag with Coke, Fanta, crisps, and sweets inside.

'Bloody hell, where did you get that?' Alan pushed me up against the side of a bus, shielding both me and my bounty.

'What're you doing, china? Do you think I stole them or something?'

Alan stood back and brushed at my blazer. 'Did you?' he considered his words for a moment then said, 'Sorry, man. Not sure what came over me.'

I put an arm around his shoulder. 'Follow me, dipstick, and I shall reveal all.'

'Wow. Hi, Mrs Wilde,' Alan said.

'Hello Alan, nice to see you again. Would you care to join Rorke and me at the front of the bus?'

'Yeah, sure thing.' Alan punched my shoulder. 'Can you believe it?' He spun on his heels to fetch his luggage.

We changed our army escort on the outskirts of the city and hurtled through the barren countryside. I dozed despite the clamour of the schoolboys catching up on the months spent in their respective schools. Boarding school receded with each kilometre. I recalled the early days at Plumtree School, my first contact with the seniors, and how I learnt to melt into the collective. Somehow, it didn't seem so bad now. My mind glossed over the hardships. My memory steered me to the good times we shared and to the close calls we all laughed over.

Should I be planning to run away? What if, I or worse still, Alan got hurt?

The comforting hand of my mother lay on my shoulder. The reassuring smell of her perfume soothed any lingering insecurities. Hour upon hour passed, with the buses stopping once at the Halfway Hotel. There, we refreshed ourselves in the reservoir cum swimming pool, stretched our legs, used the restrooms, and replenished supplies. All accompanied by the never-ending drone of military machinery.

The sun slid to the familiar rugged horizon of *kopjes* and ghoulish, silhouetted baobab trees. My pulse raced at the thought of seeing my chameleon companion again.

I'll leave at dawn tomorrow in search of Bow.

Minutes passed like hours.

Will my father and my sister be waiting for the bus? What about Themba and his family?

Anxiety replaced excitement.

Will it be as I left it?

'Wake up dopey, we're almost there,' Alan said as he dug me in the side. I detected the strain on my best-friend's face — puffy red eyes, the slight downturn of his mouth and the gaunt cheeks of fatigue.

'What are you looking at?' he asked.

'Nothing, just thinking about school. But stuff it, let's enjoy the weekend.'

'Too right.' Alan broke into a smile, which I hadn't seen in a while. 'Will Jannie be, okay?'

'I hope so, poor bugger. I'll call him from home tonight.'

Welcome to Wankie, a concrete sign dressed up with the Lions, Rotary, and Round Table charity insignias, greeted us. Chaos ensued as the occupants burst into raucous joy, threw empty containers, and began good-humoured wrestling.

'Okay, settle. Pick up the rubbish and put it into these black packets,' Mum said, as she held up a roll of dustbin bags.

The bus negotiated the last stop and turned into the junior school grounds and shuddered to a halt. Applause erupted, followed by a risqué rendition of *For He's a Jolly Good Fellow,* for the driver. Goosebumps covered me from head to foot. Dozens of cars hooted, and countless parents waved, cheering for the return of their sons.

'Check you later, china. Thanks, Mrs Wilde,' Alan said as he pushed the back of my head and opened the door to an avalanche of kids disembarking.

Mum held a hand to my chest. 'Sit awhile. Wait for the crowd to thin out.'

I peered out of the window and watched families reunite while I kept a lookout for my father and Cara. 'There they are,' I called out at last.

'Dear, did you think they'd miss your homecoming?' She clicked her tongue. I leapt off the coach and charged into my father's arms. We hugged and laughed until my father stiffened and pulled back.

'Evening, Gerald, Mavis,' my dad said to a couple standing close by.

'Hello, inspector, going to be a lovely evening,' Gerald replied.

'Isn't it just?'

It was important for my father to keep up appearances. Public displays of sentiment were taboo, not that he invited private ones.

'Hi, Rory.' Cara grabbed me around the waist and squeezed. 'You know I've been counting the days on a calendar?'

'Cool, I told you I'd be home soon.'

'It wasn't soon. It was forever.' Tears filled her eyes.

'Don't worry, I'm home now.'

'I know, but you'll be leaving again shortly.' An awkward silence fell until Mum joined us. 'Right guys, are we ready to go? Dad, have you got Rory's bag?'

'No, I thought you were getting it.'

She glared at him before he dodged off in search of the case. 'Jump in, your father won't be too long,' she mumbled something about him being married to the police force and how he forgot nothing in that regard. The boot slammed and rocked the car.

'Okay, got it, let's go home,' Dad said as he jumped behind the wheel and gave a cheerful smile. 'Others are looking forward to seeing you. We mustn't keep them waiting.' He winked at me in the rear-view mirror.

I chuckled in anticipation.

I can get through this.

Chapter Eight

The streetlights blazed. Twilight succumbed to the darkness and the night settled. It was great to be home.

'Themba has cooked you a homecoming supper, so I trust you're hungry,' Mum said from the front seat.

'I'm starving Mum.'

'We've planned little for the weekend, my boy. Thought you might want to unwind,' my father added.

'Sounds perfect, Dad.'

Cara sat in the back next to me, clinging to her doll and watching my every move.

'What's wrong?' I asked her.

'Nothing,' she said as she hugged her baby tighter and yawned. 'Will you play with me tomorrow?'

'Depends.'

'My friend at school said that you won't play with me now that you are at big school.' She looked at me with large brown eyes, her blonde shoulder-length hair brushed and banded with a *Sesame Street* ribbon for the occasion.

'We'll think of something, don't worry,' I said.

She was right. I didn't want to play with my sister anymore.

Familiar landmarks flashed by, yet they were distant to me now.

Another lifetime? I closed my eyes. I'm just tired.

When the car turned into the entrance Themba and family waved from the bottom of the backyard, I stuck my head out and returned their welcome for all it was worth.

'Can I say hi?' I asked.

Dad couldn't refuse, even though he didn't approve of me mixing with the servants.

'If you must, my boy, but be quick. I'm famished. Tell Themba we'll eat as soon as he's ready.'

'Such a racist,' Mum said under her sigh.

'Don't be so goddamn naïve. Everyone harbours racial

sentiments,' Dad replied as he climbed out of the car.

The softness of the bed and crispness of home linen drew an inner fulfilment. A distant cockerel declared the dawn. I peeped from under my pillow at the first rays of light before I leapt out of bed and rummaged for clothes while I brushed my teeth.

I tiptoed to the kitchen and filled a water bottle, opened the fridge, and helped myself to a piece of leftover-grilled steak. A waft of air chilled me as I sat on the step, pulling on my *veldskoen.* 'I hope you're there, Bow,' I said aloud. 'I'm coming for you.' Just then, a hiss from the end of the garden attracted my attention. I waved to Themba, who motioned me over.

'Howzit *jaha,* it's good to see you again. My head tells me your arrival is nothing but a dream.' He put an arm around me. 'Now I can see it is true. Come, let us drink sweet tea.' We sat beside the embers of last evening's fire, where Themba poured two large enamel mugs of scalding brew from a black three-legged pot and added lashings of brown sugar.

'The sun is strong once more and the sombre clouds have taken refuge,' he declared as he toasted my return. We sat savouring the syrupy beverage while I shared my adventures at school. Themba listened, peering at me over the brim of his cup.

'Themba?' I said, eager to continue sitting and chatting but torn to go in search of Bow.

'*Manje, manje, insizwa.* Let us enjoy this gift of time and share a moment, young man. It shall last but a minute.' White teeth filled his face as his eyes danced.

Not sure what he meant, I nodded as we marvelled at the sunrise in silence.

'Come now.' Themba tossed the dregs of his mug into the fire and slapped his legs. 'We both have things to do. You must revisit your kingdom and I must begin work.' He clapped his hands and stood. '*Size sibonane njalo,*' he said, promising to meet on the morrow.

'Thanks for the tea. Goodbye, Precious,' I said to Themba's wife, who was washing dishes in the outside concrete tub. She gave a cheerful wave, then berated her husband for keeping me too long. He flashed me a grin and retreated into the dwelling.

Bow was nowhere to be seen, so I strolled on to my thousand-year-old baobab refuge. 'That's strange.' I stroked her smooth-waxed trunk. 'What's going on, my girl? No one's been to visit you, hey?' I detected a sadness. 'Don't worry, I'll be back soon, but first I must find Bow.' I patted her once more, then started down the slope.

My search for my chameleon proved unsuccessful, but I didn't fuss. Sometimes it took days to find Bow. A tad crestfallen and feeling cheated by the morning, I went home for lunch. Cara was waiting on the back steps with a mop of shaggy hair, barefoot and still embracing her doll. 'Hi Rory, are you ready to play now?'

'Depends on what it is.'

'It's up to you. We can play inside or out here in the backyard.'

'Okay, get your things.'

Cara returned with a large kaross, arranged her dolls on it, and laid out the tea set.

I humoured her while I made a catapult from a well-chosen Y-shaped stick. Using a razor blade, I sliced an inner tyre tube into half-inch strips and bound these to the stalk. I attached the two loose ends to a square piece of leather cut from the tongue of an old shoe. I assessed the slingshot by holding the stick in one hand and pulling the skin section with the other across my chest.

'Wow, that looks great. Don't you dare shoot birds with that,' Cara said.

'Nah, just target practice. Watch this.' I placed a round pebble into the leather pouch and aimed. The stone whistled through the air and smashed into the branches of a nearby tree. 'Not too shabby, hey?'

'It's okay.' Cara went back to her toys.

I enjoyed the time spent with my sister in the garden that afternoon. She wanted to be near her brother, plying me with orange squash and cookies. It didn't matter to her I wasn't taking an active role in her make-believe world. It was enough that I was nearby.

'How's boarding school?' Cara asked out of nowhere.

'It's okay,' I replied as I toyed with my new weapon.

'No, Rory. How is it really?'

'Why are you so worried, anyway?'

'Just am. I hear the stories at school. You've changed since you've been away.'

'What do you mean changed?'

'Doesn't matter.' She mumbled and returned to her toys.

I got up and walked around the garden, taking pot-shots.

So, I am not the same. Everything I missed at home is now strange. I'm a visitor in my home.

'Rorke!' Mother yelled from the backdoor.

'Coming, Mum.'

'Your dad and I have a Lions' Club meeting this evening. Do you wish to join us? Cara's staying at her friend's.'

'That's okay, I'll hang out here at home.'

'If that's what you want, dear. I'll ask Themba to cook you something nice for supper.' She vanished into the house.

Great, I'll spend time with Themba and get answers. I didn't care for what has going on of late, least of all the clandestine exploits of everyone, including those of Themba.

The twenty-year-old yellow Renault drove out of the driveway; my parents dressed to the nines and on their way to the charity meeting. Cara waved from the back window. 'See you soon,' she called out.

Moments later, Themba appeared from the swing fly-door as he removed his white apron. 'Come over when you are ready, Mr Rory. I must go to the cafe for snuff.'

'Okay, I'll have a wash then join you.'

I bathed, enjoying the privacy of an empty house. Then I walked through to my bedroom and lay naked on the cool sheets and read my *Beano* and *Archie* comics.

Dusk turned to night in the minutes it took to stroll to Themba's impoverished home. Outside, a fire licked a metre into the air, illuminating the surroundings with a soft glow. Themba sat on his stump while the rest of the family prepared the meal.

'*Sawubona umsizwa,*' he bid me a good evening. 'Sit, take your place while we wait.'

'Thanks, Themba. Hi, Precious, how are you?'

'Fine, Mr Rory,' she said, avoiding eye contact.

'Come on, woman, hurry. Our guest has arrived,' Themba

said, pretending to scold her.

She responded with a torrent of incoherent words. I joined in the laughter, familiar with their displays of matrimonial humour, yet aware of the undercurrent of paternal dominance.

The menfolk chatted around the fire while Precious and her daughter Beauty prepared *sadza,* boiled cabbage and meat. Curious as to the whereabouts of my rival, I steered the conversation to more important issues. 'Is Sipho not joining us tonight?' I asked.

Themba's chest heaved. 'You are right, it is time we talked.' He stood up and presented his carton of traditional beer to the fire and made a toast. 'Let the *indaba* begin,' he said with Thespian drama.

I grinned at the performance, nodding my approval. 'So where is Sipho? He's not staying away because of me, is he?'

'I wish he were.' Themba looked me in the eye before turning to the glow of embers.

'His bitterness had made him choose a dangerous path.' He wiped away a tear and turned back to me. 'Yes, my friend, we can no longer pretend nothing is happening in this land of ours.' His voice cracked despite attempts at profoundness. I waited in silence for Themba to continue.

'At least let us talk, even if no-one else wishes to. What I am going to say could put me and my family in terrible danger, but I can trust you, *jaha.*'

I nodded.

Themba stretched across and set a hand on my forehead. 'Yes, *ngane zami.*' He used a phrase reserved for one's son. 'We understand conflict is commonplace. Not just here, but everywhere.'

I raised my eyebrows at him.

'The Blackman seeks self-rule; the Whiteman feels he is not ready, and fears being chased from his land. Both are sound arguments.' Themba stopped to make sure he hadn't lost me. 'Do you see the problem?'

I shook my head, not sure if I did.

'It is outside intervention. The communists exploit the continent by pretending to support the locals, which encourages the West to aid the minorities so they might hold on to their own profits. Neither of them cares for Africa or its people.'

91

Themba hung his head, then gave me a long, thoughtful look. 'Do you understand what I am saying, *jaha?*'

'I... I guess so. But we have enough room.'

'That is true, *jaha,* but adults do not see clear like children do.' Themba got up and headed into his house. 'I will show you words from two men who have taken up the fight.' He brought back an ageing scrapbook of newspaper clippings. 'Read these *jaha.* To see what we are facing.'

I took the book and read the first article.

I have fought against white domination, and I have fought against black domination. I have cherished the ideal of a democratic society in which all persons live together in harmony and with equal opportunities. It is an ideal which I hope to live for and to achieve. But if needs be, it is an ideal for which I am prepared to die. **Nelson Mandela's speech delivered from the dock, Rivonia Treason Trial, 20 April 1964, South Africa.**

The hairs on my neck bristled. Themba waved me on to the next clipping with impatience.

In the lives of most nations there comes a time when a stand has to be made for principles, whatever the consequences. This moment has come to Rhodesia ... the decision which we have taken today is a refusal by Rhodesians to sell their birth right. And even if we were to surrender, does anyone believe that Rhodesia would be the last target of the communists in the Afro-Asian bloc. We have struck a blow to preserve justice, civilisation, and Christianity — and in the spirit of this belief we have assumed our sovereign independence. **Ian Smith's Unilateral Declaration of Independence on the eleventh of November 1965.**

Precious interjected by taking the binder from me. 'Come, my Impi warriors, time to eat,' she said in a soft, empathetic manner.

'You are right, my dear, enough for one day.' Themba's mood lightened.

A little shaken, but relieved it was over, I followed in the merriment.

I will keep my questions for another time.

Ignoring the indoctrinated alarm bells that rang in the back of my mind.

After an enjoyable meal, the woman cleared up and prepared the baby while Themba savoured a nightcap and I sipped tea. A shower of sparks spewed towards the low canopy of stars as I broke the silence. 'Has Sipho become a terrorist? A freedom fighter?'

Themba didn't respond at first, but gazed into the darkness.

Not willing to push the issue, I changed tack. 'I met Ticky at school. You asked him to look out for me?'

Themba's eyes focused on my face. 'I will tell you, *jaha*, but you must promise not to judge. What I have to say puts many at risk.'

I swallowed hard, half wishing I had kept my mouth shut. 'I swear.' I kissed two fingers and gestured heavenward.

'Come, let us walk. This is for our ears only. We must learn to trust no one, including family.' Themba took a deep breath. 'Especially the family.'

He threw a rough grey blanket over my shoulders, and we walked into the night. 'These are dangerous times made more difficult by the war between communism and imperialism. If they left us alone to sort out our problems, things would be better.' Themba rested his chin on top of my head.

'I understand, but why the fighting? Why the killing?'

'Because *jaha*, the stakes are high. Men of greed and self-interest have joined the struggle. But we must be strong. Our Gods and ancestors have sent us a leader who will end the madness. The problem is everyone, be they black or white, East, or West, because they think, only they have the answer.' He wavered. 'Mandela talks of hope.' We stood in silence.

'My only son, Sipho, says he knows how to solve the problem. I fear I have lost him to the armed struggle.' Themba wiped his tears. 'To make matters worse, I am in danger of losing you too, *jaha*.'

'No way, Themba, I won't run away to fight.'

'You won't have to. They will come for you when you are ripe.' A collective shiver ran through our bodies.

'It is time to return to our families, Mr Rory. To protect them from such concerns.'

'No problem, I won't say a word. And Ticky?'

'Never mind him. He is there to watch my other son. It is hard to deal with men drunk on power.'

'Thank you, Themba.'

'Ah, there you both are.' Precious fussed over our return. 'You must go back home, Mr Rory, your parents are returning.'

'Okay, thanks for having me.'

'You are always welcome, *umfana wami* — my son,' Themba said.

Precious squinted up at her husband and shook her head. 'Too much beer again, hey *skellum*?' She ushered Themba into the shack and waved goodnight.

Indoors, I took a quick shower, tossed my clothes into the wash basket to conceal the smell of the wood fire and gravy stains and climbed into bed.

Why has my life changed? Is this what being an adult means?

I cared little for politics and worried about being drawn into the turmoil. My thoughts raced around in my head.

How did Precious know my parents were heading home? Had Sipho joined the armed struggle? There is more happening than I realise.

Ten minutes later, headlights from my parent's car lit up the room. I surrendered to a night of restless sleep.

Next morning Mum stuck her head through the doorway and smiled at me as I sorted through my collection of comics. 'Hi Rory, I thought you'd be up by now.'

'I'm just looking for something.' The butterflies returned to my belly. One more night remained of my long weekend before the return trip to boarding school.

'Well, whatever, you get up to make sure you're home before five. We're going to the police club for a barbeque. I'll be out later having my hair done.' She hugged me. 'Don't stay out all day. Be nice if we spent the afternoon together.'

'Okay.' I embraced her.

I wasted over an hour hunting for Bow, then gave up and

headed back. I didn't feel like the bush today. Tears constricted my throat.

Why can't things be different? What have I done to deserve this? I must run away if I don't want to go back. But I'll put this at risk as well.

I meandered off the hill in time to meet the neighbours returning from church on their Sunday best. Their wreck of a car didn't match their self-importance. I waved as they pulled into the driveway next door, where Sid pleaded with his mother, then ran over to me. The echoes of his mother's orders followed. 'Don't get dirty, Sid. You still have Sunday school.' She threw me a disapproving look, stuck her nose in the air and strode off into the house.

'Rory Wilde, what are you doing?' Sid asked.

Not wanting to add to Sid's unease, I kept my opinions to myself, but couldn't stop a smile.

'I know. I know,' he said as he looked down at his ill-fitting tweed coat and brown corduroy slacks that didn't quite reach his scuffed black shoes. 'What can I do? It's not worth the hassle.' He believed his explanation less than I.

'Don't worry, your secret's safe with me. But what the hell's this?' I ruffled my fingers through Sid's hair.

'Don't, man. My old man took ages getting it right,' he said, trying to push his locks back into place.

'But what's in your hair?'

'*Brylcreem.*'

He reminded me of a chic scarecrow. More *Worzel Gummidge* than me.

'How's your half-term been?'

We chatted until Sid's mother swaggered over to us.

'Rory, please pardon us; we have to go to church. Perhaps, next time *you*'ll come with us?' She raised her eyebrows, stressing keywords.

'A slim chance, Mrs Bunsen. Enjoy your praying.'

She stiffened with indignation.

'Come Sidney.' She took hold of her son by his neck and mumbled something under her breath about how the neighbourhood was slipping and there was a growing band of ragamuffins.

I plodded home for lunch, scrutinising the culverts for

whatnots and signs of life. Religion? I just don't get it. It's everywhere, but everyone uses it as a threat. That's why it goes so well with war.

Perfume, hairspray, and aftershave choked the house as the family prepared for the evening barbecue. The antics started hours earlier and built to a crescendo with the approaching deadline.

'I hope you're ready. I don't have time to check that you are presentable,' Mum said to me before turning her attention back to my sister, who was resisting any suggestion to wear a frock.

My father emerged in a billow of steam from the bathroom. It would be minutes before anyone entered the improvised sauna.

I stayed out of everyone's way. They would calm down at the party. Until then, they served bedlam with a generous helping of squabbling.

'Is everyone ready? Rory, let me look at you.' Mum stared in disbelief. 'My goodness, you clean up well. That school is doing you good.' She kissed my forehead. 'Very dapper, my boy.' I wore my best-dress school grey trousers, a collared shirt and polished shoes. I had even pulled on a pair of socks for the celebration.

The family drove to the police station and joined the dozen vehicles outside the officer's canteen. 'What's the occasion, Mum?' I asked. I enjoyed my father's workplace with the fancy law enforcement vehicles and gadgets.

'Two lads are being transferred to the border and we're throwing them a farewell party.'

Already aware of the answer, I just wanted to hear it from my parent's mouth. 'Why are they going to the border?'

'To keep us safe from men who want to take over our country, dear.'

'Why do they want the country?'

'You know very well. I'm not getting into one of your discussions.' Mum walked away.

When I opened the car door, music was playing inside the standalone-prefabricated social club, opposite the grander building that was the station. Tendrils of smoke wafted across the lawn from the half forty-four-gallon drum fires, tended by men holding brown bottles of beer.

Inside, a man in a red fez, a pristine-white uniform, and matching cummerbund served drinks over a swank bar. The musical clink of glasses and cheerful babble fused with cigarette smoke, and the benevolent sounds of The Carpenters. I waited for my father to return with drinks, then escaped outside with a bottle of cola.

'Are you coming, Cara?'

'Later,' she said. She preferred to sit with the adults on such occasions.

Outside, the three police officers tending to the fire soon forgot I was lurking among them.

'So, boys, when do you guys leave?' the older man asked as he swigged on his beer.

'We're on tomorrow's train to Salisbury.' The stockier of the other two men replied.

'How lucky are you guys to be seeing some action? Shit, I wish I could join you,' the senior man said, wearing his three stripes of authority over the others.

The younger men glanced at each other. 'You're right, sergeant, we're lucky guys.' The stocky policeman agreed. The third man remained silent, bobbing his head with each word spoken.

The sergeant took another gulp, oblivious to the sarcasm. 'In my early days, I'd be at the border. Not dillydallying around here.'

He swayed onto the rear of his heels and belched, looking pleased with himself.

'Nice one, sarge, we're in mixed company.' the other two said in unison.

'No-one heard me. Anyway, this is our canteen. I haven't got time to chew the cud with you, arseholes. I need another beer and damn quick.' He sauntered off, negotiating the steps with intoxicated deliberation.

I sat under a half-drum barbecue watching the red-hot embers drop through the air holes and listened to the men talk.

'Bloody fool, what is it with old farts and war?'

His hitherto quiet friend shrugged his shoulders and said,

'Something to do with a limp *pipi*, I guess.'

'Who knows? Let's meet our entourage of fans preparing to send their vanquishers to battle.'

'Shit, listen to you.' The silent soldier sniffed, heading to the canteen.

I sat alone. The luminous tube outside the door flickered to the muted echoes of the party. The heat from the fire warmed my face, my backside cold from the dew-chilled earth.

Everyone put on brave fronts, yet no one admitted to it. I battled to understand the air of dogged resignation. The greater the intensity of the conflict, the more entrenched each side became. Themba's words rang true. The future of Rhodesia, Africa, and the planet was dire.

Bow rested after the strenuous climb and surveyed his kingdom. The treacherous terrain proved difficult. I giggled and crossed my eyes at him. 'Quite a climb, hey?' Bow's powerful toes gripped my scalp. 'Here, let me help you,' I said as I presented a hand to my buddy, who wrapped his tail around one of my fingers for anchorage. I held him up to my nose. 'It's great to see you. You know it worried me when I couldn't find you.' Bow's globular eyes settled on me before roving again. I leant against the cool granite and stroked his chin. The sunrise was igniting our wonderland as pristine light illuminated swarms of tiny insects beginning their quest for another day.

'You hungry, Bow?' I placed him on a low-lying branch, making sure he had a proper hold before I let go. 'Wait here, let's see if I can catch breakfast.' Bow stood open-mouthed while I darted back and forth. 'How's this look, Bow?' I smacked my lips, animating the tasty morsel in my fingers. 'What's that in your mouth?' I asked him, but Bow looked elsewhere, feigning innocence, despite the lacewing protruding from his lips. 'Don't think I can't see it. You see me running around like a lunatic trying to catch your breakfast and you're busy snacking.' I wagged a finger. 'And take that smirk off your face. Shame on you.' I plonked on my backside and dug a biscuit from my pocket. 'Do you want to try one?' I offered in reconciliation. Bow refused, turning his head. 'I'm not surprised, you pig.' I ate in silence, watching the land transform as the light changed in my heaven.

This time tomorrow, I'll be on the bus back to Plumtree School.

I gave Bow a smile. 'Wish we could stay here forever.' I wore a brave face as I savoured the freshness of the earth, the soft touch of the dawn breeze, the chatter of the wild birds, the tantalising views, and the delightful taste for life. Yet an indefinable sixth sense nagged at my soul. It was time for goodbyes. Starting with Bow.

Chapter Nine

I began my trek back to school. The twelve-hour expedition passed in a blur of misery and regret. The bus shaped time-machine transported us from paradise to the terrors of dystopia.

'Hi, china, how was the trip?' Alan asked as he put an arm around my shoulder. 'We must get on the same bus, man.' He shoved me into a nearby hedge.

'You bastard.' I disentangled myself and gave chase.

'Great to see you again,' he said.

'You too, dumbass.'

Before realising it, and to our misfortune, we pulled into the school grounds in front of the Beit Hall at Plumtree School.

'Howzit, Rory. Howzit, Alan. How were the hols?' Jannie asked, shaking our hands.

I returned the welcome. A pang of guilt shot through me.

How pathetic am I? Wrapped up in self-pity when he didn't even get to see his folks?

'How did you get on, Jannie?' I asked.

'*Ja, nee,* okay, but quiet without you pricks.' He smacked the back of his hands together, self-conscious of the attention. 'We *braaied* the first night and Sunday we fished with Mr Stenk.'

'Sounds cool,' Alan said as he waited to hear more from Jannie.

'We talked about the Springbok and Welsh rugby. Sir agrees the Southern Hemisphere plays a better game,' Jannie said as he ducked and dived into a make-believe game.

The half-term exeat became nothing more than a memory as we reacquainted, listening to one another reliving our antics. Jannie scoffed treats brought back for him by us as he hung on every detail.

We buried ourselves in the preparation for the sports' gala.

A weekend for parents to watch the inter-house athletics and catch up with the teachers. The annual musical production on the final night closed festivities. This meant re-landscaping of the gardens by reprobates and volunteers interested in agriculture.

Tractors driven by farmer's sons cut the vast tracts of the playing fields. Lawn mowers clattered across manicured terraces, harmonising with the snipping of hand-held clippers. Teams of students turned flower beds, swept the roads and paths. We polished kilometres of red verandas and floors until it was nigh impossible to tell reflection from substance.

Plays and recitals filled the air: Extra-mural clubs, and societies perfected their specialities, ranging from woodwork to the debating society. It was an intense three weeks of hard work in between class and sporting commitments. Blisters, grazes, bruises, and aching limbs abounded. None too soon, the looming event dawned.

The parents slept in the pupils' beds and used their amenities, while we boys camped in every available nook and cranny. It was the highlight of the school calendar for parent and boy. The folks loved the pomp and ceremony. The kids treasured the diversion and the opportunity for freedom. I expected families to arrive early on Friday morning. The younger boys tore around, unable to contain themselves. Our gang dissipated as each of our family arrived.

I sat alone under the palm trees. My stomach churned with each billow of dust from an approaching automobile.

Where are they? It's ten o'clock? They should have been here ages ago.

The comings and goings of the guests further increased my misery with their hugs and kisses, tuck boxes, smiles, perfume, and colour.

Come on, where are you guys?

By noon, the reunited families made their way to the dining-hall for refreshment. I remained where I was.

Just in case Mum and Dad show.

Joviality thrived. Hand in hand, kin sauntered through the gardens, enjoying their surrounds and one another's company.

It's two o'clock, I hope nothing's happened. Maybe Dad got held up. It's a long way to come. Did the car break down?

My excitement swelled to utter panic. My anticipation stumbled, and my gut ached.

'Hey Rory, you still waiting?' Mr Aspen asked me.

'Yep. Hi, Mr Aspen, Mrs Aspen.'

'Hello,' Mrs Aspen said. 'Alan tells me your parents should be here by now.' Her snow-white hair and pale skin ghostlike.

'Yes, Ma'am,' I answered as I struggled to contain my emotions.

She put both arms around me. 'Don't worry, my boy, they'll be here soon. I'm sure. Come and join us. I have goodies in the car. If there's no sign of them by four, then I'll ask Mr Winker if we can use the phone. All right?' She wiped away my tears before the others noticed, except for Alan, who knew me too well. He held my collar in comfort as we headed for the car.

I gave my well-wishers the slip and returned to the hostel.

They might turn up.

I crouched on the far side of the dirt road to avoid the attentions of colleagues. They meant well, but their questions irritated me. I kept vigilance across the same fields we snuck over months earlier. Fine dust lay at my feet. I pulled a shoot from a tuft of grass and sucked at the sweet moisture from the stem then used it to steer a persistent ant away from the clutches of an antlion — a conical trap in the soft sand, which collapsed on itself the more the victim struggled. The fierce creature, known as the curly whirly, devoured insects that stumbled into the cone pit. It never ceased to amaze me how these ugly, archaic larvae transformed into a striking dragonfly.

It must be after four o'clock. What could have happened? Were they ambushed on the way? Or in an accident?

The sinking sun ignited golden specks of dust, activating the twilight of pyrotechnics. A soft whistle from a dense thicket of shrubbery behind me drew my attention.

'Sawubona, umfana.'

'Is that you, Ticky?'

'Over here.'

I pressed my way into the undergrowth. 'Where are you? His lack of response troubled me. Stop playing the fool.' In a small clearing, I found a plastic bottle of chilled water, fresh peanut butter sandwiches, and an orange wrapped in brown paper. 'What the…' My eyes flicked around. Not a rustle. Nor even the snap of a twig. Unsettled, I stuffed the bounty into my shirt and returned to the open road.

How did Themba find out? Did he tell Ticky, or did he do it on his own?

I ripped off a hefty bite and washed the bread down with the refreshing liquid.

He must be aware Mum and Dad aren't here yet.

I wiped my face with the back of my hand and held my belly to expel unwanted wind.

It can't be bad, Ticky would have said.

'Wilde, there you are. Mr Winker is searching for you,' an out-of-breath, second year, called out.

I crossed the lawn to the housemaster's office and peeped from behind the door. 'Are you looking for me, sir?'

'Hold on, Mrs Wilde, I assume this is him now,' Mr Winker said into the large black earpiece as he signalled to me with his free arm. 'Here you are, Mrs Wilde.' He tapped my back and left.

'Hi, Mum.'

'Hello, dear, just a quick call to say your father has delayed us.'

My heartbeat with relief while my head blamed my dad.

'But don't worry, we're on our way. We should arrive within the hour.'

'What, today, Mum?'

'You never listen to what I'm saying? Rory, can you hear me?'

'Sure, I'll see you now, now. Bye Mum.'

'Rory? Rory?'

I replaced the receiver and looked around the room, where I spotted a drum full of bamboo canes.

So that's what he uses for punishment. Nice of Winker to give me privacy. He's strange, although he can be kind sometimes.

My thoughts shifted back to my folks. I slipped out of the office and glided along the red-polished veranda and down the steps to resume the lone vigil.

The next couple of days were bliss without being home. I

showed my parents to their beds in the vacated dormitories, one for the mums, the other for dads. The visitors freshened up and met for sundowners at the front of the house. Coloured lights ran the length of the building and through the gardens. White-clothed tables formed a makeshift bar. Immaculate waiters served drinks to the elegant suits and ball gowns. Cordial music played from speakers strapped to palm trees; the polite murmur of conversation broken by gracious laughter. The colonial shindig in its glory was in full sway. My stomach swirled as I digested the atmosphere; I seldom came across such a splendid gathering, except the local annual police ball in Wankie village.

Our gang gathered in the shadows.

'Isn't this cool, man?' Alan asked.

'*Baie mooi.* Beautiful,' Jannie translated his words.

'We need some of that?' Vinny said. We followed his eyes to an ice-filled galvanised bath overflowing with beer bottles.

'You're off your rocker. If the masters don't catch us, the seniors will,' Alan said, raising his shoulders.

'I suppose you are right,' Vinny said.

We sniggered, more from relief than humour.

'Let's get back to our parents,' I said.

Alan punched my arm 'Okay, check you at the concert.'

'Cool, see you later,' I replied. I returned to my folks, who were busy chatting with other grown-ups. I missed Cara with a feeling that followed me throughout my life. She loved the razzmatazz. My eyes danced across the fiesta, marvelling at the sights and sounds, intrigued at how the seniors partook in the festivities and, in doing so, gave us youngsters a break from their torment. Out of the corner of my eye, beyond the spectacle, I caught a movement in the shadows.

Ticky, is that you? I scrunched up my face. Can't be. What does he want here?

The watch on my father's wrist read seven-thirty. The social gathering advanced to the dining room, which had tables dressed in green and white linen adorned with cutlery and decorations. Mid-formers in their best dress welcomed the guests with regal decorum and showed them to their seats.

'Okay, will we see you afterwards?' Mum asked as me as

she followed the server. 'Where are you boys dining?'

'Over there, Mum.'

'Oh. What fun. You're eating outside — a picnic.' Mum kissed me on my way. 'It's a pity the boys can't join us,' she said to Dad as I hesitated close by. 'They could do with bulking up.'

'Don't worry, they prefer to be with their friends?' Dad replied. 'What a spread.' His eyes lit up at the fare before him.

My folks glided towards the glamour with dubitable airs and graces while I headed for the tables under the trees. On each stood an urn of tea and a tray of coagulated hamburgers.

Pity we can't fish for our supper. There's enough bait.

I found the Gaul table, keeping an eye out for my buddies.

After dinner, we meandered up to the Beit Hall for the evening's entertainment. From my position in the fly tower, I had an aerial view of the stage, and although I was not in the production, I got goosebumps with the opening chords of the Gilbert and Sullivan play. Acting was not my thing. Apart from the fear of making an idiot of myself, being tone deaf saved me from dressing up in costume. Many of my *amis de guerre* was less fortunate, press-ganged into the extravaganza, some to play the fairer sex. I peered from above as the cast took their places behind the maroon-velvet drapery. The first bars of *H.M.S. Pinafore* raised the curtain to rapturous applause. I scaled down from the rafters to join the backstage crew and prepare for a scenery change.

At interval, while the audience partook of sherry, tea, and scones, I slipped away.

This is my last chance to plan my escape. If I go ahead with it.

I climbed back up to my perch. No one else wanted to scale the heights, hence I got the job of adjusting the lights and declining the props. Waiting on the next scene change and bored by the show, I poked behind a beam where I found a tatty piece of folded paper with the word *private* scrawled on it. I slipped the note into my breast pocket to deal with a prop malfunction that kept me busy until the end of the production. The crew tidied up afterwards, and it was my task to close once everyone left. The empty stage was eerie, and when a rat scurried across the floorboards, I fled too.

I rolled into my sleeping bag and folded my towel for a pillow. The games room, my games room, had become temporary accommodation for those who had surrendered their beds. We lined the walls like sardines, without as much as a gap between blankets. Alan sat on his bedding, leaning against the whitewashed sides. 'So, are your folks enjoying their stay?' he asked me.

'I suppose so. It's the sort of thing they go for,' I replied as I tried to find enough space to sleep. Mr Winker interrupted our conversation.

'Evening gentlemen how was your day?' he asked. His face flushed under the stark fluorescents; his beady eyes scoured the room for anomalies. Without pausing, he continued with less than perfect diction. 'Get an enjoyable night's sleep. Tomorrow is an important day of athletics,' he slurred, and lifted a finger so close to his eyes it caused him to squint. 'Oh, yes, and don't let me catch anybody out of this room tonight. Anyone caught further than that tree will have some explaining to do.' He pointed the same digit at a large jacaranda ten paces from the games room, which doubled as a urinal until the morning.

He looks half-pissed. Must have overdone it tonight. Hope he gets a hangover.

Sleep did not happen. The games room sweltered, smelt of dirty socks and disagreeable emissions. I picked my way over bodies towards the exit to relieve myself. Afterwards, I lay on the lawn, reluctant to go inside. Covered by a blanket of winking stars, a light breeze enveloped me. I viewed the heavens in search of its zodiac signs, taking consolation from the bold Southern Cross. The sound of the evening insects steadied my heart and calmed my mind into a blissful slumber. 'Better than Gilbert and whatever his name is, who write those musical plays.' I drifted off into a deep sleep.

'*Insizwa*, wake up. Can you hear me, *umfana?*' A gentle shake of my shoulder woke me.

'What is it? Who's there?' I tried to focus. Panic shot through my chest.

'It is me, Ticky.'

'What do you...? What's going...? Is everything all right?' I cleared my head.

'Don't worry. All is fine. I found you lying here and thought you might be ill or even dead.'

'Well, I'm neither.'

'I'm glad to hear that. Themba would have had my balls for garters.'

His mixed metaphor brought a smile to my lips. The dining-hall assistant checked over his shoulder and ducked. 'Time, I went, *umfana*. It is unwise to stay in one place for long. Themba sends his wishes.' Ticky prepared to leave before turning back. 'It is not safe to sleep outside anymore. *Size sibonane futhi* — until we meet again,' he hissed and disappeared into the darkness.

In the morning, I would seek Ticky in the dining hall and ask him what was going on and if he would help me escape. I resumed my position on the grass and gave in to the sounds of the African night and read the note I had found in the rafters.

An Enigma

Immortality a prevailing appeal
Death the only certain relief
Propagation to our singular legacy

Guilty of inflating our being
Lifelong games of burying our self
Keeping all at length
Resolved only by protégé

Afraid of offering our trueness
Revealing open windows
to our soul

Bound by a millennium of
prejudice and unknown
Daunted by the anarchy of history
and uncertainty of change
Paranoid to survive in the present

> *Ritual and cults*
> *crutches to our vulnerability*
> *Joy in the masked eyes*
> *of selfishness and perversion*
> *Enlightenment the natural saviour*

Signed by John and dated 1941.

Must be a schoolboy from long ago. Thirty-four years. He didn't sound happy either.

The following morning, we were up with the sparrows, to prepare the athletics track for the inter-house competition. But I snuck off to the school hall and retraced my steps into the rafters above the stage. I replaced John's poem and etched *Unknown Scholar 1941* with a penknife I had borrowed from Jannie and made my peace with John's memory.

At the racetrack, we drew white lines for lanes, hung red and blue bunting and placed chairs along the embankment. Students from the young scientist club checked the tannoy with intermittent chords of Deep Purple's *Smoke on the Water*. My job was to rake the inner field where the shot-put, discus, and javelin events were to take place. The sun peeped over the horizon; birds were in full voice and the lake wore a crochet of mist.

'Going to be a superb day, hey?' Alan said, flushed with exertion.

'You can say that again. Hope Gaul wins. Otherwise, Stenk will shit himself,' I replied.

'Too right.'

The public address system crackled into life, this time with the universal, 'one, two, testing one, two.'

The nimbus of Mr Winker and prefects materialised from behind the embankment. 'Look out. Prince of darkness is here,' Alan said. We returned to our tasks as orders shattered the calm. The tournament was that of a carnival. A hotchpotch of civilian clothing, a bouquet of perfumes and candy, with the euphoria of cordite and rousing applause.

After lunch, I changed into my athletic gear and went to the track for the three thousand metre event.

Wish I hadn't eaten so much junk food.

I was the fourth member of the four-man House squad. Not because of my ability, but because the faster athletes chose other races. 'On your marks, get set…' We jostled for position behind the white line. I stood back from the more eager players. The starting pistol set us off. I steered away from the tussle, protecting my bare feet from the lethal running spikes of the serious runners. The competitiveness, the hammering of my heart, the distant cheer of the crowd and the agony, all wrapped in slow motion. Shattered by pounding feet, elbows, and breathlessness. I surged forward to join my orange-vested counterparts with my lungs protesting at the effort.

'Well done! The team came second,' Alan and Jannie said in unison.

Flat on my back, I managed a smile, gulping air to clear my vision of tiny-black dots. Mother rushed towards me with her arms extended. 'That's my boy. That's my child.' Father sat in the stands, wearing a smug mask of contentment — basking in my glory.

That evening, parents and guests, along with the entire village, attended the school ball. We showered, ate under the trees, and retired early. I surrendered to the onset of weariness and before long, the games room beat to the rhythm of sleep.

Next morning, the four of us stood beneath the fig tree outside the chapel. Vinny was the first to speak. 'So, what's a commemoration service?'

'Giving thanks or something to do with war,' Alan said.

'It must be war. Check out the uniforms, china,' Jannie joined in. Men in full parade uniform mingled with women in Sunday hats and frocks.

'Those hats outdo the ladies,' I said as I pointed to a group of soldiers wearing splendid headgear of multi coloured berets and slouch hats. The others tittered, hiding their lips behind their sleeves.

'Are those ostriches feathers sticking out?' Alan asked, pointing out the plumes that decked the ceremonial headdress.

'Maybe, or a peacock,' I said.

The chapel heaved with people; every pew crammed to

hold the extended flock. By nine o'clock, the claustrophobic congregation waited in stifled expectation. The stirring notes of *Reveille* on a lone bugle caught the collective breath of the worshippers. I observed stern-faced soldiers and tearful spouses as the final strains played out. I flattened the hairs on my neck and glanced at my friend Alan; it covered his forearms in goosebumps. The reverend welcomed everyone with a prayer and invited us to take our seats.

'We gather here today to commemorate those brave men and women who gave their lives in the fight against evil. Many old boys of this school paid the ultimate sacrifice, defending our beliefs and rights in the First and Second World Wars.' He paused a moment as his face darkened, turning solemn. 'Once more, we call on our sons to protect us and our country.' His voice broke. 'And we remember those who have perished in that endeavour.'

The blood drained from my face and a flood of adrenalin raced through my heart. Dry mouthed, I listened as the head boy read a list of names, starting from when the insurgencies began in the sixties to the current year of 1975. Woman dabbed their eyes, and the men cleared their throats. A sense of helplessness overwhelmed me as the remembrance service continued until the *Last Post* sounded in the distance. I waited until the adults exited the chapel, grave-faced soldiers supporting an unsteady mother by the elbows.

Not one of them bothered with us boys as they passed.

Chapter Ten

The weeks dragged, waiting for the end of term. Life returned to the usual ducking and diving to avoid harassment, while exams added to our misery. I rolled my pencil between my forefinger and thumb, studying my last test paper.

It's over. Tomorrow we go home for a month. I can't wait.

I surveyed the classroom, wary of the adjudicator's attention. A thin man with brushed-back hair and horned-rim spectacles perched on a gigantic nose. He limped the aisles, his squeaking-plastic shoes filled the hall, apart from the odd fretful cough and scratch of lead on paper. His round shoulders sported an ill-fitting cardigan, while his beady eyes darted in search of trickery.

He deserves his nickname, does Mr Butterworth. Buzzard suits him.

I rubbed my eyelids with the back of my hands and stifled a yawn. My mind mooched over a week of packing trunks and buying of train tickets. The seniors became more hostile with the end of the term in sight.

After my swim, I'll try to find Ticky. Next term will be here before we realise it. By then, I must be ready. Wonder if Alan is still keen to run away with me? I'm not fussed either way.

The teachers left us to our own devices. They were too busy marking exam papers. We convinced two coaches to watch over the swimming session for the afternoon. I disrobed, careful not to wrinkle my uniform, grabbed a towel, and traipsed to the pools. The gang had yet to arrive. So, I slipped into the water and rested at the side, allowing the silky coolness to embrace me. The chlorine helped clear my sinus.

This time tomorrow we will be on the train homeward bound. With tears threatening, I slithered back into the pool. Why am I crying, idiot? We're going home.

That afternoon we played water polo, which developed into

tag, yet was more dunking than catching.

I picked my way through the thorns to the dining hall to find Ticky. The clatter of utensils greeted me as I poked my head around the door where cooks hollered at their assistants who battled dishwashers. Steam wafted from ovens and black cauldrons, knives chopped, spoons swirled, and scourers scraped. Boiled cabbage and carbolic floors mixed with the putrid garbage from the outside bins. Lunch was in full swing, everyone too busy to notice me snooping. Unable to locate Ticky inside, I perched on the steps and considered my next move.

'You can't sit there boss, chef will report you,' a cheerful face beamed at me. 'Can I help you?'

I jumped up and moved away from the entrance. 'Maybe. I'm looking for Ticky.'

The man wiped his hands on his filthy apron and bent forward. 'See the bushes behind that building? You might find him there. It's where smokers take a break, but don't say I told you.' He winked, took a deep breath, and disappeared into the busy gallery.

I eyed the outhouse where the kitchen staff changed for work, ate, and used ablutions. Such places were taboo by the school and the parents of white children across the country. I snuck in and made my way to the rear until I heard voices. In two minds about what to do, I held my ground, fighting between an inbred fear and extreme curiosity. Before I realised what was happening, a huge hand swooped and deposited me in the middle of a large clearing.

'What do we have here?' someone boomed. Half a dozen men slouched, smoking, and sipping tea in the dingy green hue beneath the foliage.

'What you want around here, boy?' one said through his teeth.

'Are you looking for trouble?' another asked.

I shook my head, not trusting my tone of voice.

'Wenzani,' a cry broke the grim silence by asking what was happening.

No one answered, avoiding his scowl. Ticky appeared, taking me under his wing, and introduced me. *'Ake ngikwethulele indodana kaThemba* — this is Themba's son.' Joyful clapping of welcome followed a shared inhalation, each of the men lifting me into the air. Afterward, I grabbed the seat offered to me beside Ticky.

The men chatted in their native tongue, rolled raw tobacco in newspaper, which they lit on the fire. Each took a draw before passing it along. I refused the joint, the bitter smoke catching in my throat. My companions laughed and nodded in my direction, but I didn't mind. It wasn't wicked, even though I couldn't understand the language. Ticky pushed my head with a playful shove. 'Don't worry, *umfana,* he said. These men will not harm Themba's *abantwana.'*

The men sobered and saluted a clenched fist at Ticky when the kitchen siren ended their break. They stirred with laborious intent. 'Wait *umfana,* let them go.' Ticky gripped my arm. They dragged themselves back to their stations, wearing aprons and white hats.

Ticky played a local board game of diagonal lines and moveable pieces. I couldn't fathom the rules, but marvelled at the speed and ferocity.

'So, *umfana,* you are returning home soon?' Ticky looked up from his game.

'Yep.' I tried to display confidence.

Ticky picked tobacco from his teeth. 'That is good.' He hesitated. 'Tell Themba everything is fine.' He nodded.

'Okay.' I shrugged.

Ticky eyed me. 'What brings you here, anyway? The school forbids it?'

'I know.' I fidgeted, hesitant to confide in the man.

'Will you help us escape? I have plans and I need a backup. If you don't want to, it doesn't matter, we're going anyway.'

Ticky recoiled at the outburst. *'Kwenzakalani?'* he asked.

'Well, nothing specific happened. It's everything about this place. The seniors, the teachers, the food… can you… will you back us?'

'I don't know.' Ticky rubbed the rear of his head. 'Where can you run, and to who?'

'South Africa.' It sounded better in my mind.

Ticky's eyes opened wider, yet he remained silent, rolling another foul cigarette. I sat, trying to ease my numb buttocks on the stony ground.

'We'll hideaway on a train through Botswana,' I said in a whisper.

Ticky shuddered. '*iNingizimu* Africa — South Africa? What you ask is impossible. If either side finds out, I helped white boys escape to the land of apartheid, they will execute me. I have more important matters at hand.'

Feeling uneasy, I stood.

He's not Themba. That's for sure. What a scary man. I wiped my hands on my khaki shorts and bid Ticky goodbye.

He stared at me. '*Uyezwa na?* ' he said.

'Yes, I understand.' I lowered my chin.

'Good, now *suka umfana.* ' Ticky chased me away, but not before a strange premonition crossed his face.

'It will disappoint Themba,' he said as I retreated. 'And put you in grave danger.'

I marched to the hostel and almost knocked Alan over as I flung my shoes under the bed.

'What's got into you?' he asked.

'Nothing.'

'Well, it can't be nothing, bozo. Something's put you in a stinker,' Alan replied.

'I'm sorry, man. I went to the kitchen… I broke my promise to Themba.'

'What the heck is happening? What are you hiding?'

'I promised I wouldn't say.' I undressed, avoiding his stare.

Alan grabbed his towel and headed for the showers.

Idiot, now you've gone and upset your best mate.

I withdrew from the others, preparing for roll call and the term's last supper. Deep in thought and oblivious to my surroundings, I tripped and fell into a nearby hedge. My mates hooted and danced in glee and pushed me in deeper. Tears ran up my face as I struggled to extricate myself, and even though I was upside down, I recognised the footwear of the ringleaders. 'I'll kill you shits when I get out of here,' I shouted.

Alan and Jannie responded by shaking my outstretched legs.

'Bastards! Somebody help me, please. Vinny, get me out of here.' Their silence shut me up, followed by the arrival, albeit the wrong way around, of a well-polished pair of shoes.

114

'Wilde, is that you, boy?'

'Yes, Mr Winker, sir.' My legs were like flagpoles.

He shook his head. 'You're a damn fool, Wilde.'

'Yes, sir.'

'Carry on, gentlemen. Get Wilde out before he bursts a blood vessel,' he said, continuing on his way. A smile played on his lips.

The next morning, I woke before the sun and crept from the room to admire its rising. Unusual blues and yellows filled the wide African sky. My stomach was a mixture of excitement and trepidation. I was looking forward to the eight-hour wait for the connecting train in Bulawayo, where Alan and I planned to explore the city.

It's the trip to town that's the problem. It'll be full of seniors. Hope a master is on board.

I took consolation in the warmth and energy of the dawn, and solace in its promise, before returning to the dormitory to wake the rest of the gang.

'Gentlemen, let me remind you. You are representatives of this school, even during the holidays. I don't want to hear tales of reckless behaviour on the train or in the city,' Winker said as he surveyed the students from the top of the red-polished steps and emphasised his point.

'Have a marvellous time. Don't forget your woollies.' He grinned at his protégé. The horseshoe on his cheek throbbed, but not from irritation. 'Let us pray.' He asked for a safe passage and our integrity. Hundreds of teenagers finding their way home worried him. He mentioned an old dude, Christopher, the patron saint of travel, but few of us were paying attention.

The dining hall was empty. Most skipped breakfast and head straight for the station.

'Where the others?' Alan asked with a mouthful of egg sandwich.

I enlarged my eyes; my cheeks were bulging with food.

Alan giggled. 'You look just like a guinea pig.'

I held my hand to my mouth, trying not to discharge my food. 'Jannie and Vinny went on ahead to book seats on the train,' I said.

'Sweet.' Alan nodded. 'They're only going to Bulawayo, anyway.'

We ate our fill, not knowing when we would eat again.

With a sports' bag in my hand, I glanced at the row of stripped beds in the pitiful dormitory. Pillows and blankets lay folded for our return. I prayed to the heavens and exhaled. A pinball of relief and exhilaration ricocheted between my heart and my stomach.

I'm going home. Bloody hell, I'm out of here.

'Let's go china before they lock us in,' Alan said as he brushed past.

Plumtree station swarmed with schoolboys in their Sunday best as raucous laughter erupted from pockets of unperturbed seniors, while skittish juniors sought discreet hideaways. The stationmaster scuttled back and forth beneath a tattered cap as he punched the odd ticket. His long-unkempt hair matched his faded uniform. The siding was in a similar state of disrepair, with sun-brittle paintwork, bleached wood, and a potholed platform pimpled with anthills. The worn-out steam engine wheezed, dribbling ash from the corners of her ageing mouth. Further evidence of the country's crippling sanctions.

A shrill whistle startled the train into life, triggering clouds of black smoke to spew into the air. Workers removed thirsty straws of water from her bowels and gave the all-clear as the driver's mate stoked coal into the furnace of her belly.

'All aboard!' the conductor yelled above the racket. 'Nine o'clock from Mafeking to Bulawayo, leaving Plumtree in five minutes.' The man poised his green flag above his head as his commuters boarded.

'Hurry, jump on. We'll walk through the train to find the others,' Alan said as he offered me a hand from the high steps of the carriage. The locomotive shuddered and pulled away from the station with a painful groan. I forced a path through the bodies and slammed the door. The number of juniors crammed into the aisles between the couplings of the carriages puzzled me.

'What's going on?' I said into Alan's ear.

A boy in front answered over his shoulder. 'The seniors have the compartments, and they won't share them with us plebs.'

I bid farewell to the playing fields and an austere Gaul House, which peered from behind her oasis web.

Good riddance.

A lone figure stood at the school perimeter.

That Ticky' is everywhere. I returned a half-hearted wave. An army patrol trudged the face of the railway embankment with semi-automatics at the ready.

I met a bunch of boys perched on their bags, swaying with the train's movement in the corridors. 'What the hell are you doing?' a shaky voice asked.

'Finding a better spot, then I'll look for Jannie and Vinny,' I responded.

'You've got to be kidding?' the same voice replied.

Alan and I paid no attention and followed the passageway, bracing ourselves to the roll of the train.

'Don't even look into the compartments,' I said, holding my finger to my lips. 'These guys won't need an excuse...'

'Where the fuck are you two heading?'

I swung towards the fierce outcry, recognising the senior.

'Going to the toilet Minnaar, the others don't work.'

'Well, piss out the fucking window, sprog. Into the wind.' He snorted as his henchmen around him laughed.

'Don't just stand there. Fuck off before you pee your pants,' Minnaar said and dismissed us as he took a drag on a cigarette.

'Thank you,' I said. We ignored the contraband. To draw attention to it would invite disaster.

Alan stuck close as we trudged our way along the train, praying there would be no further scenes. 'The guys were right; we shouldn't do this,' he said.

'Just a few more carriages. They're more interested in smoking and getting drunk,' I replied.

'Yeah, but that means no chaperone on the train.'

I forced a path through the mournful kids. The rancid stink of inadequate latrines grew with each passing kilometre.

On reaching the end, we found the door to the next carriage locked.

'You mustn't go through there,' a haughty boy with buck teeth said.

'Why the hell not?' I asked him.

117

'That's third class, dummy.'

'What do you mean, third class?' Alan asked.

The boy's teeth protruded further as he whacked his sides and whooped with amusement and looked at his friends for encouragement. 'Will someone please tell those idiots?'

Alan and I backed away. They were lofty second-year students, a year our senior.

'Don't worry about them,' a lad piped up from the far corner. He closed his book and signalled we could open the exit door. The ground raced beneath us as the rush of fleeting signs and lights reverberated from the speed.

'See the numbers painted on the sides?' His voice was hard to hear above the wind.

'I got what you meant, but why can't we go in?' Alan asked.

'From what planet are you?' the toothy one asked.

The composed boy gave him a withering stare and caused him to cower. He then glanced at Alan, who waited for an explanation.

'Do what you want.' The boy shrugged and returned to his book.

'Let's see how it is,' I said as I pulled Alan aside.

'Didn't you hear what they said?' Alan asked. I was sure that he recognised my set chin.

'All right. All right. Can we stay for a minute to gather our wits, or at least mine?'

Alan slumped on to his holdall and I squeezed in beside him. 'Sure, why not?' he said.

The train lurched and slammed us against the walls. I untangled myself from the mass of arms and legs. Outside, soldiers shouted for identification papers and dogs barked at travellers. Teeth Boy sidled up to Alan. 'Hey, idiot. Do you see now? Third class is for the blacks, they're not tolerated in second or first-class. That's why the army is checking them in case they're terrorists.'

'But we're not allowed in there either?' I replied.

'Why go in there?' he asked.

I left it, not wishing to get into a quarrel with a supposed superior.

I sat back and recalled Themba's favourite saying,

paraphrased from his incarcerated champion. *Those who control and restrict are themselves controlled and restricted.* Themba talks so much of this Nelson Mandela. Are they friends? Wonder if I'll ever meet him.

'Take no notice,' I said as I put my hand on Alan's shoulder. Alan nodded.

'Jannie says they call it apartheid in South Africa,' I added.

'That's a strange word, hey?' Alan replied.

'Apartheid.' I wrote it in the grimy window. 'It's a made-up word.'

'What are you saying?' Alan asked.

'I think it comes from joining the words *apart* and *hate*.'

We sat in silence on the couplings between two carriages outside the lavatories. Me pondering exclusion based on age, kind, and colour, Alan with his own reflections.

The railway line split into a spaghetti of tracks on the murky outskirts of the Bulawayo station. Grime-encrusted cranes loaded their merchandise in dingy stockyards while engines gasped emissions of smoke and steam. Maintenance workers who serviced the locomotives ducked into the smog, only to resurface from the pea soup.

I sat on the bottom rung of the steps as the train crawled through the contaminated ecosystem. We waved to a bored wheel tapper who was listening for imperfections in the wheels. Black lines engraved in his face opened into a toothless grin of salutation.

Despite the heat, I shivered and vowed to work harder at school.

After several starts and stops for army patrols to climb aboard and disembark with a hostage or two, we coasted onto one of the grand Victorian platforms. Soldiers carrying giant dentist mirrors inspected the underside of each carriage for mines and booby traps.

'Let's head for civilisation,' Alan said as he rose from the top level of the steps.

'We must find Jannie and Vinny,' I replied as I looked over the bustling platform of porters, civilians, kiosks, and newspaper stands.

'*Ja*, let's hit the road.' *And don't come back no more.*

I finished the line of the Ray Charles song in my head. We headed for the turnstile.

The midday sun rescued us from the squalor. A sense of relief washed over us as we wandered the streets.

'I don't believe it,' Alan said, stopping dead in his tracks.

'What?' I followed his gaze.

'Coming out of the liquor store.' Alan pushed me against the wall to avoid detection. A peculiar little man was tottering from the shop clutching a bottle of grog wrapped in a brown paper bag.

'Is that... no, can't be?' I said as I peeked around the side of the station wall at the familiar stooped silhouette.

'Can you believe it? He was on the train.' Alan finished my sentence. 'By the looks of things, he hasn't just started on that stuff either. Last time I saw him he was invigilating exams in the hall.'

'So, there was a teacher aboard,' I added.

Buzzard slipped the bottle under his arm and staggered town wards.

'Let's see where he goes,' Alan said as he pulled me by my arm.

'Okay but stay out of sight.' We followed Buzzard until he reached a small park, where he found a bench alongside the lake. He gestured to a waif scavenging through a nearby trashcan and gave her money. He patted her head and sent her on her way. The street child bobbed a curtsy and disappeared. Buzzard lifted the brown paper bag to his lips and stared out across the water.

'I heard rumours Buzzard had a daughter, but there were problems,' Alan whispered as we watched the forlorn figure.

'Problems?'

'Yes. I believe she is of colour.' Alan grimaced at the phrase. 'You know, half black, half white.'

'Maybe that was his daughter?' I said.

We chose not to spy any longer, heading instead for the beckoning skyscrapers of the city.

Before we reached the slick high-street malls, we passed through the backstreets of the metropolis. The bright mounds and fragrances of spices and the noise of high-pitched Eastern music vied with the local delicacies and the rhythmical beat of *Africa*. Intrigued by the heaps of splendid seasonings and the colloquial names given to them, we delighted in the lavishness and diversity.

'Check this out,' I said and pointed to a card buried in a warm yellow curry mix. *Mother-in-law's tongue,* it said while another read *Durban Masala.* A line of customers queued at a nearby takeaway selling *Bunny Chow,* comprising half a loaf of bread hollowed out and filled with a curry of choice. The trader, draped in a grandiose sari, gave us a *samosa* each and shooed us on our way. We tucked into the piquant triangular snack and continued past windows exhibiting goat and chicken heads, hooves, and offal. The buzz of the city energised us.

'Come on, we must move. We have to meet Jannie at his aunt's shop,' Alan said.

'Okay, but I need the loo, first.' I pointed to an underground public convenience where a scuffle had broken out metres from the entrance. A whistle pierced the air. As we looked on, an irate police officer handcuffed the offender, and forced him to jog behind a constable as he rode away on a large, black Samson bicycle. After the kerfuffle, the toilet aide turned to me and Alan and flailed his arms.

'Why do these people chance it; they know we do not allow them inside.' He pointed to a sign above the entrance which said *Whites Only.* The attendant continued to narrate the fiasco to all within range. We paid our dues for the spic and span lavatory by inserting a one-cent piece into the slot.

***

'Hey! What took you guys so long?' Jannie called from across the wide street. 'Man, it's good to see you.' We shook hands. 'Aunty Hester is waiting. She has *koeksisters* and juice for us,' he said.

The city centre was less hectic, with more vehicles and fewer people. White couples and business executives strolled the pavements and the rich regaled outside bistros. Jannie directed us to a shop window decorated with ornate curtains and glass shelves laden with produce. A neon sign, ***Hester Se Tiusnyverheid*** — Hester's Home Industry, flashed above the door with the hand-painted slogan below — ***Traditional Boer Baking***. Although I couldn't get my tongue around the name, it thrilled me at the fare on display. Cakes of every sort and size lined one wall, cookies the other and savouries the third. Everything was fresh and packed in blown-up plastic bags so as not to spoil the toppings. Handwritten tags of the mouth-watering confectionary, *melktert*, and *Ma's chocolate cake* were among my favourites. The best for me was the *koeksisters*. Behind a counter hung the ultimate delicacy, strips of dried *biltong* and spicy *droëwors*.

A sizeable woman with a delightful face greeted us. She wore a polka-dot frock with a frilly lace collar and a pale-blue Wedgwood brooch clasped to her chest. A white-linen apron strained at her midriff; her greying hair scraped into a ponytail.

'Hallo, my *skat*,' she said as she gathered us into her saggy arms. She smelt of lavender and hot bread. 'Go through to the back and wash. I have *lekker koeksisters* for you to try.' She spoke with the same throaty accent as her nephew, Jannie.

Tannie Hester brought through a generous plate of the appetising *chow* and a jug of fresh, cold milk. I reached over and helped myself. The twist of deep-fried dough, crispy on the outside and dripping in syrup, was delicious as I licked the sweetness from my fingers.

'*Siestog* — say again,' the soft maternal 'g' reverberated in the back of her throat. 'Don't worry. It is impossible to eat *koeksister* any other way.' She pushed another one into my mouth. We gorged ourselves as Hester served her clients and chatted away to everyone.

'So, when will you and your family disappear?' a customer asked Hester.

'Well, we've sold the shop to Mrs Wessels from the embroidery club. Do you know her?' she added as she clasped her chin. 'Never mind, she's a delightful lady who loves the shop. We leave at the end of the month.'

The buyer nodded. 'I wish you the very best for your family, Mrs Buitendag. We shall miss you.'

'Ta so much, Mrs Evans, but I will see you before we go. *Mooi bly.*'

What lovely people. I wonder how Jannie feels about leaving the country.

Aunt Hester read my mind. 'Sorry, but there's nothing else to do. The family must return home,' she said to me.

'But we were born here. You, Pa, me, everybody,' Jannie added.

She paused and looked at her nephew with pained tenderness. She wiped the corner of her eye with her apron and continued. 'I know. The family has been here a hundred and fifty years. We mustn't forget our roots. We are fourth-generation farmers here in Africa and we must fight for that.' She cleared the table. 'Come, it's time to go. I must close up and bake for tomorrow.'

'Thanks, *Tannie*,' I said, unaccustomed to using the word, an affectionate mark of respect for mature ladies. I embraced her before walking out into the avenue.

'Cheers, I'll check you next term,' I said to Jannie.

'Bye, Rory. Bye, Alan Bye Vinny, enjoy the hols.' Jannie waved from his aunt's shop as we headed for the high-street to mooch. I glanced up at the city clock.

'It's only two o'clock, still another seven hours before the train leaves,' I said to the others.

Chapter Eleven

We cruised the city on foot. Outside one swanky restaurant, we avoided detection from the stiff ironing board servers who waddled back and forth under the watchful eye of the maître d'hôtel. With faces resembling the *Kilroy Was Here* character of a long nose peering over a brick wall, we feasted our saucer eyes on the banquet before us. A deluge of cakes, tarts, and canapes decorated layers of silver platters while an oasis of salads surrounded the carvery. Cut flowers, sweetened by the lavish confectionary, piqued our attention.

'Bloody hell, what is that?' I asked. 'Almost as good as *Tannie* Hester's.'

Alan wiped the drool from his bottom lip.

A girl dining with her parents spotted us from behind the wall. Her mother looked over her shoulder at what was distracting her daughter from her cream scone. Disgust cracked her porcelain face as she snapped a linen napkin in our direction. The hullabaloo attracted the snooty-beaked head server. 'Get lost, you ruffians.' His high-pitched cry matched his mincing gait. We scarpered as they chased after us along the mirror-polished corridors of the mall like veteran roller skaters and regrouped on the lower floor. We gave the penguin pursuers the slip on the escalators somewhere in the lingerie department.

'Miserable shits, what harm were we doing?' I said.

'Not sure, a bunch of bloody toffs, that's all,' Alan replied.

'Well, one day is one day,' I vowed vengeance against highbrows to myself as much as Alan.

'Forget it. Let's check out this level. We have time to kill,' Alan said.

I recognised Rodriguez's *Cold Fact* and his lilting acoustic guitar from the games room back at school. The American with Mexican heritage was born in Detroit and sang of inequality.

There's that music again. It's coming from these hippies.

Are they from the movies? Why aren't they in the army with short back and sides like all the rest?

Young people in bell-bottoms danced and worked behind the counter. Mirrored balls reflected flashing lights on psychedelic walls. I couldn't tell the staff, customers, men, or women apart, but it was the grooviest sight ever.

'Man, this is cool,' Alan said as we sidled up to the record bar. The cacophony of a Jimi Hendrix track was reverberating in my chest. Alan broke into laughter at the adrenalin-inducing discotheque. We spent the rest of our time hanging out with the hipsters.

Things will get better. This lot doesn't care about the other rubbish going on — communism, colonialism, war, and greed. Maybe they're a cult or a religion?

A woman gyrated without embarrassment in front of everyone. The message on her tight t-shirt burnt into my mind's eye. *Make Love Not War.*

'Time to go,' Alan said. 'The train is leaving soon.' We waited our turn to exit the shop through the army checkpoint.

The slight chill in the night air refreshed Alan and me as we joined the schoolboys' migration to the train terminal.

'Thank goodness for that. The city was becoming too much. I'm buggered,' Alan said as he pulled his rucksack on and slipped his hands into his blazer pockets.

'Too right, my feet are aching. Looks like there's more than just Plumtree School using the trains tonight,' I said.

'Hope that makes it better. Let's get a cola and sticky buns for the journey. Richard mentioned earlier the buffet car is expensive,' Alan said.

'Talking of which, where is that snob?' I asked.

'Huh, no doubt him and his newfound friends will have a slap-up meal on the train.'

'Yeah, but won't be as much fun, though.'

The glow from the streetlights cast eerie shadows through the tree-lined avenues. I imagined eyes watching us in the dingy, neglected back roads as we walked from the dazzling high streets. We strode in silence with our eyes peeled. The grimy station loomed in the murkiness as we picked up the pace, trying not to give in to our fears. A weathered hand reached out from a dark alley in a desperate appeal for charity. The shrill blast of a steam engine followed it. We lost our nerve and fled. I led the way as I thought a critter from the depths of the earth was following us.

When we crashed into the wall of the railway terminal, it relieved us to have escaped the dim shroud. Alan doubled over, gulping for air.

'I'll treat you to a cola,' I said as guilt tugged at my conscience.

'Cool, cheers,' Alan replied. The day cemented our friendship further.

Once we had recovered, we searched for our names on the platform information board. 'Cool, we're in the same cubicle. Check it out, no seniors.' Alan read my full name printed on the passenger list. 'I see Richard is with us, too,' he added as he slung his backpack and strode towards the waiting train. 'Oh well, not serious, it's the holidays. Come on. Let's find compartment 4065, there's still time to buy tuck.'

We found our cubicle and began settling down.

'This is great,' Alan said as he swung his arms. 'This little basin folds into a table.'

I hopped on the cushioned bench. 'These are the beds and those the bunks.' I pointed upward. 'Where are the other berths?'

Alan surveyed the room. 'Good question.'

At that moment, the door slid open, and I recognised one boy. 'Howzit Kev,' I said.

'Hey Rory, you in here with us? Cool,' he replied.

'Yep, me and Alan. He was at Wankie primary.'

'Oh shit, yeah, howzit, china.'

We shook hands.

'Thought you moved to Mazoe?' I asked Kev.

'We have. I'm staying with Giles.' Kev patted the fourth boy on the shoulder. 'My folks have gone overseas for two weeks.'

I recognised Giles but couldn't put my finger on it.

Giles nodded, then deflected our attention. 'So, which bunks do you guys have? I'll take one of the top ones, if that's okay?'

'Sure,' I said and stood back. Giles stretched, pressing against the side of the cubicle where a middle bunk descended. I lifted an eyebrow at Alan, who smiled and shook his head. A soft rap on the door distracted us. A frail lad with huge ears and a crew cut stared at us with doe eyes. 'Is this compartment D?'

'No, you rat. Now piss off,' I said.

Giles and Kev inhaled, their eyes darting between me and the door knocker.

When the urchin at the door opened his mouth to speak, I pounced. 'Don't stand there like a goldfish. Fuck off.'

'Give the poor guy a chance,' Kev intervened.

The newcomer, unable to control himself, burst into laughter and slapped my hand in greeting.

'Howzit numbnuts, how's the new school?' I said.

'Fine thanks, better than out in the sticks,' he replied.

'Guys, meet numbnuts from Milton.'

Numbnuts gave the others the two-fingered peace sign and stuck out a casual foot. I hid a smile at the sight of my short, skinny, crew cut friend trying to be smooth.

When the muffled public address system announced the imminent departure of the train to Wankie village, we gazed from the windows at the gaudy platform as it slipped away. With a whistle, the steam engine surged in a huff of vapour and soot. The conductor checked our tickets and made sure everyone was in their assigned cabins while an accompanying steward asked who needed bedding and breakfast. We were skint and declined. He chalked a number one on the cabin exit and moved to the next.

'Wonder what that means?' Alan said as he closed the door.

It opened again to show Richard. Unable to stay mad at our snooty chum, I broke the awkward silence. 'Howzit, Richard, we were just thinking about you.'

'Your bunk is that top one.' Alan made sure there was no confusion.

'One bed roll? Two dollars fifty,' the steward said from the doorway.

'That's mine, thanks. On the top bunk, please,' Richard said.

We sat like the three wise monkeys of *See no evil, hear no evil, speak no evil* except we had a fourth addition — do

127

no evil, and scrutinised the attendant, unravelling the crisped bedding. A hue of envy hung in the air as Richard climbed up, fluffed his feather pillow and without a word opened a thick dog-eared book titled *Hold My Hand I'm Dying*.

Alan shrugged. 'Let's explore, Rory. Come on.' The others remained behind, exhausted from roving the streets.

The two of us squeezed past the train attendant who was unpacking bedrolls from a storage locker. We grinned at one another with sly intent. Alan took the initiative. 'Excuse me, sir. Which way to the buffet car?' His face complimented his sugary voice.

'Well son, they don't allow kids on their own in the dining car, but you can buy refreshments from the hatch.' He pointed along the heaving aisle. Whilst distracted, I lunged into the closet, pinched a bedroll, and stuffed it under my arm and bolted with my head tucked into my shoulders, half expecting a yell of detection. When none was forthcoming, we slunk back into our compartment to the adulation of our compatriots. Richard viewed the desperados share the spoils with distaste.

I stripped to my underpants and rolled my clothes up for a pillow. Lying on my stomach, I watched the Cinemascope of life outside flash by — dense bush interrupted by empty railway sidings, orange streetlights but otherwise darkness. I was content with the chance of a good night's sleep.

We woke to the crib motion and soothing click-clack of the carriage. I pressed the last trappings of toothpaste onto my finger and rubbed my teeth. The rest splashed in lukewarm water from the tiny stainless-steel bowl in the cabin. One by one, we hushed and stuck our heads out of the windows, lost in thought as the train coughed and wheezed its way through the baobab studded granite *kopjes* of home. With leaden arms, I hauled myself further out of the window, pretending to wipe a fleck of soot from my eye. Moments later, a glint of glass in the baking sun caught my attention through the haze. 'There's the station, guys.'

Alan pulled at my shoulder. 'Where, where?'

I studied my best friend's face. 'Won't be long now, china.' Alan gazed into the wind, blinking away his tears.

The terminal that serviced the collieries and transported hundreds of tons of world-renowned bitumen coal was little more than a two-track siding. I drew back to the raucous mêlée in the passageway. Boys shoved, laughed, and yelled. I waited for the rush to pass and stuck out my head again. My thoughts on my homecoming and the prospect of seeing everyone — Themba and his family, and of looking up Bow, made my stomach churn.

When the train jolted to a halt, we disembarked, clutching our backpacks and cases.

'Hi, Mum,' I said and pecked her on the cheek before the other kids saw.

'Hello, Cara.'

'Rory?' she said in an uncertain voice as she stood as close to me as possible.

'What's wrong?' I asked her.

Cara's eyes flicked to Mum. She nodded.

'Dad's gone,' Cara said.

My heart stopped. 'Where's he gone?'

'Sweetheart, at least give your brother a chance to get home,' Mum said.

'Where's Dad?'

'They've called him up.' Mum hugged me.

'What do you mean, called him up?'

'Yes, my boy, he's gone to the Mozambique border in the north on active service for two months.'

I mulled the news over for a few seconds. 'But he's too old, surely?'

'They need him for his experience so he can train the cadets.' She embraced us and we headed for the ageing Renault and added. 'Besides, this government changes the rules to suit itself.'

Cara sat forward and peered at me in the front seat. 'Rory?'

'What?'

'Themba has also gone.'

I twisted towards my sister, who bit on her lip to hold back the tears. Empathy, flushed with a dose of anger, tore at my heart.

'Don't worry. It will be okay.' Cara touched my shoulder.

'I'm glad you're home, Rorke.'

I glanced at my mother; her white knuckles gripped the steering wheel. I chose not to pursue the issue.

Where the hell is Themba? I hope he's all right. Is it to do with the fighting? What if he and Dad are on opposite sides? I leant against the side window; the vibrations of the glass tickled my nose as I perused the sidewalks.

It wasn't long before we pulled into the entrance.

'Empty your clothes into the wash. Our temporary boy will be here tomorrow,' Mum said as we battled our way into the house with my large-black tin trunk.

'I can smell your socks from here.' Mum wrinkled her nose at me.

'Mum?' I blushed.

'Right, that should do it,' Mother said as she wiped her reddened hands. 'Kids. I must get back to work. I'll bring something home for supper.'

I waved to the car disappearing out of the driveway and cast a look at Themba's *khaya* at the bottom of the garden. An eerie silence swathed the once-bustling home of my confidant. The brushed dirt courtyard sported weeds as a dripping tap stained the outside cement washbasin. Cobwebs claimed the corners of the twin-room dwelling. The soot above the extinct fire was no longer black. The faint perfume of their existence clung to the surrounds — smoke, carbolic soap and whitewash on the walls sparked fond memories. I plonked myself on the tree trunk next to Themba's, where we had spent many hours together. The hive of the family's social being was hushed.

Where are you, Themba? What happened? What is going on?

'Hello, sir,' said a man standing halfway down the driveway.

'Morning,' I replied.

'My name is Tshabalala. I am here to help the madam clean the house.' He clapped his hands in the conventional greeting.

'Oh, okay.' I walked inside with the substitute domestic worker.

Tshabalala changed into his white apron and made himself a mug of tea before setting about the housework. Aware of

130

my attention, he straightened up from sweeping the floor and smiled. 'Do you miss Themba?'

I nodded, not wanting to confide in the stranger. He looked old enough to be Themba's father.

'That is good, you must. I am only helping him out. I am not taking his job.'

'Where did he go?'

'He needs to take care of things. His family is with their *ubuntu* while he is away. He asked me to tell you not to worry.'

'Thanks.'

'Good, now can we be friends, Mr Rory.' He held out his right hand, supported at the elbow by his left, in the traditional mark of respect. I shook his hand and looked him in the eyes. He seems nice enough.

When Cara popped out to visit her friends across the road, I headed up the *kopje* in search of Bow. I stopped halfway and surveyed my dominion, taking in the sights, sounds, and smells. I strutted on up to where I'd last seen my pal. The sun was warm on my back. 'Bow, where are you?' I scratched through the undergrowth on my hands and knees. 'Show yourself. It's me, Rory. I'm here.' I paused and scrutinised the bush, spitting out specks of dust. Debris filled my blonde hair. I brushed a cobweb tickling the side of my face, then sat cross-legged in silence as I hoped for a hint of movement. 'Bow, stop messing around. I know you're here, somewhere,' I said before I meandered up the hill, muttering to myself. 'Well, it's up to you, Bow. I'm going to the village. You can wait for your bugs.' I placed a handful of insects into my breast pocket and headed for town.

I was a kilometre down the road when the earth shook, accompanied by a deep rumbling.

What the hell was that?

The ribbon of tarmac disappeared into the distant heat haze. On the horizon, a puff of dust rose into the air.

It's not from the mines; they're in the opposite direction. I recalled Wankie's infamous mine disaster years earlier. The larger the world had ever seen; it killed four hundred and twenty-six miners. The town would never be the same. I plucked a fresh shoot of grass, placing it in the corner of my mouth, and sat on a painted road marker.

Puffs of smoke from diesel engines choked the air as a fleet of armoured cars hurtled past with such force, it almost knocked me over. The unique V-shaped trucks, the first in the world, withstood the blast of landmines. Out the rear of each camouflaged vehicle, officers clutching weapons faced one another. A full five minutes passed before the roar of the convoy dissipated. I waved to each truck and received a salute from soldiers who noticed me on the side of the highway. It reminded me of movie *Kelly's Heroes*. I hummed the theme song from *Burning Bridges* as I marched in the middle of the road. My thoughts turned to my father, who would also be in uniform, then to Themba and his whereabouts — the lump in my throat grew.

At the shops, I ran the outside tap until the water cooled enough to drink, then made myself comfortable under the canopy of the small shopping centre.

Some things never change.

Mr Nicolaou still wore his greasy apron as he held a spatula in his sausage-like fingers. Perspiration rolled down his jowls as he deep-fried takeaways. Skeletal, Mr Kloppers leant against the doorway of his butchery, chatting to Mr Pereira, who was busy checking his fresh produce. Mr Winterbottom, a young pimply faced man who ran the town's grocery store, sat in his office scribbling away. The bank's solemn visitors slipped in and out of the tinted-glass facia. Two liquor stores flanked the centre. One housed a dubious crowd playing pool with distorted blaring music, while the other doubled as the town pharmacy. I couldn't work out the mysterious shop with the words *TOTE* painted above it.

Must be a bank, because those leaving look sadder than when they went in.

Mr Pereira beckoned from across the car park. 'Is that you, young Master Wilde? I see you're back. Come here.'

I acknowledged the short, dark-haired man and headed towards the greengrocer with its awnings in the colours of Portugal. 'Hi, Mr Pereira.'

'Never mind, *hi, Mr Pereira*. He poked me in the ribs. How skinny you've got, amigo.'

'Do your mother a favour and choose five-fresh fruits and

bring them to me. *Rapido meu garoto* — hurry my boy.' He crossed his arms across his rotund chest as he winked at Mr Kloppers the butcher. Inside the shop were wooden boxes loaded with mountains of produce of every shape and colour. I grabbed my favourite ones and went back outside.

'*Bom Menino.* What did you find?' He held the items in the air.

'Tell me the name of each *fruta.*' His deep brown eyes matched his Mediterranean skin.

'Orange, banana, granadilla, lemon, and an avo.' I rattled off the names.

'Never shorten their names. What is the proper name for this?'

'Avocado?'

'Avocado, what?' Mr Pereira said, raising his thick eyebrows.

Embarrassed, I shrugged and glanced at the watchful butcher.

Mr Pereira softened. 'Avocado pear and you are right to choose it as a fruit.' He ruffled my hair. 'Now get a bag of each and take them home to your *mãe* and give her *meus cumprimentos* — my regards.'

I tied the bags together and bid farewell to the shopkeepers. When Mr Kloppers ducked into his shop, he returned with a brown paper bag. 'Here's *biltong.* Now on your way.'

'Wow, thanks, sir.' The spicy strips of beef or game were my favourite snack.

I walked to the back of the centre where there were more shops reserved for the non-white trader. I waved to the old cobbler, who sat on the porch outside Gulab's haberdashery, pumping the manual Singer sewing machine with his foot. The man, with a wizened face, tipped his trilby and gave a toothy grin. '*Namaste,* Rorke Wilde.'

'*Kem chhe?*' I asked.

'The birds are still singing,' he said as he raised a gnarled finger to the heavens.

I continued past the rolls of fabric displayed in the window. A few paces further on, black youths propping up the far end of the porch eyed me with disdain. I hurried on, ignoring the jeers behind me.

133

I bet they're Sipho's friends. No wonder Themba worries about his son.

I readjusted the groceries on the cycle rack and prepared for the three-kilometre ride home.

Mum wrapped her arms around me the minute I walked through the door. 'Hi. Did you have a pleasant afternoon?' she asked as she planted a kiss on my forehead. 'I'm glad you made it home before dark. Cara, draw the curtains, darling, and I'll dish up.'

I headed to the lounge-cum-dining room to find the girls beaming.

'Sit, Rory,' they said in unison.

I pulled up a chair without taking my eyes off them. My mother disappeared into the kitchen and brought out a large, fat-stained brown bag.

'Guess what I got for supper?' she said.

I shrugged.

Mum shook out plate-sized beef burgers wrapped in a greaseproof paper that had **Kansas Roadhouse** strewn across it.

'Cool.' I licked my lips and my eyes bulged at the size of the patty in front of me. I peeled off the top half of the bun and showed my sister. 'And it's got cheese too.'

Cara squealed and dived into the kitchen for a family-size cola.

'Cool, man,' I mumbled through an oversized mouthful.

Mum threw up her hands in mock despair.

Afterwards, we sat in the lounge. I sprawled out on the couch as Cara chatted to Sally-Anne, her red-haired doll. Mother sat with her legs curled under her as she read and sipped tea. Before I gave in to an over-full belly, a twinge tugged at my heart upon seeing my father's empty armchair.

Hope Themba is okay.

Then I thought about Jannie and his pain at having to leave the country and I whispered *Tannie* Hester's saying before I drifted off. *'Magie vol, ogies toe.'* I imagined her closing her eyes and rubbing her tummy.

Chapter Twelve

After another fruitless attempt at locating Bow, I traipsed down the *kopje* to Alan's place. The dawn mist, implying winter, was on its way, succumbing to the belligerent sun.

'Wake up, you lazy shit,' I said to Alan.

He pulled his dishevelled head from under the pillows and peered through puffy eyes.

I stripped back his blanket and flopped into a rattan chair. 'Time to make a move. The frog's gone, so we're on our own.'

'The frog?' Alan asked.

'Yup. Your folk's Citroen isn't in the drive. Let's get out of here.'

'Okay, okay, I'm up.' Alan scratched his crotch and stumbled to the toilet. 'So, what's the plan?' he asked over the sound of his Victoria Falls.

'Why don't we ride out to that new army camp?'

'What? But that's kilometres away.'

'So, we'll take rations. We've gone further than that.'

'Cool, let's do it.' Alan splashed his face and changed.

We raided the pantry and took baked beans, bread, and a sachet of Kool Aid, all of which we loaded onto the carriers on the rear of our bicycles.

'Sixpence? Tell Mum I'll be home for supper. So, don't bother about lunch. Thanks,' Alan said to the servant as he waved without looking back.

We crossed the hills by clicking into first gear and grinding upward, then we hurtled along in third, with one eye on our speedometers, with disregard to the consequences of falling onto the tarmac at breakneck speeds or the possibility of oncoming traffic.

We swerved to a halt on top of the final *kopje* and found a shady place to rest and plan our descent. The barracks below covered twenty rugby fields with row upon row of tents and an array of trucks. The soldiers, ant-like, scurried back and forth.

Whitewashed rocks encircled an immaculate parade ground at the entrance to the encampment. A limp-green and white Rhodesian flag hung in the centre.

'They're busy. Not a good idea to bother them,' Alan said as he swiped at a fly.

I took another hard look, then swung back to my accomplice. 'I wonder how close we can get.'

'Are you crazy?'

We peered over the precipice once more.

'It'll be great. They won't notice us,' I added.

'Those are soldiers. If they catch us, they'll throw us in a pit, or shoot us as spies, or both.'

I swallowed hard. 'You've been watching too many movies. I reckon...' We devised a plan and set off.

Our khakis masked us amid the tufts of dry savannah, as did the ant mounds that reached heavenward in reverence to Mother Nature. We scrutinised the nearest sentry, careful not to poke our eyes out on the vicious two-inch white thorns.

'This is where things get tricky,' I said from behind the *wag-n-bietjie* tree.

'No shit, Sherlock.' Alan's face flushed from leopard-crawling. 'You're not well. Do you know that?'

The guard wiped his brow, took a nip out of the water bottle from around his waist, then continued his patrol. Each step discharged a puff of dust.

'Okay, now's our chance,' I said.

'This is madness.' Despite ongoing protestations, Alan followed and doubled over as we headed for the blind spot behind the guardhouse. Around the corner the same, but now angry, soldier stood waiting with folded arms across his chest. He carted us by the scruff of our necks; our feet weren't touching the ground.

'Sir, these are the lads who infiltrated the camp.' The sentry's forearm, which was larger than my waist, sported a tattoo of a proud eagle among the silverware of menacing daggers, obscured my vision. He dropped us in front of a tent where a man at a typewriter sat at a makeshift desk.

'Thank you, sergeant,' a soft, well-spoken voice said. 'You can leave them with me.'

'Are you sure? They're slippery scallywags, sir.' The

sergeant winked.

'That's all right, my good man. I'll show these lads around and teach them what they can expect when they're old enough to serve their country. We need everyone to do their bit and appreciate what Rhodesia requires of them.' He saluted and turned to us. 'Right lads, let me show you the camp. Be sure to listen to everything. No exceptions.'

I covered my ears at the roar of artillery. Blue smoke swirled and the caustic smell of cordite burnt my nostrils. The terrain erupted from the impact of the high-velocity shells that shredded all in their path. I hooted, a noise that was feeble by comparison — I screamed louder. The rush of adrenalin kicked in.

'Check it out, china,' I said, prodding Alan from his self-induced cocoon.

Alan mustered a grin and flipped onto his back as he waited for the line of prone soldiers alongside to exhaust their semi-automatic magazines. A muffled calm followed. Our ears hummed. The world held its breath — the silence absolute.

'That was cool, hey?' I announced as I foresaw the all-clear from the instructor. 'Let's get closer.'

'Bloody hell, that was loud,' Alan said as he opened and closed his jaw and wriggled a finger in each ear. The targets, depicting evil foes charging, perished in an instant, as if it was a nuclear catastrophe. We headed for the carnage in search of spent cartridges on the firing range.

The squad huddled in small groups in what little shade was available. Gas burners hissed and water boiled for lunch. Alan opened a ration pack given to us by the sergeant.

We sat to one side, away from the squaddies. 'Bully beef, tea, powdered milk, sugar,' Alan read the faded labels. 'What's this?' I took the silver tube from Alan. 'Looks like toothpaste,' I said, as I unscrewed the top and squeezed the contents onto my finger. 'No, it's butter.'

'Are you boys looking or cooking?' the sergeant asked, his shadow blotting out the sun.

'Cooking, sir,' I said.

'Well, open those damn mess tins and get cracking.'

I grabbed the iron vessel, unfolding the handle and turned it into a saucepan. Alan tried to lever the tin of food with a penknife, to no avail.

'Give me that knife.' The soldier used his giant hands. 'Here. The rest's up to you.' He gave the utensil back to Alan. 'What you got there, son?' His enormous, sun-tanned face showed signs of kindness. I offered him the brass casings we had collected earlier. 'Well, that's mighty interesting. Can you tell one from another?' he asked.

We shook our heads.

'Well then, I'll tell you. Permission to join the camp.' A sign of respect when joining another soldier's place of rest, irrespective of rank.

'Pass me one of each size,' he said as he waited for me to re-join my friend. 'Thank you. Now read the casing. 7.62 mm, right?' he continued. 'This one is also 7.62 mm, but shorter. Do you see that?'

Again, we nodded.

'The longer 7.62 mm casing is from an army issue Belgium FN rifle or MAG machine gun. The shorter version was the Kalashnikov AK-47 assault rifle and RPD machine gun — communist weapons used by our enemy.' His face hardened and his lips thinned.

Alan fidgeted.

'This is a 9 mm shell from a Browning Parabellum pistol. This .303-inch casing is for our Browning machine guns, not to mention our second world war Lee-Enfield single-shot rifles.' The sergeant stood and rubbed his hands. 'If you want to know about arms and ammunition, just ask me. Don't be shy.'

We thanked him and sought shelter from the heat.

'When will they let us go?' I broke the silence.

'When we've learnt our lesson.'

'It's not so terrible. The shooting was fun.'

Alan shut his eyes and shook his head. 'What's wrong with you?' he asked. 'How can you be enjoying this?' He stirred the cauldron on our cooker, which was reducing the bully beef in water using a stock cube. We dipped in the dog biscuits to soak up the gravy, sweetened by a smidgen of Apricot jam, then washed it down with the tepid Kool Aid.

138

I watched the futile efforts of a wispy cloud to subdue the midday sun. I recalled how Ticky viewed authoritative figures with suspicion. My father was no different. He always suspected the locals.

Where did all this mistrust come from?

As if they were beads of quicksilver, the soldiers reassembled after lunch and stood in the blistering heat. We sidled up to the troop carrier to watch. Alan leant against the bodywork but recoiled, shaking his hand. 'Shit, that's bloody hot. We could have cooked our meal on here.'

We shimmied underneath the vehicle to avoid the sun and detection. 'You'd think they'd wear shorts and a T-shirt in this heat,' Alan said.

I nodded. 'Yes, but it's about camouflage. The long sleeves and pants break up their outline in the bush.'

Alan listened with intent.

'Look, they paint the rifles green and brown, even this troop carrier,' I said as I patted the tyre tread beside me.

'What about the tyres, they're still black?' Alan said.

'Maybe they had a puncture?'

'What, six wheels?'

'Don't worry about it. Why is the troop carrier V-shaped and has extra steel?'

'To stop bullets?'

'More for protection against landmines,' I said.

'So, it can drive over booby traps?'

I nodded while I studied the soldiers, who were being given orders by the sergeant.

'And the tyres…?' Alan said.

'Never mind the bloody colour. Let's move before they run us over,' I said as I squirmed from under the vehicle, thankful I didn't have to discuss the conundrum of the tyres.

'There you are you little buggers. Jump into the Land Rover, your day's not over,' the sergeant said.

I pointed at the troop carrier, but the sergeant wasn't interested. 'Don't even try it, Sunshine. That's reserved for actual soldiers,' he said.

We bounced around in the utility's tail like snooker balls as the driver negotiated the bumpy, anthill-endowed terrain. We giggled and clung to the sides of the canopy.

'This is better than the park. You look like a clown,' Alan said as he spat an insect into the wind.

'You do too, china,' I replied.

We hurtled into the rear of the cab as it skidded to a standstill. From the back of the vehicle, we watched soldiers performing manoeuvres on the drill square.

'Lads, I have a task for you,' the sergeant said as he marched us across the camp to the mess tent. 'See those drums? I want them cleaned out before you go home.'

We filled buckets with water from the mobile bowser and approached the half dozen forty-four-gallon drums.

I dropped my bucket. 'Shit, what stinks?' I said.

Alan buried his nose in the crook of his arm. 'You're right. It is shit.'

I held my breath and peered into the drum, where I found a congealed mass of rotting food.

'You have got to be kidding,' Alan said. 'That's disgusting.'

'It's infested with maggots.'

'No way, man. Forget it,' Alan said.

'We must. If we don't want our folks to know.'

'Yes, but...' Alan closed his mouth. He picked up the bucket and tossed it into the barrel. 'It isn't fair. It's your fault, Rorke Wilde. We would never have come here if you hadn't mentioned it.'

I ignored him; guilt played its part.

'Hold on. Hold on, you two.' A skinny man with a potbelly approached us as he wiped his palms on a grubby apron. 'Take off your clothes otherwise you'll stink all day.' He displayed gapped teeth. 'Call me chef,' he added as he yanked off our clothes down to our boxer shorts and hang them on a tree. 'That's better. Now get moving; I must prepare dinner.' Chef returned to the food tent, smearing his hands on his apron.

'He looks pregnant,' Alan said.

'Never mind that. 'Let's get finished.'

We scraped and washed until the sergeant reappeared. 'Not bad. Now get yourselves to the shower. It's sixteen hundred and time to get you home.'

We grabbed our clothes as we ran through the gauntlet of mocking soldiers. The icy water from the outdoor shower took our breaths away but brought respite to body and mind.

Once dressed, the sergeant beckoned us. 'Put your bikes in the troop carrier and climb in. You're going home.'

Alan checked me out.

'What's wrong, boys? Why the hell are you waiting?' the sergeant asked us.

We tore off to the guard hut where our cycles were.

'Can you believe it?' Alan said.

'We're soldiers now.' I announced to my friend.

This doesn't seem so bad. Cool guns and things. Maybe men enjoy fighting and killing. What if I have no choice?

An inner voice from deep within attacked my line of thought with visions of death, pain, and cruelty.

Bloody fool. Don't let them wear you down, Rorke Wilde. This just isn't right. Themba warned me of this.

***

On the final evening before returning to school, the family *braaied* dinner. Dad was busy with the fire in the half drum. The steel grill leant against the legs of the drum, holding it off the grass. Mother prepared salads and the smell of garlic bread wafted through the fly screen door of the kitchen. Meanwhile, Cara entertained her dolls around a pink table with matching chairs next to the wrought-iron outdoor set.

Mum passed a bottle of beer to Dad, who mopped his brow and took a swig.

'Rorke, we have news,' she said as she glanced at Dad.

'We do, my boy.' He took over. 'The police force has transferred me. We'll be leaving Wankie while you're at school next term. It is why I'm home early from border duty.'

'What? Again?'

'You know it's every couple of years, dear. We've been here almost three,' Mum said.

'I thought because Dad was in charge we would stay here longer?'

'Afraid not, son. We are moving North to Mangula in Mashonaland near the Kariba Dam.'

'That's the opposite side of the country, six hundred kilos away,' I said.

'There's an overnight train and perhaps on the exeat weekends we can fly you home,' Mum said.

'My sixth town and I'm only thirteen.'

'Dear, at least you won't need to change schools this time,' she replied.

My open mouth sent my mother into a tizzy, causing her to dive back into the kitchen.

'It isn't your mum's fault,' Dad said.

'I know.'

I went inside, took Mum's hand, and brought her to the barbecue. 'If nothing else, we've got tonight.'

Tomorrow the nightmare of school starts. I knew this would happen and it's one reason I followed my Wankie friends to Plumtree. At least we are together.

The lights from our prefabricated home cast a glow where we cooked over the coals. The African night was alive with the chirp of insects and the beat of drums from a nearby *kraal*. Sparks joined the milky way with each waft of breeze.

'So why Mangula, Dad?' I asked.

'They've promoted me, son. After this one I'll pick up bigger towns, not sleepy *dorps*. Better for us. More so as you two get older.' He pointed to Cara resting against Mum's shins.

I nodded and sipped on my Coke.

'The war is hotting up and Mangula is right in the middle. They expect the police to help fight the war and keep law and order.' Dad's face showed all. 'It's difficult to balance warfare and civil duties,' he said, more to himself than anyone else.

Mum dabbed a tissue on either side of her nose. 'We'll be fine guys, you'll see,' she said, with her eyes brimming.

The next term passed as the first. We grasped how best to survive in an environment both hostile and boring. School life, the immediate threat, adapting to civil war, the greater concern. The move to a new town meant fitting in again. Difficult when you've been away at boarding school.

Life at Mangula was a time of personal loneliness as I spent my holidays in the isolated copper-mining town. I turned inwards and went for lengthy walks with my new best friend after losing Bow — a fine dog named Pilot that my parents gave me to ease my boredom. He was a red-pedigree boxer with a demeanour and deviance that suited my own. Our treks through the bush got me to thinking about the times we lived and to write them down on paper.

In 1978, the family moved once more. This time to the tobacco-farming village of Karoi, less than a hundred kilometres from Mangula. It was closer to the Zambian border, from where one faction of the freedom fighters, backed by the Russians, operated. Themba country and soon after arriving in our new town, and to my utmost joy, he re-joined the household.

Our new home adjoined the police station, along with another three that housed officers from the army and the home guard on a nearby piece of land commissioned to accommodate anti-landmine troop carriers. The rugby field across the road from us was used to land Bell helicopters. It was there that I stumbled over my first body in a tin coffin. They stacked it with other caskets in the baking sun in the station's backyard. It was a sight that stayed with me for time immemorial.

In another three years, I would leave school and do my national service. I would be one of those soldiers who outnumbered the police at the Karoi station.

We travelled to and from the country's capital, Salisbury by convoy, where the vehicles and a stick of soldiers guarded civilians against ambush. Armed men, women, and children occupied each car with handguns, shotguns and automatic weapons at the ready. We were at war — it was survival. A generation lost their youth, if not their lives. And the world looked on, not understanding or choosing not to. The defensive laager mentality of white Africa was once more in practice.

The school Sunday exeats ceased — the bush became a no-go. Three-metre-high, security fencing sealed the school grounds and defended by the national guard patrols, a version of the dad's army during the Second World War.

Evening prayers in the prep-room became announcements of boys killed in action, some only nineteen years old. They equipped prefects with .303 Enfield's in case of attack. At fifteen years of age, the school armed us when the seniors left after their exams. Trained to evacuate if attacked and where to take cover should we face a mortar barrage. We spent several nights in the washrooms lying on the concrete floors listening

to the firefights and tracer bullets lighting the sky clutching
our weapons. Fear was an everyday emotion. Our darkest hour
approached — the resultant silence from the rest of humanity
was deafening. The name *Hunyani,* anglicised from the Shona
word *Manyame* meaning sad, would change the country and
its people forever. A pivotal point in Southern African history
marking the end of the beginning.

Chapter Thirteen

The 3rd of September 1978 started off as any other Sunday. Spring was in the air, and the birds were in full song. Mum and Dad lazed around in the lounge, reading, or listening to the wireless.

That evening, as Mum prepared dinner, the phone shrilled. 'Hello? Yes, he is. Hold on, please.' She stuck her head through the doorway. 'Dear, it's for you,' she called out to Dad. 'Sounds urgent.'

'Why always on a Sunday? No rest for the wicked, I suppose,' Father said as he dragged himself up from his chair and lumbered to the telephone in the hall.

'Hello.'

'What?'

'Flight 825?'

Followed by a silence that lasted forever. He replaced the earpiece, staring down at it, then said to himself. *'Hunyani?'*

'What is it?' Mum asked.

'Something's cropped up.' Dad threw on a tunic and hugged my mother. 'A civilian plane has crashed near here.'

'An accident?'

'We're not sure yet. The pilot said it was engine failure. I'll catch you later, don't wait up.' Boney M's the *Rivers of Babylon* played in background.

We ate dinner in silence as we listened to the clatter of helicopters and the drone of planes. Bedtime came and still there was no sign of my father. The night buzzed — all was not well.

I woke to the sound of pounding on the front door and voices arguing. Before I cleared my head, an arm stretched through my window and pulled aside the curtains. I was fifteen years old and six feet tall.

'What the fuck are you doing?' I shouted as I leapt towards the opening. 'Mum, are you okay?' I called out.

'Is your father at home?' a stranger with a microphone who was intruding through the window asked.

'Tell him we want to speak to him,' said another as a television camera turned towards me.

'Fuck off,' I shouted and slammed the louvre windows and ran through to the lounge where I found Dad forcing the front door closed as Mum kicked at feet that were trying to prevent that from happening. Once shut, Dad spoke into his two-way radio. 'The international press is here. They smell something. I'll be up in five minutes. Over.' He hugged Mum again, then ruffled my hair. 'I'll see you guys later. Whatever you do, don't open the doors or speak to anyone.' He left dressed in the same clothes he'd worn yesterday.

'I hope they haven't woken Cara,' Mum said as she crept to her room to check and then closed her door.

I peered at the melee of vans, television cameras, and the journalist through the curtains.

'All hell is breaking loose,' Mum whispered. 'Something too terrible has happened.' Tears streamed down her cheeks.

'The plane?'

She nodded, biting her lip.

When the blade slap of helicopters drew my attention, I snuck out of the door, hoping the press wouldn't resume their assault. Outside, the military had pushed them behind police tape.

I headed across the deserted road; everyone was too busy to bother with a teenage boy. V-shaped landmine-proof vehicles and armoured trucks were trundling in from the outskirts of town. The blank expressions of the soldiers hinted at the scale of the incident. At other times, we waved and joked with one another.

I perched on the fence around the rugby field when the night sky was lit up with flashing blue lights and an ordnance of off-road trucks screeched to a halt metres away. A helicopter landed frothing medics, soldiers, and officials onto the makeshift landing pad. Nearby, the press surged, restrained by the camouflaged personnel. The reception party plucked civilians from the chopper into waiting Red Cross vehicles. Two of the survivors climbed into the back of a truck, their expressions forever etched in my conscience — a mother and daughter looked straight through me — living a nightmare only they could see, the puzzlement, the vulnerability, and the wretched despair was a sight I never wish to witness again. My stomach turned, my head spun, I dropped to my knees and puked.

A pair of hands slid beneath my armpits and raised me to my feet. Themba took me home and sat me on the steps outside the kitchen door. He placed a mug of hot tea beside me and left me be.

I don't recall how long I sat there, but my next recollection was of Themba shaking my shoulder. 'Come inside and lock the door behind you.' He gestured towards the house with his eyes.

Without question, I followed. I hadn't seen him in this mood.

'Your mother and father are at the station with the rest of the officers. They'll come home for something to eat, then return to the operations room,' he said.

'What's going on?' I asked.

His face softened, then turned stony. 'Now is not the time. A plane crashed near here. That is all we know.'

'Why are we locking the doors?'

'Just to be safe. These are troubling times.'

'Ngiyabonga ukuza kwakho ngekhaya baba wami.' I spoke in broken *isiNdebele* — thank you for coming home, my father.

Themba cupped my face with his hand, unable to say a word.

A few hours later, when keys rattled in the back door, I heard Mum speaking.

'Hi Themba,' she said. 'Is everything okay?'

'Yes, madam, it has been very quiet.'

'Where are the kids?'

'In their rooms. Shall I get them?'

'No, I want to keep everything as normal as possible. Mr Wilde will be here in a few minutes, then we'll have dinner.'

'Okay, madam. I'll serve up the food when you are ready.' Then there was a minute of whispering, but I couldn't hear because of the air con. I turned it off and opened the louvre windows in my room. The night was hushed. Apprehension crept through the trees on the far side of the garden. The drone from the police camp continued unabated — the world was not at peace.

A further set of keys in the kitchen door announced Dad's arrival.

'Hi guys, a quick change, then we'll eat. I need to get back.' The strain in his voice was obvious. He popped his head into my bedroom. 'Hi. How are you doing?' He looked worse than he sounded.

'I'm good, Dad.' I was lying in the top corner of my bed, clutching my pillow.

'That's good. You ready for a bite?'

'Not really,' I replied.

Dad sat on the side of the mattress. 'Listen, son, these are tough times; I need you to be strong. We cannot allow others to change our lives. If we do, they will win.' He reached over and gave my leg a light punch, then ducked out.

I sat for a minute. Who are they? Who are the others? Why don't they just talk this whole thing through? What is each side hoping to gain?

Themba placed the macaroni cheese in front of my mother. She dished up and passed the first plate to my father.

'Dad, I'm not hungry,' Cara, who was sitting on the opposite side of me, said.

'Try some, my dear. You'll feel better with food in your tummy.'

'But Mum...?'

'Ouch!' she squealed. 'Mum, Rory kicked me under the table.'

'Don't you dare lay a finger on your sister again.' Dad had a go at me.

'Oh, leave him be. He hardly touched her.' Mum retaliated in my defence.

I flicked a bit of cheese sauce from the end of my fork which hit Cara between the eyes.

'Rory, that's not funny.' She let out a high-pitched screech.

'You little shit.' Dad leant across the table and clipped me behind the ear.

'Don't you hit him; you bully.' Mum added to the pandemonium.

Everyone was up in arms shouting and remonstrating, no one listening at all.

Once again, Themba saved me by restoring the peace with a jug of iced water. A rare treat at mealtimes. We listened to the radio and for a moment, normality returned.

Themba was dishing up the apple crumble and custard when the kitchen door shook, followed by thumping on the front one. Mum glanced at Dad.

'Who can that be?' she asked.

Dad rose to his feet and grabbed the semi-automatic. He slid against the wall and peeked through the window.

'Who is it, dear?'

'I'm not sure. Everyone, get under the table. You too, Themba,' Dad said.

The hammering grew louder, as did the rattling of the doorknobs. Dad again kept to the wall as he did with the kitchen door earlier, this time a spotlight flashed into his face.

'Oh shit...' It was rare that Dad ever swore in front of us. He crouched on one knee and signalled to us under the table. 'It's just the press. Come out from under there. I'll get rid of them.'

'Right kids into the lounge, let's see what's on TV,' Mum said.

We dived onto the settee with relief and left Dad to deal with the baying rabble.

'I'll talk to you guys once you stop harassing my family,' he yelled through the letter slot in the door. Though the battering stopped, the commotion continued. A medley of headlights played on our wall.

Dad came into the lounge. 'How do I look?' he asked.

Mum got up, adjusted his tie, and tapped at the polished-gold buttons on his tunic. 'Be careful, dear. They sound a rowdy bunch.'

'I've dealt with their likes. I'll be back in an hour. Just want to nip up to the ops room to see how things are going.' He headed for the kitchen door.

'Okay, dear. See you when I see you. Say bye to your father, Cara.'

'Bye, Daddy.' She hugged him and climbed back onto the settee with the book she was reading.

The door squeaked open as father tried to leave the house, but a mob of reporters with microphones, cameras, and lights burst their way in.

'Mum! Mum!' Cara shouted as she dived into my mother's arms.

Dad attempted to fend them off, but the weight of numbers forced him back.

'Inspector Wilde was it an accident or an act of war?' a correspondent asked as he shoved a microphone into Dad's face.

'I believe there were survivors...' the reporter continued. 'Our sources say ZIPRA terrorists shot down the plane with a SAM 7 heat-seeking missile.?'

'Inspector Wilde, *Scope Magazine,* South Africa here. Is it true they murdered the survivors after it crash landed?' Another reporter interrupted.

Dad's face turned ashen; they drowned his voice out before he could answer.

'We've heard there's been incidents of rape.' The tabloid writer pushed forward.

Mother launched herself from her seat and cocked the rifle that had been lying next to her. The loading mechanism silenced the baying mob.

'You have five seconds to leave my home. You are scaring my children and for that I will not hesitate to shoot the whole goddam lot of you!' Mum's face turned blood red. There was no misreading that she meant business.

'Themba, help me get these low-life out of here,' Dad said as he rallied.

'Yes, sir.' Themba man-handled the rabble from the residence, by which time Dad's officers arrived and took control.

Mum normalised the house by drying Cara's tears and running a bath and filling it with bath salts and scent.

'Right, sweetheart. Jump in the bath and try to relax. It's over now,' Mum said as she came back to the lounge with her arms held out.

'You were great, Mum. Would you have shot them?' I asked.
'A couple of them tempted me.' She winked, brushing my sister's hair.

'So cool,' I said as I got up and hugged my mother and my little sister. We held each other for a while, drawing strength.

Days ran into nights as we hunkered out of sight of the press and military. My parents spent most of their time at the incident room co-ordinating with the joint operations of the police, army, and the air force.

On Wednesday morning, I walked through to the kitchen. Themba was washing last night's dishes while Cara slept in her bed. Mum and Dad were long gone and wouldn't be back until the wee hours of the next morning. I ate a bowl of cornflakes as I sat on the lounge floor before turning on the radio. It was then that I caught sight of the headline on the previous day's Rhodesian Herald — **Tuesday 5 September 1978.**

SHOT AT POINT BLANK RANGE

Ten shocked and numb survivors of the Air Rhodesia Viscount disaster were ordered to their feet by terrorists in the vicinity of the crash and shot dead at point-blank range, combined operations headquarters said in a statement last night. Eyewitness reports stated that 18 of the 52 passengers survived the crash and were alive and well at 5.45 p.m. on Sunday, the report said. Of these, five escaped through thick bush to seek help from local tribespeople while 13 remained close to the aircraft. Terrorists later approached the scene and ordered the shocked and numb survivors to their feet. The terrorists then opened fire with communist-made Kalashnikov assault rifles and 10 of the passengers — as yet unnamed, but six known to be women — died in a hail of fire. The three who survived the massacre were named. They are in Kariba Hospital suffering from nothing more serious than numb feet, following the impact of the plane as it hit the ground. Combined operations headquarters were unable last night to name the terror victims. The five who made their way to nearby kraals were at the Andrew Fleming Hospital in Salisbury by nightfall yesterday. One was discharged soon after arrival. A spokesman for the hospital said it remained to be seen whether the others would spend the night at the hospital. The combined operations statement went on — on arriving at the scene of the crash this morning security force members said a starboard engine appeared to have exploded and the starboard external side of the plane was heavily scorched. The terrorists looted the plane. The wreckage of what appeared to be the missing plane was spotted by the pilot of an air force Dakota, who said there was no sign of survivors. At Kariba Airport a family anxiously awaited news of the fate of relatives who were visiting Rhodesia from Scotland. After a short discussion with military personnel, who had come off one of the Dakotas in search of the wreck, he indicated to a reporter he had been told there was little likelihood of any survivors. His relatives were not among the survivors. Also keeping vigil at the airport was a manager of a Kariba hotel, whose wife and four-year-old daughter were on the flight. His daughter was discharged from the Andrew Fleming Hospital in Salisbury last night while her mother was detained there. Her condition was said to be satisfactory. At 12.10 Air Rhodesia announced officially that the wreck had been found and that a helicopter had been sent for a closer look after the plane had been spotted from a fixed-wing aircraft. The Viscount had been missing since it took off from Kariba for Salisbury at about 5 p.m. on Sunday carrying 52 passengers and four crew. First eyewitness accounts of the wreck say that it appeared to be completely burnt out. Paratroopers and paramedics were dropped at the crash site, which is in an area heavily infested with terrorists. An air force pilot who flew over the wreck said that the only identifiable part of the plane was its tail. His impression was that the pilot had tried to land in a 400 metre patch of comparatively open bush and that, while attempting to put the plane down, hit a gulley. The Viscount apparently broke up on impact.

A rage from the depths of my very being erupted through me. My heartbeat so loud my chest heaved at the outrage welling up. I couldn't breathe and my hands shook. 'What the fuck?' I said, emphatic enough to bring Themba into the room.

He rushed over and lifted me to my feet. 'Come with me,

jaha.' He led me into the garage, where he stuffed a duffel bag full of old clothing. 'Now attack this.'

I launched my demons at the makeshift punchbag, kicking, punching, and biting it with as much force as I could muster. The beast rolled on the ground; I smashed it against the wall, trying to tear it apart.

After a short while, I lay sweating and panting. Themba helped me to my feet. Tears threatened us both.

'Fear not your anger, Chameleon, but always control it. For it will take you places you shall regret for the rest of your life.'

'Have you seen what they have done?' I asked him.

'Yes, my friend, but it was *those* people. Not all the people. The difference matters. Understand what makes some behave, how they do, and why it angers you so.'

'Sorry, I yell at you too often of late.'

'No apologies needed. Emotions are natural, more so in young warriors. Now let's have a cup of sweet tea. What do you say?' We walked inside, where we sipped our drinks and talked about Father Africa, Mother Nature, and *Ubuntu* people.

The week of Hell culminated on Friday when I sat with the family on the veranda, despite the public scrutiny and the weather. My father turned on the radio and in a melancholy silence we listened to a sermon, the words of which stayed with me forever.

Clergymen, I am frequently told, should keep out of politics. I thoroughly agree. For this reason, I will not allow politics to be preached in this cathedral. Clergy have to be reconcilers. That is no easy job. A minister of religion who has well-known political views, and allows them to come to the fore, cannot reconcile, but will alienate others, and fail in the chief part of his ministry.

For this reason, I personally am surprised at there being two clergymen in the Executive Council. It is my sincere prayer that they can act as Christ's ambassadors of reconciliation.

My own ministry began in Ghana, where Kwame Nkrumah preached: "Seek ye first the political kingdom and all these things will be added to you." We know what became of Kwame

Nkrumah. We are not to preach a political kingdom, but the kingdom of God.

Clergy are usually in the middle, shot at from both sides. It is not an enviable role. Yet times come when it is necessary to speak out, and in direct and forthright terms, like trumpets with unmistakable notes. I believe that this is one such time.

Nobody who holds sacred the dignity of human life can be anything but sickened at the events attending the crash of the Viscount Hunyani. Survivors have the greatest call on the sympathy and assistance of every other human being. The horror of the crash was bad enough, but that this should have been compounded by murder of the most savage and treacherous sort leaves us stunned with disbelief and brings revulsion in the minds of anyone deserving the name "human."

This bestiality, worse than anything in recent history, stinks in the nostrils of Heaven. But are we deafened with the voice of protest from nations which call themselves "civilised"? We are not. Like men in the story of the Good Samaritan, they "pass by, on the other side."

One listens for loud condemnation by Dr. David Owen, himself a medical doctor, trained to extend mercy and help to all in need.

One listens and the silence is deafening.

One listens for loud condemnation by the President of the United States, himself a man from the Bible-Baptist belt, and again the silence is deafening.

One listens for loud condemnation by the Pope, by the Chief Rabbi, by the Archbishop of Canterbury, by all who love the name of God.

Again the silence is deafening.

I do not believe in white supremacy. I do not believe in black supremacy either. I do not believe that anyone is better than another, until he has proved himself to be so. I believe that those who govern or who seek to govern must prove themselves worthy of the trust that will be placed in them.

One looks for real leadership One finds little in the Western world: how much less in Africa?

Who is to be blamed for this ghastly episode?

Like Pontius Pilate, the world may ask "What is truth?" What is to be believed? That depends on what your prejudices will allow you to believe, for then no evidence will convince you otherwise.

So who is to be blamed?

First, those who fired the guns. Who were they? Youths and men who, as likely as not, were until recently in church schools. This is the first terrible fact. Men who went over to the other side in a few months were so indoctrinated that all they had previously learned was obliterated. How could this happen if they had been given a truly Christian education?

Second, it is common knowledge that in large parts of the world violence is paraded on TV and cinema screens as entertainment. Films about war, murder, violence, rape devil-possession and the like are "good box-office". Peak viewing time is set aside for murderers from Belfast, Palestine, Europe, Africa and the rest, to speak before an audience of tens of millions. Thugs are given full treatment, as if deserving of respect.

Not so the victims' relations.

Who else is to be blamed?

The United Nations and their church equivalent, the WCC. I am sure they both bear blame in this. Each parade a pseudo-morality which, like all half-truths, is more dangerous than the lie direct. From the safety and comfort of New York and Geneva, high moral attitudes can safely be struck. For us in the sweat, the blood, the suffering, it is somewhat different.

Who else? The churches? Oh yes, I fear so.

For too long, too many people have been allowed to call themselves "believers" when they have been nothing of the kind. Those who believe must act. If you believe the car is going to crash, you attempt to get out. If you believe the house is on fire, you try to get help and move things quickly. If you believe a child has drunk poison, you rush him to the doctor. Belief must bring about action.

Yet churches, even in our own dangerous times, are more than half-empty all the time. We are surrounded by heathens who equate belief in God with the Western way of life. In many war areas, Africans are told to "burn their Bibles". If this call was made to us, what sort of Bibles would be handed in? Would they be dog-eared from constant use; well-thumbed and marked? Would they be pristine in their virgin loveliness, in the same box in which they were first received?

There are tens of millions of all races who call themselves believers, who never enter any house of prayer and praise. Many are folk who scream loudest against communism, yet do not themselves help to defeat these Satanic forces by means of prayer, and praise and religious witness.

For, make no mistake, if our witness were as it ought to be, men would flock to join our ranks. As it is, we are by-passed by the world, as if irrelevant.

Is anyone else to be blamed for this ghastly episode near Kariba? I think so.

Politicians throughout the world have made opportunist speeches from time to time. These add to the heap of blameworthiness, for a speech can cause wounds which may take years to heal.

The ghastliness of this ill-fated flight from Kariba will be burned upon our memories for years to come. For others, far from our borders, it is an intellectual matter, not one which affects them deeply. Here is the tragedy!

The especial danger of Marxism is its teaching that human life is cheap, expendable, of less importance than the well-being of the State. But there are men who call themselves Christians who have the same contempt for other human beings, and who treat them as being expendable.

Had we, who claim to love God, shown more real love and understanding, more patience, more trust of others, the churches would not be vilified as they are today. I have nothing but sympathy with those who are here today and whose grief we share. I have nothing but revulsion for the less-than-human act of murder which has so horrified us all.

I have nothing but amazement at the silence of so many of the political leaders of the world. I have nothing but sadness that our churches have failed so badly to practise what we preach. May God forgive us all, and may he bring all those who died so suddenly and unprepared into the light of His glorious presence.

Amen

The Silence is Deafening **by Very Rev. John da Costa, Anglican Dean of Salisbury.**

The lesson ended and the world fell silent. Not a single bird sang. Neither did a cricket trill. A mournful moon rose without the faintest sigh of a breeze. The family retreated — each to our place of solitude.

I sat on the floor in my room with the cupboard door open and looked at a copy of *Scope Magazine*. The same weekly represented by a reporter a few days earlier. A young woman with blonde hair and white teeth on the cover grinned at me with the headlines: *Prison Cell Lovers* and *Handsome Prince Andrew* stamped across her. Inside, pictures of girls with stars covering their breasts filled most of the publication, interspersed by articles on how to improve your love life and how to be popular.

For the first time in my life, I questioned my very existence.

Was there any difference between religion and politics? Is fighting all we humans do well?

I feared for my place in Africa, dismayed by the infidelity of humanity. Soon I would turn sixteen and expected to confirm my registration for national service. My flippant and attention seeking comments in Wankie years ago came back to haunt me. I had suggested to my father that I join one of the elite armed services. I hauled myself to my feet and hid the magazine beneath my shirt and slipped outside, where I lifted the lid on the garbage bin and dropped it in with no one seeing me.

'There you are, Mr Rory.' Themba's voiced startled me. 'Cheer up my friend, life has a way of working itself out.' He gave me a warm smile.

'Well, it hasn't for those poor survivors,' I said.

My anger brought grief to his face. 'No, not for them.'

'Sorry, I didn't mean to take it out on you. I'm so glad you're home.'

'That's okay, my son. Pain and hate make us behave in ways we couldn't imagine; on whatever side we find ourselves.' He tousled my hair. 'Of course, I came back for you and my family. Without whom, I am nothing.'

'What must I do? I can't take this,' I appealed to my mentor.

'Let me show you something.' Themba lead me to the garden hedge, knelt and picked up a small stick. 'Look who I have found.'

I peered into the shrubbery. 'What is it?'

'Look with care, my friend.'

'Wow. A chameleon. It's younger than Bow.'

'Yes, *jaha*, much like yourself. Now watch what happens.' Themba teased the green lizard. 'See his colours darken from anger and fear?' He asked.

'Run away, my chameleon, to live another day on your own terms. There is no shame in losing a battle to win a war,' Themba whispered as he turned his face towards me. 'Run away, *jaha*.' A tear slid down his brown cheek. '*Uhambe kuhle*, chameleon, go well.' He stood up and strode back to his quarters.

My heart thumped so hard my ears hurt.

Five months later, Flight 827 *Umniati* was downed in the same manner — **Tuesday, February 13, 1979.**

THE HERALD SALISBURY

AN Air Rhodesia Viscount with 59 people on board crashed minutes after take-off from Kariba late yesterday afternoon. There were no survivors. The full plane, which was followed soon afterwards by another carrying an overflow of passengers bound for Salisbury, came down about 46 kilometres due east of Kariba, in the Vuti Purchase Area. First news of the disaster came in a brief statement from the airline's general manager, Captain Pat Travers, which said a distress signal was made from Viscount VP-YND operating flight RH827 from Victoria Falls, Wankie and Kariba. "The location of the aircraft is known and it has been established that there are no survivors," he said. The aircraft, the Umniati was carrying 54 passengers and a crew of five. The crash site is only about 50 kilometres north-east of the spot where a sister Viscount, the Hunyani, was shot down by a terrorist missile on September 3.

Where to now? What does life offer apart from death and deception, hate and cowardice?

Something had to give.

Chapter Fourteen

I returned to boarding school for my senior years between 1979 and 1981. It was less gruelling than the junior years of bullying and testosterone. With each year as we climbed the ladder of seniority, this meant a decrease in misery from teacher and senior alike. First-year students were the sludge. The second years were in a position to deflect attention. Third year was middle ground, where their loyalties changed to enable seniors rather than protecting the juniors. There were fewer traditions, such as not asking to cross a patch of grass or take a shortcut. Where students would stand straight and yell for permission. 'Can I please walk on the grass?' Three times in succession if a senior didn't give verbal approval. The number of buttons displayed the passing years on our blazer. First years were all buttoned. Second years had one undone until the fourth year, when the jacket could be open. The soft rawhide *veldskoen* was the shoe of prestige for year four and above, replacing the polished shoes. Fifth and sixth years were the seniors. A mob who ran the school, be it in the open or by subterfuge.

I viewed members of the opposite sex as a curious sect with strange behaviour and ideals, and apart from family, I had little to do with them. Instead, I threw myself into sport and strove for educational excellence. Alas, the latter didn't go well. So, the adulation of sport sufficed despite the limitations of career choice.

The war continued, with political aspirations to move the country to majority rule without the radicals. Abel Muzorewa, a Methodist bishop, became the country's first black prime minister of Zimbabwe Rhodesia after a whites' only referendum came back with an overwhelming eighty-five per cent agreeing to accept change. Within a year, they returned the country to the British crown to prepare for a one man one vote election and an independent Zimbabwe. My father pulled strings so I could return to school for another year to avoid doing my national service during an uncertain and vulnerable time.

I left school with the prospect of a transformed country, or so we imagined — one where everybody had equal rights and peace had returned. An opportunity to launch a career in a fair society and take part in a nation embraced by the world.

On my last day at Plumtree School, I wondered about the grounds. Most of us survived the persecution, the war, and ourselves. My thoughts turned to those who weren't so lucky. I ended up in the rafters above the stage in the Beit Hall, where I sat in silence and stared at the words *Unknown Scholar* I had etched six years earlier. The poem written by John during the Second World War was still there, albeit the paper curling and yellow.

Tough times. Makes what I went through seem trivial.

My first job was at a bank, counting cash and adding up hundreds of cheques. By the second day, I knew it was one field that didn't suit me; I found it inane and pointless, although others there loved what they did. I don't use the term lightly because the accountants, clerks, and assistants were consummate professionals and their attention to detail impressive. My brain was unaccustomed and uninspired by the rationale, preferring the obscurity, the freedom of conjecture, and the thrill of the unknown. I struggled to be part of a team in such proximity to one another. In error, I blamed it on my boarding school experience.

Two months later, I resigned and accepted a job with the local Cold Storage Commission as an accounts clerk. A far better place, so I thought, where mates and players from the town's rugby team worked. The work was a side-line to the socialising — the eighties were in full flight, skinny white *Lee* jeans and pink *Wrangler* shirts in the fashion. Mullets and bouffant hair thrived along with the English pop scene, Wham, Duran Duran, Madonna, and Prince, while Michael Jackson's career in the U.S.A. was taking off.

Carefree days at discos where alcohol and cheap cigarettes overshadowed the threats of nuclear obliteration from the Cold War, apartheid, and world starvation.

In 1984, my self-induced foggy view on life came to a crashing halt with the accusations that me and my supervisor had stolen the company's wages. My work colleagues watched the police load me into the back of their van where I sat while they investigated.

'Exciting news listeners,' the DJ on the radio, which was playing in the cab, said. 'Here is the promised *Band Aid* song *Do They Know It's Christmas*? To raise money for those starving kids in Ethiopia. Listen up, folks.' I recognised a few of the artists.

But say a prayer, pray for the other ones

At Christmas time it's hard, but when you're having fun.

There's a world outside your window

And it's a world of dread and fear.

Where the only water flowing

Is the bitter sting of tears?

'It's written by Midge Ure and Bob Geldof from the Boomtown Rats people. Buy yourself the record. It will save lives,' the jockey said before he went on to the next song.

An officer climbed in and turned off the radio.

Keys jangled in the cell door, followed by the clunk of the lock. I dared not move, perplexed by who the guards were after and what they wanted. The other inmates stirred or coughed. There were twenty-two of us with our heads against the four walls and our feet facing the centre of the three-by-three metre cell. There wasn't an inch of empty floor except in one corner where the latrine was — a mere hole in the cement that flushed from the outside.

With my eyes clenched, I inhaled shallow breaths as I pleaded with the heavens that they weren't after me. Stories abounded of other prisoners disappearing in the small hours. In the political climate of the day, uncertainty prevailed. Rhodesia was now Zimbabwe. The enemy, the new government. The military was in turmoil after being purged, and the previous regime's officer in charge of the station where I was held was my father. Retribution was the order of the time. I did not lose the irony and imminent danger to myself.

The cell door opened, and a uniformed arm stretched through the gap above my head. There was a crinkle of paper and the plop of an object landing near my face. The door shut with the sliding of the bolts to lock it. No one moved.

It smelt of chocolate. I was still debating what to do when an inmate tiptoed over everyone's legs and draped a thin blanket over my feet before returning to his space. Phineas, my co-worker, detained for the same reason as me, lay beside me. 'Be strong, Chameleon. All is not what it seems,' he said.

How did he know Themba's pet name for me?

The noise of the wrapper and shape of it confirmed a warden had dropped a chocolate bar. My mind raced.

Was it Dad or Themba?

The welcome rays of light through the rusty bars brought with them a new faith that sanity might prevail. Wardens flung open the steel doors and crashed dustbin's lids together.

'Assemble outside you thieves and traitors,' a warden shouted and pointed to the fenced courtyard. A pot of porridge was boiling over coals in the far corner, next to a tap with a stack of enamel plates and mugs. When the wardens moved on to the adjoining cellblock, everyone helped themselves to breakfast.

We sucked in the fresh air after the confines of the earlier night, our bodies aching from the solid concrete floors and threadbare blankets. Food turned my stomach and the queue at the long drop didn't help. We relieved ourselves against the single tree in the courtyard.

The morning traffic passed by the fence as people went about their business. My chest tightened as the hairs on my neck rose. I fetched the chocolate bar from under the pillow before going outside again, taking heart that there might be hope.

Phineas was washing beneath the spigot and rubbing his face with his hands. 'How was last night?' he asked, not waiting for a response. 'This is politics, you know.' He straightened. 'You are white. I speak isiNdebele. Your father was a police officer; mine was a soldier. We were on the wrong side.'

Choosing not to answer, I kicked at the dirt.

Wonder what he meant when he called me Chameleon? How could he know? Was it a coincidence? I didn't ask. Of late, trust was not my strongest inclination.

Phineas lifted my chin with his finger. 'Stand proud, believe in yourself and others,' he said as he handed over his John Lennon glasses and stuck his head beneath the tap. His thin frame and short stature belied the leadership he displayed at work and now, here. He wasn't much older than me, but far wiser and street-smart.

Hangers-on leant against the security fence to get closer to their loved ones. A young mother peered through the diamond-shaped wire as she bounced and consoled a baby strapped to her back. An officer sat on a chair nearby to stop contraband from being passed through the fence. No one was yet a felon. These were the holding cells before we faced the magistrate. Today was Saturday — the courts closed until Monday.

When Dad arrived, he convinced those in charge to allow him to speak to me through the fence.

'I've got this in hand. Most of these officers worked with me before the change,' he said, then hesitated, unsure what to do next. 'Did you get the chocolate bar?' he asked as he stroked his dishevelled hair. He still saw himself as an Elvis lookalike. He had the same black rings under his eyes.

'Yes, thank you,' I said.

'Themba arranged that. We are in luck. He has organised people to watch out for you. I'm just sorry we can't get you out.' Dad paused again. 'Mum's at home, and I don't want your sister to see you like this. We must be careful not to make it worse. It's in our interests to run this as low key as possible.' He glanced around to make sure no one was eavesdropping. 'It's important to keep your head low. Do as you're told and keep to yourself.'

'Okay.'

'They say you guys stole from the wages.'

Unsure if this was a statement or a question, I waited for him to continue.

'This isn't true, is it? We're looking into it. The consensus is the investigators have taken shortcuts to boost their political standings. It will backfire. Look, I don't want to hang around in case we draw attention to who we are. It's all happening in the background.'

'That's okay,' I said before I followed the rest of the inmates back into the cell.

How could my father question whether I stole the money?

The jailers allowed an hour for exercise and fresh air. Inside, unrecognisable faces sat against the walls. A confused and unwell old man cowered in a corner. Most were in their thirties, but one was a teenager. They chatted among themselves.

'Sit, brother,' a voice said, its owner an emancipated middle-aged African gentleman with a face full of scars made space against the wall. 'Sleep here tonight, away from the door.'

Phineas nodded his approval.

We spent the day in silence; each deep in thought of our freedom or confinement, be it criminal or political. The youngest entertained himself by watching a column of ants crawl over his finger in their search for food. He hummed to himself, safe in his world. The old man drifted in and out of consciousness. Awake, he murmured about evil spirits and ancestral influences. Asleep, he grinned and called out to his children and his wife as he coughed and spluttered.

In the courtyard, a group played a perplexing game with stones, where each player picked up a pebble and tossed it into the air while moving another. I stared up at the barred window and deliberated on a future after freedom.

It was time to leave this town, this country, and my beloved Africa.

I had thoughts of a life in England, the place Mum and Dad still called home despite a lifetime in Rhodesia. A flicker of hope turned to excitement.

Lookout London, Belfast, Cardiff, here I come.

A welcome respite from the tedium came when wardens dumped food inside the door. Stale bread, with a scraping of what resembled — but didn't taste like — peanut butter, made palatable with a warm mug of over-sweetened tea. The likes I never tasted again.

When the door opened for the afternoon break, our brains

leapt at the prospect. Our bodies, though, didn't follow, but limped and hobbled behind. Time became irrelevant. Days flowed into nights and dusk turned to light. A lifetime in a few days. Tomorrow, we could state our case for a chance of freedom. Until then, we chatted, laughed, and told our favourite stories. Phineas sat in one corner singing to himself. His soft alto tone floated up through the soiled area, cleansing it. The hairs on my forearms rose with each verse as another voice joined. Until all but one of us sang in perfect harmony — my white voice could add no value — and before long, everyone was on their feet, swaying. Twenty-two inmates stood in a circle with arms folded around each other's shoulders. I have always envied the natural talent in African cultures with their impeccable rhythm. To be part of and included was a rare privilege — the glint of hope in their eyes, the joy in their voices and the goodwill in their movement.

On Monday morning, the birds woke me from my stupor. The plaque on my teeth was as rough as my stubble. My hair like *Play-Doh*. I plucked gunk from the corners of my eyes.

'Don't worry,' Phineas said. 'The judge has seen far worse than us in his courtroom.' He pulled a face and joined the line at the tap. He showed the same quiet confidence at the office when the pressure was on. His colleagues and bosses were the opposite and were very hard on Phineas, the supervisor.

'Right, you bandits, we leave in five minutes,' a voice blasted from behind the fence. 'Here's your tea. There's no time for breakfast.'

We folded our blankets and headed towards the barbed-wire gate. A police officer slapped on handcuffs and man-handled us into an open truck. They hung our shoes over our cuffs, which dug into the soft flesh of my wrists. Regardless, I showed no sign of suffering, weakness, or duress.

The village courthouse was less than a kilometre away. A small group broke from the milling crowd on our arrival. Most were family members. Others were curiosity seekers. A plain clothes detective with one hand inside his jacket studied us from behind sunglasses. The austere-whitewashed justice building with its daunting manicured gardens waited for us. An icy shiver ran down my spine.

A young police officer, led our chain gang into a room where there was nothing other than wooden benches around the walls and a single metal desk at one end. Red-scuffed floors bore the years of neglect and high traffic.

What tales it could tell. The cruelty it hid. Justice and injustice alike. I sensed the room's history.

'Sit, gents. We'll call you up one at a time to the table to complete the paperwork,' the officer said and disappeared from the room.

'Where's the lawyer?' a prisoner called after him.

He peeped from behind the door, mumbled something under his breath, and locked after him.

'You don't get lawyers anymore, unless you can afford to hire one,' an older cellmate said.

'The two boys will have them,' another hinted.

Phineas leant forward and faced our accuser. 'That is not our fault. Like most things, it's beyond our control.'

'Sorry, but someone is responsible?' the first said.

'Now is not the time. Maybe we are all to blame.' Phineas put his finger to his lips, and the group fell silent.

'Rorke Wilde, how do you plead?' the magistrate said.

I looked at the lawyer that my family had hired.

'Not guilty, sir. 'I said my well-rehearsed and advised response.

The judge peered at me from behind a raised bench. He examined several papers, then turned to the advocate. 'Defence, what is your position?'

'We propose the State drops the case, Your Honour. There is no evidence, let alone proof.'

The magistrate's eyes darted across the room. 'Prosecutor, what is your argument?'

'Remand him in custody until the investigation is complete.'

My blood drained to my feet and my eyes blurred.

The judge raised his voice. 'Can I see both councils, please?' the magistrate said in a loud voice. The lawyers approached the bench, and the three spoke in quiet tones until the magistrate called an end to proceedings and collected his papers. He waited for the lawyers to return to their places, then turned his attention to me. 'Rorke Wilde, I am withdrawing your case pending further investigation. You are free to go.' He banged his hammer, then peered at the prosecutor, almost threatening. 'I will watch this with interest.' He leant forward over the edge of the bench. 'Do we agree on the same outcome for Wilde's colleague?'

I was free for now but confused; a sense of vulnerability engulfed me, the sudden open spaces daunting. Mum took hold of me and marched me along as quickly as she was able. 'You're safe now,' she said once we were beside the car. Then she crinkled her nose. 'Let's get you into a bath. That is an interesting odour you have, young man.' She threw her arms around me. Her smile belied the tears and pain on her face. 'Dad is paying your bail, then we can get out of here.'

Cara held onto me until father returned with Phineas in tow.

'Look who I found.' Dad grinned and shook Phineas's hand.

'Thank you, Mr Wilde. I promise to repay the debt.'

'That's all right. You are a wonderful friend to Rory. Come on, I'll drop you at the bus station.'

'Thanks.' Phineas turned to me. 'Bye Rory, I'll see you soon.'

'Cheers.'

Dad and Phineas headed off down the street.

'Your dad paid his bail, too. His parents couldn't get up here and he's short of cash. Payday is just around the corner,' Mother said as she and Cara herded me into the car.

I was aware of the fuss and bother, but it meant nothing. My brain was numb. Poor Phineas, who now had to endure a five-hundred-kilometre bus journey home.

My tears welled. I sobbed, for myself, for Phineas, for the men in the cell, for the country and above all for my family.

Once we were home, Themba ran me a bath without saying a word. He was not himself. Not the confident person I admired. Something was bothering him.

I left it there, too tired to ask.

During the next week, I soaked in baths to rid myself of the smells, to remove the tattoos of pain engrained in me and to ease my anguish. Every time I ventured out of the house, my stomach churned, and fear gripped whenever a marked vehicle or someone in uniform approached.

I reported for work the following Monday, as per my father's suggestion that it would bode well with the court. The company gave us our normal duties, which included paying out the weekly wages. Phineas and I sat on our first Thursday back, counting out the money and placing it in brown pay packets, whereupon the receiver signed their name or placed a thumbprint using the ink pad provided. Phineas clapped his hands at completion and looked through his thick-round glasses. 'That's it, Rory. Are you ready for tomorrow?'

'As ready as I'll ever be.'

'Good. Let's put this in the safe and go home.' The two of us carried the case, relieved that the company had decided on a security guard to escort us and stand watch overnight.

'Sharp, I'll see you tomorrow,' Phineas waved. 'Thanks for the lift.'

'Sure thing, Phineas, anytime.' I raised my hand off the steering wheel of my Morris Minor. 'Cheers.'

The next morning, we assembled our camping tables on the front lawn outside the company's office with the open wage trunk and set up.

The blast of the hooter announced tea break. It was time for the employees to collect their wages.

'Name and number,' Phineas asked the first person.

'*Ngiyabonga kakhulu* — thank you very much,' the man dressed in white overalls called out in Shona as sweat dripped down his face.

'Sign here,' Phineas said, as he showed him the space on the pay packet.

The worker was counting it to make sure he got what he signed for when a woman approached and snatched it from him.

'Aww Ma, every week you take the money.'

'We have mouths to feed and bills to pay, husband. If I leave this with you to walk home with, we shall see you in three days without even a penny to your name.' She wiped his face and gave his cheek a light slap. 'Now, have your tea. We will get you at home.' The man scurried away to the caterwauling of the ladies.

The workers in the queue were apprehensive about the ritual. Sometimes one made a dash for it. Only to have their partners or wives run them down and confiscate their wages. It was an arrangement agreed upon by management and union because the road home was fraught with *shebeens* offering alcohol and other dubious distractions.

The procedure took us most of the day, and while we were busy sorting the empty pay packets into alphabetical order, Phineas spotted our general manager approaching in his blue trilby hat and jacket too tight to close. His designer leather shoes were without traction. He slid and stumbled on the uneven grass, his legs as thin as stork's, his oversized belly rendering him top-heavy.

'Watch out, here comes the boss,' Phineas said.

'Oh shit, wonder what he wants?'

'Ha, I'm glad I found you two before the weekend,' he said and asked us to sit. 'No need to worry. I realise the tough time you have both been through.' Wearing a pin-striped suit, he perched a buttock on the table and folded his arms. 'It seems the police have caught the thief who stole the wages.'

Phineas jumped up and interrupted him. 'Who was it? How did they…'

'I don't have the details, I'm afraid,' he replied. 'But I believe a night security guard found the keys in a certain desk drawer,' the older man continued. 'I will hold someone accountable for that, leaving safe keys lying around…'

'Sir?' Phineas spoke to attract his attention.

'Oh, I'm sorry lads.' He grinned. 'So that's it. They'll drop the charges against you at the hearing.'

'How did they catch him?' I asked.

The general manager stared at me. 'His wife threw him under the bus. Told us she hadn't seen him for a week and that he'd been spending up a storm in the village. Stupid bugger.'

We thanked the boss, then ran to collect our belongings and jumped into the car. Phineas wound down the window and howled into the wind as the needle crept up to the fifty mile per hour mark on the ageing speedometer. We laughed aloud, waving at every pedestrian in sight.

'Stop here. My treat,' Phineas said as he pointed to the local convenience store and then dived inside.

Alone, I pumped the steering wheel with my palms, stoked that at last we would be free. I climbed out of the vehicle and kicked the wheels, then attacked the chassis.

Angry?

No, furious — it was time to vent.

'Here you are,' Phineas said as he passed me a glass bottle of cola and a Chelsea bun.

'Thanks man, it's so good to be free.' I beamed back at him.

'It is? Maybe one day for us all.' He pointed his bottle at me, then climbed into the passenger seat.

'I'm sorry, Phineas. I didn't mean to upset you.'

'That's okay,' he said as he reached across to tap bottles in a silent toast to our freedom. 'Let the anger go. It will cause you pain and suffering. It is not an emotion to hold on to Chameleon.'

'How do you know…?'

Phineas slammed the door and waved goodbye. 'Next time, catch you later, man.' He disappeared down the street.

'What the hell is happening?' I said aloud as I drove off in the opposite direction and then pulled over because of me over-revving the engine by not changing gears in time. I turned off the car and stumbled onto a granite rock nearby and sat observing vehicles, including buses negotiate a cart being hauled by a donkey. Images of school life and war flashed through my mind as the smells of the African savannah filled my senses.

'What have I got that you want?' I asked aloud. Then I stood up and roared at the heavens. 'What the hell is there to lose?'

A wisp of air lifted my fringe as it kissed my cheek. My Africa wished me well. I would leave her to find out what lay beyond her warm embrace.

I had decided.

Chapter Fifteen

I rebounded from the horror of the trial and mulled over what was next. I considered South Africa but didn't fancy being drafted into two years of military service and couldn't foresee a future any different from Rhodesia or Zimbabwe.

Been there, done that. Thank you. Themba speaks of this Madiba, but what are the chances the minority government will release him?

The third choice was to join my extended family in the United Kingdom. Apart from the odd letter and Christmas card, the clans hadn't kept close contact, so the prospects weren't tempting.

With the war over, my father had resigned from the police and was now a loss prevention officer for a national retail chain where he spent much of his time travelling.

Sunday evening after Dad left on one of his trips, the rest of the family sat on the stoep. Cara was listening to her Sony Walkman and Mum, as usual, sifted through a stack of romance novels.

'Mum, can we talk?' I said.

'What's wrong?'

I paused, unsure how to broach this.

'Say what's on your mind. Better out than in.' My mother gave an uneasy smile.

'All right. I have two questions.'

'Well, fire away. One at a time, my boy. What's the first?'

'I want to see the world.'

Her face contorted with a range of emotions.

'Yes, my son. It's been a long while coming.' Her voice was croaky. She got up, hugged me, and returned to her seat with hands resting in her lap. 'Tell me more. Where are you thinking of going?' She pulled a tissue from her sleeve and cleaned her reading glasses.

'I'm not sure. Ireland, where the Wilde's are, or to your folk?'

Mother drew in a lengthy breath. 'Those are probabilities. It might help if we chat about the trip we took when you were younger. To see what you recall and what you've forgotten.'

'Sounds like a plan. Thanks, Mum.'

Caro pulled her earphones. 'What are you talking about?'

'Just chatting to Mum.'

'Where did she go?'

'To make a pot of tea.'

'Looks like you're in the shit.' Caro gave me a look and replaced her earphones, listening to her favourite group, Wham.

She would be the hardest to tell I was moving overseas.

Mum pushed the tea trolley onto the veranda. 'Right, now where do we start? I've put cookies on your saucer.' She handed me the brew.

'Thanks, but sit and quit your fussing,' I said.

She glowered at me, then grinned. 'Okay, I'm ready. Where shall I begin? Oh, I know. On the plane. It was 1972, well, early seventies. You were ten, Cara five. Now tell me what you remember,' Mum said to me.

The Emerald Isle approached through the porthole window as the jet descended into Aldergrove Airport, contrasting with the ocean and the murky sky. I recalled Neil Armstrong landing on the moon three years earlier, except the picture now wasn't as fuzzy. The captain welcomed us to Belfast and reminded us about security precautions and the risks of Ireland's troubles.

'One small step for Rory, one giant leap for mankind.' I yelled, leaping from the bottom rung of the steps onto the airstrip. Dad clipped me with a playful but embarrassing slap behind the ear as passengers laughed.

After an uneventful yet tiresome journey, we pulled up to my grandparent's house.

'Well, hello there. If my eyes don't deceive my sweet, sweet grandchildren,' Granny Wilde said as she opened the bungalow door and approached the taxi with open arms. 'Oh, my goodness, you must be so exhausted. The kettle is on, and brunch is waiting if you're hungry.' She smiled broadly as I took in her rosy cheeks and blue-rinsed bun on top of her head. She gave us a cuddle, then called to Dad. 'At last, the clan is together. A grand day, so it is.' She pushed her glasses back up her nose and headed indoors with us under each of her arms.

'Grandpa, they're here!' she shrieked out of the kitchen window.

Grandpa dropped his garden fork and raised a glove in greeting and started towards us. He combed his lengthy strands of white hair back with his fingers after removing his hat to protect his pasty, vein blemished face and shook hands with my dad, then hugged Mum. *'Bout ye?'*

'I'm fine. How are you, Dad?' Mum pecked his cheek.

'How many mums and dads have you got?' Caro asked.

'Two, Grandpa Wilde and Grandad Morgan in Wales, dear,' Mum replied.

We gathered at the kitchen table while Granny poured the tea and served scrambled eggs, sausages, bacon, and soda bread. She sat at one end and Grandpa at the other — both were grinning.

Grandpa raised his cup. The crow's feet around his eyes fashioned in a permanent smile. 'Welcome to *Norn Iron.*' His thick Belfast accent was referring to Northern Ireland. 'Your mother's up to *high doh* since she heard you're coming.'

'Sure, this is right. I am very excited, so I am.' Granny's Wilde's grey eyes flickered. 'It is so nice to see you and my wee grandchildren. Oh Mammy, what a grand day.' The Irish brogue was heavy with emotion. 'Eat up everybody.'

Cara and my parents napped with the onset of jetlag. Unable to sleep, I explored.

'Where are you going?' Grandpa asked.

'To check out the backyard,' I replied.

'Well, that will be fine. So, it will.' A swirl of smoke drifted over him. 'I'll finish my pipe, then you and I can have a dander down the street. What do you say?' He tapped his pipe on his shoe as he sat in the dark patterned armchair.

'Okay, Grandpa, I'll be outside.'

The chilly, dank weather greeted me. Within minutes I had seen all there was in the well-manicured backyard, with its sweet-smelling flowerbeds, ornate vegetable patch and short mown grass. The closeness of the neighbours puzzled me. Everyone lived on top of one another, and the houses had double storeys.

Grandpa emerged dressed in a waxed jacket and gumboots. 'I'm *foundered*, so I am. How about you, lad?'

My blank expression invited an explanation.

'Aren't you chilly? Maybe put on extra clothing?'

'No, that's okay Grandpa, let's go,' I replied. I didn't want to disturb everyone's rest.

We strolled along the lane with houses on one side and open fields on the other, as I told my grandfather about life in Southern Africa. Then I asked a question that led to silence before he answered. 'It's a troublesome thing to explain, lad. The country is at war with itself, with one *buck eejit* after another making it worse, with acts of violence against the innocent.'

'Like Africa, Grandpa?'

He reflected on my question before nodding. '*Ats us Naï* — that's us now. Time for home. It's a wee bit Baltic right now.' He gripped the rear of my neck as we headed up the driveway. 'How old are ye now, my boy?'

'I'll be ten soon.'

'Is that right? Well, I never.'

Granny Wilde fed us all day long, starting with a full Irish breakfast, followed by sandwiches at morning tea, lunch at one o'clock, a three-course high tea, ending with a light supper of something on toast before bedtime.

We laughed and spoke of the different worlds in which we lived.

On the first Friday evening, Caro and I watched *Top of the Pops* on a colour television. Grandpa and Dad smoked. One a pipe, the other a cigar. They made plans for Dad to meet the locals, including the provincial constabulary, while Granny and Mum chatted, read, and knitted all at once.

On Saturday morning granny woke me up with a cup of tea. 'Up you get, big lad. Today will be a cracker. So, it will.'

'What are we doing?' I asked as my eyes flew open.

'Make your bed and we'll have a yarn at breakfast. Hurry

now.'

Once I was at the kitchen counter, my grandmother divulged her news. 'We are going to the shops in Belfast, after which Grandpa is treating us to lunch at his mucker's pub. It is a cracker of a place and he's a sound *oul-lad*. You'll see if he isn't.'

'Sounds great, kids, eat up and brush your teeth,' Mum said, hurrying us along. 'Don't want to keep Grandpa waiting now, do we?'

The rolling hills and picture postcard villages with wisps of smoke emanating from the chimneys gave way to roadblocks and the burnt-out shells of city buildings. The conflict scattered mounds of rubble through the roads of Belfast. On the sides of buses and on pavements, they wrote graffiti demonising the British Government over threats against the Irish Republican Army (IRA). Armed soldiers mingled with shoppers, bankers, and teachers going about their business.

We parked in the city centre and strolled towards the high street, where the army searched us for explosives and paraphernalia. Tall gates closed off the roads, obliging the public to queue in single file for inspection by terse officials.

The weather matched the mood in the streets — bleak and spitting with rain. A troop carrier rumbled down the street with a man perched on top with binoculars. A line of gun barrels protruding from within suggested he wasn't alone.

I remember it was odd to see everyone shopping as if it was normal and they weren't afraid, and I said so to Grandpa.

'They're just very brave people. Scared all right, lad, but they will not change their lifestyles, otherwise the other side wins.'

'I don't understand why they are blowing up their own communities and things, Grandpa?'

'Aye, it does my head in too.' He placed his walking stick between his legs and dug out his pipe and lit it as we stood at the start of the first queue.

'Is that you, Ma?' he called out to his wife. 'You take the ladies into that *naff* line, and I'll show the boys through this one, so I will.'

'Okay, *aul-lad*. C'mere ladies, a line for boys and one for the girls.' She beckoned my mother and sister. 'Once inside, we'll do some grand shopping.'

The line moved along at a rate, although the woman's one was slower. I squinted into the dim shadows of the checkpoint. Soldiers scanned people and patted clothing; most were let through while they tapped others on the shoulder for closer inspection.

'Close yer gob, *mingers*, and git yourselves over this side,' a sergeant yelled at a small group who wore bell-bottom jeans and had long unkempt hair and scruffy beards.

'Shut your bake,' a woman retaliated.

An uneasy silence seized the crowd, causing tensions to rise until the gathering burst into laughter. They shook the sergeant's hand, lit cigarettes, and chatted while they continued through the rigmarole.

'Get your lazy holes out of here,' the sergeant said as he man-handle them out. He slapped their shoulders and turned back to the line; his face returned to its former unnerving expression.

'*Friggin' eejits*,' Granny said as she held a hand to her mouth.

'Language, Ma,' Grandpa called out from the other line as he raised his eyebrows.

'Oh dear, I'm sorry wee girl. Your granny forgot herself.' She covered Cara's ears and blushed.

'Been awhile since I have seen such a *reddener*, Mammy,' Grandpa said and gave a hearty laugh.

'*Youse*, keep the roar down.' Granny rolled her eyes in mock fury.

We followed the same routine on every street. Before long, we too joined the lines because the extraordinary became the norm. In mid-afternoon, we ended our spree and hurried to the car to be in time for lunch at Grandpa's friend's pub.

On the outskirts of the capital, the tranquillity of the countryside resumed. Grandpa turned into a narrow lane where a building stood with a sign creaking in the wind.

'*Ballypadraig?*' I read aloud. '*Fine Irish stout.*'

'Yes,' Dad said. 'It means Patrick's Place.'

'I didn't know you had a pub?' I said.

'Padraig is a typical Irish name, and alas, the bar is not mine.' Dad reached for the handle to let us out.

'What's stout?' I asked.

'It's a black beer, my boy. Have you heard of *Guinness?*' Dad replied.

I shook my head.

'There are fewer famous names than *Kilkenny* and *Murphy's.*'

'You're too young to trouble yourself with beer, so you are,' Granny said as she grabbed my hand and led us into the lobby.

We sat in a room of five or six tables and chairs where a paisley lounge suite stood in front of the communal hearth. The wooden walls displayed sketches by artists past. Aged Toby jugs, and other random pub artefacts filled the shelves. Large beams ran the length of the ceiling, joining pillars that held the roof. The carpet bore scorch marks and threadbare patches from decades of traffic. Stained-glass windows with four-leaf clovers and leprechauns completed the décor of the interior.

The adults settled upon a tray of battered cod and chips while I wandered to have a closer look around the tavern. Through glass doors I watched a buffoonery of men. Some leant on the timber bar where beer was being pulled by levers. Bartenders arranged the poured glasses on top of the bar to settle, and I observed the beige foam transform into the black stout of *Guinness*. Clouds of smoke from pipes, cigarettes, and cigars wafted across the den. They flicked ash and butt ends into trough ashtrays at the men's feet. I looked for spittoons like I'd seen in John Wayne movies, but to no avail, so I decided not to enter. They were a scary mob who roared with laughter and swore — not dissimilar to the green-bearded leprechauns on the tinted windows above me. I could make out the remnants of a sign *Men Only*, etched into the door. That's weird. Why aren't woman allowed?

We ate until not a single chip remained or we left a half lemon unsqueezed. Talking and teasing one another as we deepened our bonds.

The owner of the pub walked in as we readied to leave. 'I thought I saw a *minger* through the *windee*,' he blustered

178

towards Grandpa with his hand outstretched.

'Well, I'll be darned if it ain't my *aul-mucker*. How are ye, lad?' Grandpa struggled to his feet and shook hands.

'*Bout ye* big lad? Been a few years.'

'That it has. That it has,' Grandpa said as he sat down again and waved my father over to join them.

'Right kids, jackets on, we'll meet the lads in the car,' Granny said as she took us towards the exit.

A few days later, our parents surprised us with news.

'We're into the second week of our holiday, kids. It's time to talk about you going to school.' Dad dropped the bombshell on us one night after dinner.

'School?' I cried out in shock.

'You didn't expect to go three months without school?' Mum interjected.

'Well, yeah?' I said.

'Too bad. On Monday, Cara is going to nursery school, and you are attending central primary.'

'But Mum,' I protested

'No buts, Rory,' Dad said.

'Okay.' I blinked slowly and sat back with my arms crossed.

'School starts at nine o'clock and finishes at three-thirty. On Friday, it's two-thirty, isn't it?' Mum looked at Dad. He shrugged.

'All day?' I asked. 'Back home. We finish school at lunchtime.'

'That's because you start earlier,' Mum said as she cut the conversation short by turning to Granny, who was sitting nearby knitting.

The school in the centre of the village reminded me of a prison with security fencing, barbed wire, and cameras at every turn. With brick walls in a uniform design, four storeys high, and barred windows and loudspeakers everywhere.

Scholars skulked in small groups, children kicked a football, while others played with a skipping rope on a tarred playground. A depressed pot plant stood guard at the facade next to the entrance, which was neglected and polluted with the debris of unwanted lunches. Traffic hooted and roared up and

179

down the four streets encircling the grounds; the smell of fossil fuel and rubber hung in the air.

However, my classroom was a treat with vast windows, despite the grenade shields, which lit up the art adorning the walls. Communal Formica desks in the prime colours of red, blue, and yellow seated eight students. Lessons were fun and interactive compared to the isolated single-wooden desk back home.

Break times were not as enjoyable. There, I confronted our differences and managed my solitude. Most of the scholars tolerated my accent, others laughed. A cluster of morons nicknamed me Albino — the white African. The teachers spoke of *the Troubles*, as did the posters and the threat of suspicious parcels and safety procedures in case of explosions and armed assaults.

In the six weeks of my Irish schooling, I made the most of it by doing the best I was able. I lay low in the group exercises and did what they expected of me so as not to draw attention to myself. By adapting to my surroundings, I became a chameleon.

I delighted in the liberating arts of the Irish curriculum. For the first time in longer than my memory, I didn't partake in sports on grassless schoolyards. Nor did I try to understand their fixation that the individual was more important than the team in their pursuit of sports, especially the beloved football.

With each week that passed, I became more introverted as I imagined life back home. Missing with every ounce of my ten-year-old body, Mother Nature, and the diversity of African people.

In my last days at the school, I lost my cool — unable to cope. Frustrated at being the outsider — angry at the ignorance. Depressed because there was no way out.

The authorities thought it was time to call my parents.

Mum found me clutching the security fencing with my cheek, pushed hard up against the wire, looking out.

'He's like a caged animal,' the schoolteacher said.

When Mum agreed, the teacher asked for clarification.

Mum stared at her as she stroked the back of my neck. 'He's an African. We've locked him in a cage on this island for too long.'

The teacher looked at me and then offered to leave us alone.

'Hey Rory, it's me, Mum. We're sorry and you're right. It's time to go home.' She hugged me as she hummed a tune. I let go of the fence. We left more than a school that day.

That evening, over dinner, the family discussed the day's events, including my meltdown.

'A penny for your thoughts, Rorke Wilde?' Granny said, as she gave me one of her smiles. 'Tell us how you are, big lad.'

'It's safer to go back home to Africa. Here, they blow up their own buildings because of religion; they don't like foreigners and they won't allow Mums and sisters into the pubs. There are no wild animals, and everybody lives on top of each other,' I said. 'No wonder the sun doesn't shine here.'

'That is not everyone, fella,' Grandpa said.

'He's dead-on and I am *scundered* about how this country acts,' Granny said to her husband. 'Catch yourself on and smell the roses, *oul-Lad*. We have some way to go. So, we have.'

'Aye, *Norn Iron* is not pretty right now, Ma,' Grandpa said, dispirited by the notion. He turned off the television, which was reporting on the McGurk's Bar bombing. Fifteen civilians killed because they were Catholic and as revenge for the protestants shot the day before.

Mum and Dad looked at each other, then announced our return home.

We would leave for Wales after Christmas before flying to Rhodesia. I leapt into the air and danced around the lounge. Caro joined me, more in spirit than understanding. Three generations laughed and clapped; We set aside the outside world for the evening as we planned for our first Christmas with family — perhaps it would be a white one weather permitting. Carols replaced the news on the TV — Granny sang along. For a short while, we enjoyed ourselves as a clan.

Caro interrupted my reminiscing when she turned off her Walkman and got off the couch. 'You guys still talking? Anyone want something from the kitchen? Hope there're some cookies left.'

'In the bottom drawer, sweetheart,' Mum called after her. 'I don't suppose you remember our trip to Ireland, dear; you were only five?' Mum asked her.

'Just from the photos you showed me.'

Mum turned to me and shook her head. 'They were tough times with hard choices. Your dad was thinking of moving.'

'So not a long holiday, then?'

'A bit of both.'

'Was it because of me we came back to Africa?'

Mum smiled. 'Not at all, my boy. You were miserable, but that would have changed the longer we stayed.'

'So, what was the decider?'

'I'll tell you after I go to the loo.' Mum stretched and disappeared into the hallway. On her return, she pulled on a cardigan and rubbed a hand through my hair, then sat down. 'Remember Dad, Grandpa, and the owner talking at the *Ballypadraig* pub while we waited in the car?'

'Yup.'

'Well, one of his sons was a police officer in the Royal Ulster Constabulary in Belfast.'

'And?' I asked.

'Okay, I'll start from the beginning.'

'He invited your father to visit the depot for a day in the office and another on the beat. In return, Dad would talk about his escapades in Southern Africa with the British South Africa Police. A week later, your dad took a bus into the city, excited at the prospect but concerned. Being a rural police officer, he preferred the country to urban policing. He returned the first day exhausted yet thrilled at the three t's, as he called them, technology, training, and tactics from the control rooms at the station.'

'So, if he enjoyed it, why didn't we stay?' I asked.

Mum removed her glasses and cleaned them with a tissue in silence. When she replaced them, she stared out of the window before she continued. 'The second day he got back late. It worried us sick and minutes before your grandpa was about to call his friend from *Ballypadraig*, your father knocked at the front door. It was around seven-thirty when we opened the door to find him with his shirt hanging out and his tie loose around his neck.' Mum shook her head at the memory and proceeded in a quieter voice. 'And you know your father. He is never untidy, let alone unruly, but that night he was tipsy.'

'Dad? Drunk?' I said in a louder than usual tone.

'It is not a laughing matter, Rory. Your dad was in a state.'

'Sorry Mum, just the thought of Dad being drunk is funny. Tell me about the second day.'

'Granny pulled your father off the front step, but not before checking the neighbours weren't peeping through their curtains. She sat him in the kitchen and there he stayed, limp, staring at nothing with his hands resting in his lap. Granny poured him a mug of hot tea and threw a rug around his shoulders and sat opposite him in silence, waiting until he was ready. It must have been an hour if it wasn't two before he regained his colour. Granny and Grandpa were in the laundry engaging in small talk when your dad looked up and gave a vacant smile.'

'Sorry Mammy, sorry Daddy. I forget myself. Thank you for the tea and for what you've done for me and my family.'

Mum dabbed at her eyes. 'With that, your father stood up, hugged everyone, and went for a shower. We never spoke of that day again.'

'So, we don't know what happened,' I said as I put out my hands, palms facing upward.

'No, dear. He won't speak about it. He has seen so much in the police force. Maybe one day he'll tell you if you ask.' Mum left the room while I digested Dad's ordeal in Belfast all those years ago.

We were sipping tea and eating cookies when Mum spoke. 'Now Rory, what's the other question you have for me?'

'Am I named after the battle of Rorke's Drift in South Africa between the British and the Zulu?'

'Why do you ask?'

'It's the one thing I remember about that trip to the UK.'

'Go on, dear.' Mum nodded at me.

'It was when we were in Wales with the family. Grandad and your sister always spoke of it. Something about Welsh heroes brave stand against the odds.' I shrugged my shoulders, unsure of the detail but concerned by the connection.

'First, that's a coincidence. Don't worry yourself over it.' She batted her eyelids, not missing a step. 'The 24th regiment, which later became the South Wales Borderers who train in the hills near Brecon, was ordered to defend Rorke's Drift in the Anglo-Zulu war in 1879. Thousands of Zulus against a hundred soldiers.' Mum's eyes lit up with pride.

'Why did the British invade Zululand?'

'I'm not sure. To open the country. To help the locals?' Her eyes avoided mine.

'Armed soldiers against people with spears?'

'Don't start that nonsense, please. If you want to know more, read it in history books.' She stood up and thrust the tea trolley into the kitchen.

'Have the Zulus written a history book telling their side of the story?' I asked after her.

'Don't be silly. Sometimes you are hard work, and second, Rorke is Irish for champion. Now be a Rorke and give your poor mother a break.'

Alone in the house, I was going through the cupboards in the spare bedroom to pack what I needed for abroad. In a bag with a tag marked *holidays* on it, I came across my old British passport. There were photographs which I recognised. Underneath was a page from a newspaper, which I assumed was the lining for the case. I straightened it out and my eyes caught the headline. *Teenage Girl Killed by Rubber Bullet.* My heart stopped as I read the dates. Dad was on the streets of Belfast in the 1973 Troubles.

Was he there?

I repacked the suitcase and the press cutting, having decided never to mention it to anyone.

I would go to London to start afresh. Wales was a less violent option, and it was right next door to England. I would call my Welsh cousins and my aunt and take them up on their offer to stay until I found a place for myself.

It's the eighties in London and this time for real. I'm on my way.

Chapter Sixteen

I wasn't keen on goodbyes and cared even less for farewells. So, I kept my plans to myself. The dawn before we left for the airport, Themba woke me up with a breakfast tray of tea and toast.

'Good morning, my son,' he said as he waited at the foot of my bed.

'Hi.' An awkward silence hovered between us. 'It's my last day.'

'No, *jaha*. It is your first.'

'Thank you. Thank you for everything.'

He raised the palms of his hands to quieten me. 'Show me how thankful you are, Chameleon. Seek the world and be the difference. Life is about miracles. Large and small. Relish those moments, for they are visions that stay with us forever.'

'I will try. Thank you. I wanted to buy you and Precious a going away present.'

'You are our gift, Zulu warrior,' Themba said. 'Now, let us celebrate your first day with untold joy. Tomorrow we will call on our memories to ward off the agony of absence.'

***

The green grass of England beckoned as the jet landed at Heathrow Airport — a far cry from Harare International Airfield, where passengers walked across the runway to reach their plane.

Exhausted after the sixteen-hour flight, the terminal reminded me of a Benny Hill scene with people rushing behind one another, in time to elevator music. Electric carts trundled along never-ending passageways. The whirring snakes and ladders of escalators. Flashing lights and the constant bing bong of public announcements. All it needed was the closing

Yakety Sax theme tune.

I hauled myself through customs, then passport control, and picked up my suitcase from the luggage carousel. 'Welcome to London,' a woman called out as the sliding doors revealed the stark reality of an English winter.

Outside, my Welsh cousins greeted me. 'Hello boyo, it's been a few years. Since 1973, me thinks?' Evan shook my hand and lifted my case. A sprinkling of grey in his goatee heralding the ten years since my last visit.

'Hi, good to see you both,' I said.

'Hiya Rory,' Terry, the younger by five years, said and gave me a man hug. His red highlighted mullet and puffy long-sleeved shirt tucked into his matching skin-tight blue jeans with white branded sneakers finished his trendy appearance.

'Right.' Evan looked in the car park. 'Where is the motor?'

'Somewhere up by the toilets,' Terry said in his Welsh Valley accent.

'Oh aye, that's right. Come on, then *butts*.'

We walked for an eternity in an endless car park.

'It's up over by yer,' Terry said and pointed to a newish blue Ford Cortina.

We loaded the car and jumped in. I settled in the backseat to sneak a nap on the three-hour journey to Cwmbran — *Valley of the Crows* — in Wales.

'Where are we?' I asked, waking as the engine slowed down to navigate an impressive bridge.

Terry turned in the passenger seat. 'Welcome back, boyo. Had a good snooze? This is the Severn Bridge. It separates England from Wales.'

'Wow, it's huge.'

'Tidy mun, aye,' Evan said. 'Almost two kilometres 'an all.'

We joined the queue and paid the toll to the cashier in the booth. 'Just picking up our African cuz from Heathrow. How are you, luv?' Evan asked. The two chatted, but I didn't understand a word.

'Ok, traaaa, see you next time,' he said at last.

'Aye, see you then,' she said with a wide grin. 'Traaaa.' She beckoned the car behind.

'Traaaa.' Evan checked me out in the review mirror. 'We

charge the bloody English to come into Wales.' He laughed as
he glanced at his brother sitting next to him.

'Cheers Drive,' Terry said, as they roared with laughter at a
private joke.

'How long before we get to Cwmbran?' I asked over the
beat of *Two Tribes* by Frankie Goes to Hollywood.

'We're not going by there, *butt*,' Evan said. 'What it is.
We live in Pontypool, but I'll not lie to you. It's easier to say
Cwmbran, which everyone knows.'

'Now, in a minute,' Terry interjected. 'Half an hour. Leave
Rory alone, Evan. He'll find out soon enough about the English
and the Welsh.'

I sat back and admired the rolling hills of the valleys framed
by the Brecon Beacons. I was not in the mood.

On our arrival in Pontypool, my mum's sister was waiting at
the door. 'Rory Wilde, as I live and breathe,' she said, as she
swept me to her bosom and hugged me with all her might.

'Hi, Aunty,' I mumbled.

'Stand here while I look at you.' She held my arms, then
looked me up and down.

'Where's Uncle?' I asked.

'Oh, he's indoors, but I got to be honest with you. He's not
well.' She shook her head and plucked the dishtowel from her
shoulder. 'Come on then, inside for a cuppa. I've embarrassed
you enough.'

We left our shoes outside the door and traipsed into the tiny
house; the lounge filled with a three-piece suite with a box
television in the corner.

'We'll pop your things upstairs. Mum looks *chopsy*. She
wants to tell you all the news,' Terry said, as they charged up
the narrow stairs to the bedrooms.

'Hi Uncle, how are you doing?' I said.

He shook my hand with both of his. 'Grand boyo, good to
see you again. How is your mother?'

'We're fine, thanks.'

'Great. Oops yer Aunty wants to feed yer.' His eyes flicked
to my aunt, who was clutching a tea tray. 'Where to, Mam?' he
asked.

'Over by here.' She pointed to a three-legged table.

'Can I interest you in a piece of Welsh Rarebit, Rory dear?' Aunty asked.

'That's cheese on toast, what are you talking about?' Uncle said from behind his newspaper.

'Just ignore him. I won't lie to you, but he's been in a mood of late. Haven't you, Daddy-O?'

'Aye. Sorry, son. Times are tough with the recession.' He said.

'Here's your tea, dear.' Aunty handed him a cup with a biscuit on the saucer. He placed it on the periodical on his lap.

'What it is, boyo. Your best bet is back across the Severn Bridge in England. Here the coal mines are closing. Not much in the valleys these days. Thatcher is making sure of that. I'm not trying to get rid of you. You're welcome to stay. Even if you decide to commute.' He sat on the edge of his chair and tapped my shoulder. 'We'll do what we can. That includes the truth.'

'Thanks Uncle, thanks Aunty, I appreciate your kindness.'

'No needs for thank you's. Now you know. All right *butt?*' Uncle turned on the television and slumped into the lounger to watch the rugby. 'We have the best flag in the world. Fact. It's got a freaking dragon on it,' he said to no one in particular.

'Come dear, let him be,' Aunty said before she took me on a tour of the house.

My uncle was right. It was in Cirencester Gloucestershire that I found my first job, albeit part time. It was cheaper to rent a flat than travel an hour and a half to and from Pontypool — never mind the toll fee.

Cirencester, in the heart of the Cotswolds, is the picturesque town many imagine of a typical English village. They make the buildings from local limestone in the same fashion as the Romans constructed the hot springs in Bath. Pastural land surrounded the town and is the home of the Royal Agricultural University, where I met up with old schoolmates from Plumtree. Cirencester also has strong royal connections because of its proximity to Highgrove House, where Prince Charles and Princess Diana lived; and it is also close to Badminton House, of the Badminton Horse Trials. I didn't feel the need to conform to protocol or act according to my station in life. For me, anything was possible — a loose cannon to most.

My job became full-time with frequent trips to London, Birmingham, and Bristol in a company van to deliver and collect goods. My official title was store person. Technology was advancing by introducing barcodes so products and computers could talk to one another.

If I got a penny for every person who said technology would never take off. A billionaire, if it included, why can't the youngsters just read the labels?

Although it wasn't an important job, it was a means to an end. I enjoyed meeting people from every walk of life, their accents and how their behaviour differed from town to town — sometimes street by the street fascinated me. It was the late eighties and Britain was coming out of the slump, led by the irrepressible Margaret Thatcher. I followed my dreams of watching Formula One drivers Mansell, Senna, and Prost at Silverstone and Liverpool Football Club at its finest playing Arsenal at Wembley Stadium, and the Welsh were in a fine voice at the rugby match against Scotland at Cardiff Arms Park.

A chance to catch up on a lost childhood without fear or guilt because I was one of the many. Something I hadn't experienced before. I loved pop concerts with the likes of Foreigner, Tina Turner, Bee Gees, Elton John, and a little-known band INXS who were the curtain raiser of the greatest concert of all time, *A Kind of Magic* — Queen — again at Wembley stadium. I watched the enigmatic Freddie Mercury control one hundred thousand people, lifting them and bringing them back down with the operatic ballad that is *Bohemian Rhapsody*.

Prime Minister Margaret Thatcher had made it practical for families to buy their own homes with subsidies for first-time buyers and enabling tenants to purchase their council house for next to nothing. I bought my first home at twenty-two. It was a one bedroom upstairs, downstairs starter-home that cost eighteen thousand pounds — cheaper than renting and a sound investment today if I had held onto it, but that sacrifice was too great. Not for the investor, but for the underprivileged. Compared to the houses back in Africa, it was a broom cupboard.

My job led to a career that paid the bills and provided

opportunities made possible because of an education which involved more than regurgitating information.

I take no pride in these accomplishments. They fulfilled a necessity and contributed little to my happiness. With an empty soul, it was time for change. What form that would take? I didn't know. I was still as desolate as the day I left my Africa. Weekends spent lying on the rug tuning in to the rhythms of Johnny Clegg and *Ladysmith Mambazo*, state-of-the-art technology, fast foods, and a first world country offered little by comparison. And I missed the camaraderie of my Themba.

Years later, I lay in the same spot on the carpet listening to Nelson Mandela's speech after they released him from twenty-seven years of imprisonment. His words remain with me forever.

"As I walked out of the door towards the gate that would lead to my freedom, If I didn't leave my bitterness and hatred behind, I'd still be in prison." Later, he emerged from the Cape Town City Hall to an impatient crowd of over one hundred thousand people.

"I greet you all in the name of peace, democracy and freedom for all. I stand here before you not as a prophet, but as a humble servant of you, the people. Your tireless and heroic sacrifices have made it possible for me to be here today. I therefore place the remaining years of my life in your hands." Mandela closed by repeating a famous line from an address he'd given at his trial in 1964.

"I have fought against white domination, and I have fought against black domination," he said. *"I have cherished the ideal of a democratic society in which all persons live together in harmony and with equal opportunities. It is an ideal for which I hope to live for and to achieve. But, if need be, it is an ideal for which I am prepared to die."*

I cried again, this time for myself — I cried for my nation of birth — I cried for Africa's Madiba, Nelson Rolihlahla Mandela, to deliver for South Africa. I sat on the floor in my lounge until the television station closed to the snowy hiss of the screen — excited at the prospect of a new South Africa — terrified because I must return to Africa. A decision which was not understood by my family or appreciated by friends.

'Why turn your back on a successful career and a lovely home in the Cotswolds?' one friend said. 'What is in South Africa that you don't have here? What about your family? You're putting them at risk?' Questions I didn't have the answers to. It was something I had to do.

The nineties marked the perfect opportunity for me to move on. Many companies in South Africa had shown an interest in my skills. The government was more than willing to offer me permanent residence before I had even set foot in the country. That based no doubt on the colour of my skin rather than what I might contribute towards a new era. One advantage was I had close family there. I resigned my position and sold my home and spent the last few weeks on a trip to the Greek islands before I underwent a week of farewells.

The day before I flew out, Evan posed a question in his singsong accent. 'So, boyo, what is it about our fair island you don't like?'

'There's nothing wrong with it. I just want to go back to Africa.'

'Drop the diplomatic bullshit, ole *butt*. Tell us plain and simple,' he slurred as everyone sat on the patio enjoying snacks and a farewell drink.

'Okay, if that's what you want.' I leant forward with my elbows resting on my knees and my eyes on the ground. 'This is not a country where I want my children to live. The schools have no playing fields apart from cement car parks and far too many kids hang around street corners, sniffing, drinking, and smoking.' I looked about the room, all focussed on me. Terry was sitting in one corner, nodding his head.

'Tidy darts, cousin, bullseye,' he said as he raised his glass and toasted me in Welsh. '*Lechyd da* — Good health.'

'Cheers,' the assembled company responded in unison.

The country did me proud. The people, once you became acquainted, were salt of the earth folk, who did the best they could considering their circumstances. As an outsider who shares their heritage, I knew that the feudal system was alive and well, with the middle class duped into believing that they deserved their lot. They were still the working class. With another subclass that drained the kingdom of its essence. Gone was the stiff upper lip and, for God and country, replaced by a forever growing narcissistic culture of what's in it for me. The jewels of the crown have emigrated to the colonies, where they meet reluctance and disdain because of a lingering delusion that they still believe they rule the world. Difficult to hear. The seven-year-chafe ended with many fond memories of associations and a land drenched in tradition and a nation blinded by credence.

The early 1990s brought change to the planet. President de Klerk addressed the South African apartheid government on February 2, 1991.

"The government will accord the process of negotiation the highest priority. The aim is a totally new and just constitutional dispensation in which every inhabitant will enjoy equal rights, treatment, and opportunity in every sphere of endeavour — constitutional, social and economic."

The nineties promised a new world order. After decades of nuclear threat, the next generation expressed themselves through electronic new-wave music. A revolution was afoot that would alter life forever. It was the time of change — the last throws of the Cold War and dissolution of the Soviet Union. The launch of the Hubble Space Telescope. Birth of the World Wide Web and with it the Information Age was born. The Los Angeles riots left sixty dead after the acquittal of police officers — some things never change. Desert Storm and the Gulf War in the Middle East ended. The release of Mandela instigated my return, and the fall of the Berlin wall a year later justified my decision. Hope springs eternal.

So why shouldn't I go back?

I negotiated my way through the security checks and intensity of Heathrow Airport in London, where I boarded the plane and took off for Jan Smuts International Airport. England's green and pleasant land fell away. Sleep was not a choice. I sat with my eyes closed and replayed my life, then tried to imagine where I wanted it to go.

As the airplane descended, the dry savannah contrasted with the glint of the Johannesburg skyline scarred by the gold mine dumps. The airport was quiet, surveillance was non-existent, and a lackadaisical demeanour welcomed me back to Africa.

***

Two decades passed, during which I was fortunate enough to raise children and pay off debts. My family live all over the world — part of a vast diaspora in Africa, Europe, and Australasia. Not by choice, but by the continued political instability in my beloved Africa. The superpowers continue to exploit the continent's natural resources, and poor leadership forces the skilled to seek opportunities elsewhere on the planet.

Seventeen years on from my arrival, the new South Africa was no longer the Rainbow Nation welcoming diversity. Mandela had become a wistful memory of a dream that never endured. The world was in deep recession. The exodus continued to grow. Corruption and xenophobia were rampant.

As I drove my kids to college on Monday morning, the radio report said they had turned the town hall into a place of safety for immigrants fleeing from another onslaught on their possessions, homes, and lives. I passed by on my way home, concerned that the violence might spread to the suburbs. The plight of these poor people spilling onto the sidewalks dispelled any thoughts of self-preservation. Mothers, dozens of women, feeding their children in the gutters, while toddlers sat on the pavements in tattered clothing. I had seen the pictures on television over the past week, yet nothing prepared me for this. It was time to put aside political agendas and concern myself on a humanitarian level.

I pulled over in my luxury car and headed towards the dishevelled congregation, who paid me little attention. A sense of walking among ghosts turned me cold. The large wooden doors of the old colonial hall in the high-street grated open. I took my chance and ducked inside, without hindrance, past the doorkeeper into the empty main entrance but for a small gang of conscripts cleaning. I approached a group who appeared in charge of proceedings; they greeted me with an unexpected exuberance. A young, fresh-faced man from the Salvation Army with a pleasant demeanour shook my hand. Two ladies from the Red Cross, one from the church and another in a private capacity, completed the band. A slim, well-dressed man, nicknamed Comrade, joined us along with our local council member, trailed by a brusque police officer.

Instead of focusing on the discussion, I studied the faces in our small circle. The holy lady talked ten to the dozen, touching each person's arm, and spoke to the anxious citizen who scribbled lengthy lists, insisting upon structure. The Red Cross team moved on, more concerned with sleeping arrangements and medication. The Salvation Army leader did his best to listen to everyone. The police officer laid down the law in a manner that made us cringe. His only concern was the safety of the terrified hordes. The councillor objected to the police officer's lack of political correctness and threatened to report him. He pulled at the breast pocket of his immaculate suit, searching for what resembled Mao's *Little Red Book*. I scanned the officer's pockets, half expecting to find a copy of Hitler's *Mein Kampf*.

Their passion re-ignited the embers of my burnt African pride. Our modest group of diverse Africans was here for a common cause, to aid those afflicted. Instead of a halo forming above my head, I became depressed and exhausted. No warm fuzzy feelings washed over me at my perceived goodwill. A thankless vocation that only the dedicated endured.

I collected clothing and food that I had brought with me. In doing so, I thought I recognised someone but shrugged it off and continued to help vehicles offload their wares when a voice from behind spoke. 'Is that a Chameleon I see?'

I froze.

I know that voice. It cannot be. Your mind is playing tricks on you, Rorke Wilde. A different country? Another universe? Am I hearing things?

'Turn around, young man. Have you forgotten me?'

I remained rooted to the ground, afraid to turn in case it wasn't who I expected it to be.

'It's okay, my friend. I am here.' The eyes were the same —
the rest was of an older man I knew very well. A sadness set in,
the corners of his lips turned downward, his face harrowed with
permanent lines from years of hardship and pain. No longer
endowed with muscle but bones that creaked, yet he still didn't
miss a thing as his gaze saw everything.

'Themba. I have missed you, *u Khulu* — grandfather.'

'And I, you.' We hugged until we couldn't breathe. I lost
myself in the smell of wood fires, carbolic soap, open savannah,
and home-brewed beer — eleven years old once more.

There were no chairs. We laid out a blanket and sat on
the cement floor, told tales, and read the life stories sketched
around our eyes — Themba still had a twinkle in his eye. We
walked slower, talked with more wisdom, and laughed with the
tenderness of days past.

Someone made us a cup of tea each. Whom it was, I am not
sure, because we didn't pay them attention or thank them for
their kindness. I dared not look away should Themba not be
there when I turned back.

We spoke of the past and shared our experiences since the
last time we met.

'Tell me about your wife and family, jaha.' Themba asked.

'Rose is my wife. A beautiful woman inside and out,' I said.

Themba smiled at the cliché, but knew it to be true. 'You are
indeed a lucky man. Tell me more.'

"She means everything to me,' I continued. 'We have
had our challenges and our highs, but wouldn't change it for
anything.' I paused and watched the pride on my old friend's
face.

'I look forward to meeting her. What about children?'

'Yes. Our youngest is Chelsea—*a laat lammetjie.*'

'The late lamb hey?' Themba translated the Afrikaans
phrase.

I nodded and changed the subject.

'So, what are you doing now?' I asked.

'I live in *Umgodi* village, *jaha.*'

His calling me his son warmed my very essence after all
these years. 'Is your family there with you?'

Themba's face twisted in pain and a deep sadness. 'No,
alone.' He closed his eyes, then broke into a wide grin. 'Let me

195

tell you about my nephew, Lucky. Lucky Ndlovu. Elephant by name, elephant by nature.' The smile didn't reach his eyes, but I resisted the urge to ask why. Instead, I listened to my hero.

The hall lit up, accompanied by the rumble of food trollies.

'Time to eat. Will you join us, *jaha?*' Themba asked.

'I am no longer a boy, but thank you. I would love to.'

'That you are, for you still have a story to tell, Chameleon.'

'I do?'

'*Yebo* and one day you shall share that wisdom, whether either of us is still on this earth or not.' He raised his head to the heavens.

'So where are Lucky and his grandmother? Can I meet them?' I changed the topic, unsure how to take Themba's foretelling.

'His grandmother, my sister, has passed. She was burnt while asleep by xenophobic gangs.' Themba hung his head to hide his grief. 'But that is not everything, master Rory. My nephew Lucky Ndlovu, son of my sister, is unwell.'

I stared at the back of Themba's salt and pepper hair as it slipped lower into his lap. 'Themba, I'm so sorry. Where is he? What's wrong?'

'He's recovering in Baragwanath hospital and in a few weeks will move to a place of care.' The old man straightened up, with tears streaming down his face. 'Now is not the time. Let us enjoy each other's company and relish this gift that life has given us.'

Three decades vanished in a heartbeat. We relived the good times and skipped the bad; we laughed and cried hidden tears. The town hall filled with the waiting homeless families; we helped where we were able and ate *sadza* and gravy until the carers announced it was time for the visitors to leave.

'Why don't you come home with me? A hot shower, a soft bed and we can talk the night away?' I said.

'Thank you, but no, my son, this is where I belong. I cannot leave my people for my comfort. Forgive me, I mean no disrespect.'

'But Themba...'

'There are no buts, my friend.' He placed two fingers on my forehead. 'We can go together to visit Lucky one day.'

'Why don't we go in the morning?' I asked as I helped my

mentor up from the floor.

He gripped my hands. 'You have grown into a fine man, *jaha.*'

'Tomorrow nine-thirty am?' I said.

'By then, the day will be old. Come now, we will make it six a.m.,' Themba's grin filled his face, then faded. 'I am tired, my body is weary, my brain cluttered. I will see you later.' He held onto me. 'Imagine a world where money is more important than healing. Where profit comes before children,' he whispered in my ear. 'What have we become?'

'Where are we going?' I asked.

'The earth is sick.'

'Nature is angry.'

'We defecate in the oceans.'

'And poison the air we breathe.'

Themba drew back with a shake of his head. '*Lihambe kuhle, jaha, Lisale kuhle.*'

'It went well. Goodbye,' I replied.

I climbed into the car and drove without direction. It was time for the chameleon to change once more. To find somewhere for his family's sake, and his own — be the difference.

Cry, the beloved country.

Mourn i-Afrika.

Rise, *abantu,* the long road to freedom continues.

Return home my scatterlings.

We must be one.

I would worry about that tomorrow.

I can't wait to meet Themba's nephew, Lucky Ndlovu.

197

Chapter Seventeen

Lucky Ndlovu lay in a cot along with dozens of other children in a ward at Baragwanath hospital just outside Soweto in Johannesburg. The south-western township is the country's largest black precinct, built to cope with the influx of people in the nineteenth century gold rush. Created by a government intent on separating the races. Home of the African National Council. *The Spear of the Nation, Umkhonto we Sizwe,* the armed resistance movement and the tragedy of school children, massacred by state troops at the Soweto uprising in 1976.

Themba clutched at my arm as we passed bed after bed of wide-eyed youngsters. They stared as we walked by, without malice, beyond accusation. A medical trolley rolled down the aisle by nurses numbed by the task before them. Yellowing posters adorned the walls, warning of Human Immunodeficiency Virus — HIV transmission and the consequences of acquired immunodeficiency syndrome — AIDS. It kills over a million people every year. A pandemic unequalled to this day, claiming over forty million lives worldwide.

'I'm sorry,' I confided to Themba, to myself, to my country, humanity, and the world. 'What have we done?'

'What haven't we done?' Themba answered. Beyond comprehension his face harrowed in pain 'Hey, Lucky, I've brought a close friend of the family,' he called to a child with their back to us.

'Salibonane malume,' a frail, raspy voice replied.

'I see you too, Lucky Ndlovu. Elephant by name. Elephant by nature.' Themba held the boy and wiped his nose.

'Umngani wakho umngumngane wami njalo,' Lucky greeted me. His head was too big for his body — his round eyes exposed his soul.

'Your friend is always my friend,' Themba translated.

I had to stop myself from snatching the boy and running

away from this netherworld — this holocaust.

Why is it we never see this on the news? Hidden rather than faced up to?

'I'm happy to meet you. Your uncle has told me so much about you,' I lied, uncertain whether to offer a hand or hug him.

Themba placed his stool close to the bed, stroked the back of Lucky's hand, and tidied the intravenous bandage on his wrist. When he leant forward to whisper in Lucky's ear, the boy turned to me. 'Should we tell him?' Themba asked with a quizzical frown and a glint in his eye.

'*Yebo,* Uncle.' Both spoke in English for my benefit.

'Go on then, my brave warrior. Put him out of his misery.' Themba snorted.

'All right, you two. What's going on?' I played along.

'Sorry, Mr Rory. We do not mean to be rude. I have... we have wonderful news.' He looked across at Themba. 'Tell him, Uncle.'

'We do. The Gods have answered our prayers and spared my sister's son, *umshana wami,* Lucky Ndlovu. Elephant by name, elephant by nature.'

I bit my tongue and waited until the two were ready to share their message. Their faces beamed, wide eyed with excitement.

Themba placed my hand with his onto Lucky's. 'We are one. Bless this moment, for it shall be my happiest.' He wiped his creased forehead. 'Our Lucky is leaving hospital; he is HIV negative. AIDS will play no part in the family, this time.' Themba thanked the heavens, the ancestors, and lady luck.

What does he mean this time, I wondered, not wanting to push the issue?

Lucky lay backward, enjoying the fuss. It would take a while to rebuild his strength. We sat and chatted, reading a child's version of *Moby Dick* until visiting hour was over.

Themba stood and brushed at an imaginary crumb on Lucky's cheek with the back of his palm. 'Tomorrow our Rory, we shall share Lucky Ndlovu's story.'

The boy closed his eyes, a smile playing on his lips.

'See you, Lucky. I can't wait to find out all about you.'

Themba took my hand and we trudged out of the ward, conscious of the children, the sickness and despair.

199

'Where are their families?'
'They have lost them to the dreaded virus, Mr Rory. Most don't even understand what kills them,' my old friend croaked.

***

At dawn the next morning, I strolled through my suburb in Germiston while the family slept. Barbed wire and high walls, alarms, and security lights surrounded homes to protect the inhabitants. A pair of Alsatians attacked at the neighbour's electric gates, safeguarding the expensive cars in the driveway, as I walked by.

What have we become? This isn't right; I cannot let the family live this way. We are in prison.

I sipped on a carton of milk bought from the corner café that was setting up shop. The owners wore guns beneath their armpits and were serving customers from behind iron bars.

What of those who have no choice and cannot leave this topsy-turvydom? Will my family follow me?

I traipsed homeward with the conviction the time had come as Themba foresaw decades earlier. I climbed into the car after securing my household on the property and headed to the town hall for my rendezvous.

Themba waited outside, dressed in tan trousers and a lime-tartan jacket with a purple kerchief in his breast pocket and a rug tucked under one arm, while he held an open scarlet umbrella in the other.

'Morning. You look amazing. Ready for the day?' I said.
'I am Mr Rory. A time of stories — of happiness.' He tipped his straw boater.

'Sounds great and I'm treating everyone to Kentucky Fried Chicken.'

'Thank the Gods. What a moment this promises to be.'

***

As I helped Lucky into the car, he looked brighter than he had the day before.

'Where are we travelling to?' he asked.

'Maureen Park, it's not far. Five k's from here?'

'Cool.'

Themba clambered into the front seat with his arm around Lucky. 'Just in case we have an accident, I'll hold on to you.'

We set off through the streets, passing the Southgate Shopping Center and the overladen mini-bus taxis. Lucky leant forward with his hands spread on the dashboard, absorbing everything around him.

The park comprising a child's playground, and lawns and trees that provided shade. Themba selected one, unrolled the rug underneath it and sat with the bucket of chicken on his lap. Lucky lay on his back with his knees up.

'This is nice, thank you, Uncle,' Lucky said.

'It is for us to thank you, Lucky Ndlovu. Elephant by name. Elephant by nature,' Themba said.

'Our privilege, Lucky. Now let's hear about you. I can't wait another second,' I said.

'Yes, Uncle, start. It is time.' Lucky propped himself on an elbow and helped himself to a drumstick.

'Ah, good times and bad make life's remembrances.' Themba peered into the distance. 'I recall when we first went to the shopping mall.'

'*Ja* Uncle, I remember. Tell that one.' Lucky's eyes lit.

'A few years ago, my dear sister, grandmother to Lucky Ndlovu. Elephant by name. Elephant, by nature, asked me to take you to the marketplace.'

'Uncle? I know you mean well, but no more elephants, please,' Lucky said.

'Sure, *umfana*. As you wish.' He rubbed his nephew's head and began his account.

As Lucky Ndlovu trotted after me, he asked how much further?

'To those buildings,' I said, squinting as the traffic hurtled by.

Lucky lifted his t-shirt over his nose to avoid the fumes and ogled at the chrome-domed building in the distance. 'It's the same as the frogs' eggs in our river. The cars are the tadpoles wriggling. Can you see them, Uncle?'

'There is no time to dream today. Walk here away from the

trucks.' I took the boy's hand. Once in the car park, I dusted Lucky's pants, then wiped his face and shaven head with my hands. The lad returned the favour, brushing the flecks from the tail of my tatty blazer. Groomed, we headed to the entrance.

'What does that say?' Lucky pointed above the gates.

'East Rand Shopping Mall.'

'Huh?' he asked.

'The home of many shops,' I said, trying to join the bustle of shoppers wary of the electric doors.

'The sun lives here too?' Lucky looked upward, spread his arms, and spun. The glass roof and fluorescent lights merged into a kaleidoscope.

I chuckled. 'The best is yet to come.'

My boy couldn't help himself other than to gawk into every window at the mannequins and wonder at the plasma screens that sprung to life to sell their wares. He laughed at the customers who danced on headphones in the music boutiques and marvelled at the goings on within the hairdressers.

A clown cavorted in the toyshop entrance, shaping balloons, and dishing them out to a party of kids.

'Do you want one?' I asked.

Lucky clapped his hands and bounced around. 'Can I also have a balloon for my little friend too?'

I shuffled forward, holding out a hand.

'Clear off, these are for customers.' The jester held the bunch to his chest.

I withdrew and raised my worn hat. 'Sorry, I thought they were for everyone?'

'If you want one, go inside and buy something.' The comic sneered.

'I have no money, Mr Clown, but I acknowledge you for your help.'

'My help?'

'Yes, sir. Now I can explain to this child why clowns have painted smiles.' Down-at-the-heel, we continued our way.

'What's that smell?' Lucky pinched his snout.

A flood of neon signs fought for dominance. Fried chicken, pizza, hamburgers, fish, and curries. The confection and spices made his nose run.

*'Hey, McDonald's.' Lucky pointed to a large yellow **M**, pleased he recognised something in this fantastical world. Albeit from magazines decorating his gran's walls.*

'Don't stare at the people eating. It is rude.' I distracted the lad away from the diners.

'They remind me of the hyena,' Lucky said as patrons pushed and shoved one another to satiate themselves.

'Come, my boy.' I guided my nephew to a department store.

'What's your favourite takeaway, Rory?' Lucky asked.

'It depends on my mood, but Kentucky Fried Chicken.' I waved a wing at him.

'Mine was McDonalds, but now I don't like clowns, so it's also KFC. Continue with the story, Uncle.'

The doors hissed open and closed, promising another realm. Inside, the shoppers surrendered to the ambience of the décor and mellow music.

'Don't touch a thing.' I spoke to Lucky out the side of my mouth. 'Be careful as we pass.'

Lucky shuffled behind me, holding onto my jacket tails until we reached the foot of an escalator.

'No, I can't. It's magic,' Lucky said, backing away.

I grasped the youngster's wrist and lunged at the moving staircase. He teetered, then found his balance, and enjoyed the world dropping away from him.

At the top, he asked, 'Can we go again?'

'Aren't you hungry?'

'Yes, but I want another ride.'

'Perhaps later.' I answered.

Themba stopped his ramblings when Lucky sat bolt upright and shook his hands in excitement. 'What is it, son?' Themba asked.

'I'm not scared of those moving steps now. I'm much older and wiser.'

'That you are. Should I continue?' Themba asked.

We nodded, our stomachs and hearts full.

Lucky and I walked to the far end of the mall, peering through windows at the theatrics of retail. Then ducked through a fire escape to the first-floor car park.

I hobbled up to a food vendor and ordered a can of cola to share with our lunch. How my feet ached that day. We sat in the shade outside the public toilets and watched the children in the arcade through a large plate-glass window.

'One day I'll work here. It's nicer than driving a taxi or being a street seller. I can bring ugogo,' Lucky said aloud to himself. He washed his fingers and wiped them on his pants.

'You're better than that. Look bigger and wider. Do not be afraid to dream. Nothing is impossible,' I said, tearing the wrap from our lunch. We dug in, folding the meal in our fingertips, discussing the day.

I refilled the soda tin from an outside tap and drank the tepid water before I returned to Lucky. 'So, what have you learnt, young man?'

'Is this where the rich live, Uncle?'

I nodded. 'The colonials before, now the privileged few.' I pondered a moment, recalling the past in my mind's eye before saying to Lucky. 'Remember, my boy, wealth does not spread, but famine does.'

Lucky rolled his eyes when I began my usual cabaret of proverbs. 'Gluttony remains. Hunger wanders. It knows no colour.'

'*Come, Uncle, we have much to do.' Lucky pulled me up, and we returned to the mall.*

'*Where are we going? I want to play with those kids.' Lucky pointed towards the arcade machines and the children he recognised at lunch.*

'*Those things eat money.' Instead, I gestured to the table and chairs. 'You can sit over there.'*

Lucky sidled up to a table to take a seat, wary of another kid who sat with his nose in a book.

'*I love Spiderman.' The boy smiled across at him.*

Lucky couldn't stop himself from sliding off the chair. He had never seen a face covered in spots with a toothless smile, ginger hair, and ears akin to wings.

'*Do you like Spiderman?' The lad showed a picture of a flying man.*

Lucky nodded. He wasn't sure what the boy meant.

'*Me too. Do you want to read with me? Sit here, we can share.' The boy invited him.*

Lucky remained rooted to the spot.

'*Okay, I'll sit by you then.' The lad pushed on the tabletop and dragged his limbs beneath him.*

Lucky wasn't sure whether to look at the boy's face, or the callipers attached to his legs.

'*My name is Eddie. What's yours?'*

'*Lucky.' He managed a whisper.*

'*Hi, Lucky.' Eddie offered a pale hand.*

Lucky shook the limp grip, lost for words.

Eddie opened the book and explained Spiderman and his superpowers. Lucky wasn't listening, instead I saw him studying his new friend.

'What a strange person I have met today. Red hair, big ears, and funny legs. What are those stains on his face?'

'They're freckles.'

Lucky pulled his palm from the boy's cheek with a start, not realising he had said the words aloud. I laughed so.

'My Mum says I must wear cream because the sun will burn my skin, or I'll get more of them.'

Initiation over, the boys settled on communicating via hand signals and the language of youth.

I left them a while together, then interrupted. 'Lucky, it's time to go. I want to buy groceries before the shops close. Say goodbye to your friend.'

'Can he come back next week, Lucky's dad?'

'Maybe Eddie.' I did not correct his assumption.

'Great, see you later.'

Unsure of what Eddie meant; Lucky responded to the tone and nodded.

'Lihambe kuhle, Lucky.'

'How?' He gawked at the Zulu farewell. 'Lisale kuhle.' Lucky grinned, tapping his friend's callipers with his foot.

Lucky peeked over his shoulder at Eddie, already buried in his books.

He lifted his hand to wave but didn't want to prolong the goodbye. Instead, he spun around and chased after me, as I headed back through the mall to fulfil my shopping list.

I stopped at the first supermarket and ducked inside. 'I need to get a few things here.'

'Can I push the cart?' Lucky asked.

'Sure, but stay close and don't bump my heels,' I said.

Lucky giggled at my scuffed shoes as they swished along the shiny tiles.

'Now, where is the soap?'

Lucky shook his head, scanning the shelves.

'I'll ask this kind person.' I shuffled across to a shop assistant filling a shelf.

'Sawubona.'

No response to my greeting.

'Hello?' I tried again.

Lucky stuck his fingers in his ears and shook his head, suggesting the woman might be hard of hearing.

The attendant peered up at me after I tapped her on the shoulder.

'I'll be with you as soon as I'm done here, sir.'

I smiled back and waited.

Finished, she turned to us. 'What do you want?'

I looked at the lady with her nose ring and dyed hair. 'I want green soap.' showing the length of the bar I wanted with my fingers.

The assistant said, 'Not in this aisle, Oupa. Lane twenty-seven, where the house cleaners are.' The derogatory use of the word grandfather apparent.

She poked a tongue at Lucky.

'Well, thank you,' I said.

'Don't thank me, it's my job.' She called after us.

'Why is that lady's hair yellow?' Lucky asked.

'I'm not sure, my boy.'

'I thought only white people have yellow hair?' Lucky said.

'Here it is.' I selected a stick of carbolic soap. 'It's fifty cents less. Now, where do they sell the snuff? I mustn't forget ugogo's gel.'

On our way home, Lucky stopped at the toy store now that the clown had gone.

The late afternoon sunlight caused us to quicken our pace.

'Lucky, Lucky.' A voice called.

'Over here.' A hand waved from an expensive, unfamiliar vehicle. Eddie peered out the window.

'Who calls your name?' I squinted into the sunset.

'The ear's that the sun shines through,' Lucky muttered, waving back.

I repressed a smile.

Eddie struggled out of the truck. 'This is Lucky. The one I told you about, Mum.'

'Pleased to meet you guys. Thank you for your time with Eddie,' his mother, draped in gold, said to us.

'It's a pleasure, Mrs Eddie.' Her make-up reminding me of the clown's.

'Can I offer you two a lift home?'

'Wonderful.' I shoved Lucky into the pickup before she changed her mind.

'Can I also go in the back?'

'Eddie, I don't.... Oh, all right, but don't sit on the sides,' Mother said.

'Cool.'

I helped Eddie up, then hopped on the back and banged the roof that we were ready.

'Thanks for a great day.' Lucky hugged my leg.

'You warm an old man's heart. What else have you learned today?'

Lucky answered, 'You can't tell where your friends come from or how they look.'

'True, my warrior. It takes the colours of the leaves to make a tree.'

Eddie, unable to understand the language, butted in with the only Zulu word in his vocabulary.

'Sala kuhle.' His red hair flickered in the wind; his blue eyes danced.

The three of us laughed until our sides hurt, appreciating the freedom of the breeze as the car hurtled home. Each with our reason.

Themba paused his storytelling. We sat in silence, enjoying the outdoors, each of us deep in our own thoughts and dreams. A sense of inequality ate at my soul. Guilt rose with the bile in my stomach. Aware of the disparity in Africa had changed little.

Maybe it will be better elsewhere in the world.

'Just look at him, Mr Rory. I am confused what our lesson is, least of all for a young boy,' Themba said.

'I'm not sure. It is what it is,' I said.

'No, *jaha,* that can't be so. Every culture talks of the same force but uses different names — Hinduism and Buddhism talk of Karma; Islam of Kismet and the Bible warns us we reap what we sow. Nature works the same. With every action, there is an equal and opposite reaction.'

'Isaac Newton's third law of motion,' I said.

'Mr Rory, your schooling, although painful, has paid off.'

'Alan also has a saying he likes to use,' I said.

'I remember your best friend from Wankie days. How is he?' Themba asked.

'I don't know. Haven't spoken to him since boarding school.'

'That is a shame, *jaha.* Take the time to seek him out.' Themba suggested.

'You know, I might just do that.'

'Well, are you going to share his words of wisdom?'

'Not sure about the wisdom part,' I said.

'Share it anyway, *jaha.*'

'If you fart in the shower, you have only yourself to blame.' We laughed harder than the phrase deserved.

We listened to the birds and enjoyed the light breeze while Lucky slept. Kids played in the jungle gym, and a few kicked a football.

'Mr Rory?' Themba asked, his head propped up on his one hand as he lay on the rug.

'Yes, my friend.'

'Tell me more about your life here in South Africa.'

'It's not very interesting. It's one of privilege and a selective vision I am not proud of.'

'A worthwhile journey if you can see the error of your ways.'

'Only if you promise to tell me more of yours and Lucky's.'

Themba lay back on the rug and held his nephew — young and old. The strains of *World in Union* sung by P J Powers and Ladysmith Black Mambazo played from a vehicle in the car park nearby. Memories leapt to mind as I sifted through which to share.

'Tell me one that pains you and another that brings joy, for then *jaha* we maintain the balance,' Themba said under his breath.

'The experience I have in mind offered both. The anguish of the moment brought a happiness I never imagined,' I replied.

'Go on, *jaha*. I do not sleep. I lie here, content and at peace with myself. Share your story, Chameleon. Share it now.'

'Her name was Lethabo. A sinewy woman an inch above five feet, with a shaved head and the largest round earrings I have ever seen. My youngest daughter, Chelsea, called her Letty and the rest of us copied. We employed her as our housecleaner, and like you, she became part of the family.'

'Like me or better than me?' Themba raised his head and winked at me.

I ignored the remark and went on with my story.

'Letty? I have news for you,' Rose said.

'Madam, tell me quick. What is it?'

'I'm pregnant.'

The two ladies hugged one another in a frenzy of ohs and ahs. Rose's red hair covering Letty's as they looked into each other's eyes — one set brown, the other green.

'*Ouma. Ouma.*' Letty ran from the kitchen down the hallway in search of Rose's mother.

'What is it, Letty? What's the noise?' *Ouma* asked from the end of her bed, where she was eating breakfast. 'Can't you see I'm watching *Egoli,* my favourite soap?'

'Miss Rose is pregnant.' Letty spun around and gave me a hug. 'Mr Rory, we are having a baby.'

'Yes, Letty we are.'

'Madam, we have work to do.' She took Rose's hand and marched her back to the breakfast nook.

The months following were about the baby. Letty took charge of the functional side, my wife, the emotional reality of running both a family and a business — **Cobblers Bar and Grill**, a local Irish pub in Germiston.

The baby shower came and went. Chelsea's birth changed our lives forever. Life was grand. She hit all her stages of development and influenced all under her spell. Letty was no different.

'Chelsea, breakfast is ready,' Letty said as she waited for the two-year-old dressed up in Mum's shoes and wearing my T-shirt tucked into my underpants. Standard attire for the time of day.

'You look lovely, Chelsea,' Letty said and lifted her onto the stool. Chelsea's platinum curls, rosy cheeks complimented her emerald eyes. They sat and ate pap and milk sweetened with a teaspoon of honey and drank mugs of milky tea. The two were inseparable. Chelsea helped with the housework, although it took Letty longer to finish every day because of Chelsea's attempts to help. She helped Letty wash the dishes in suds that always overflowed onto the lino floor. She swept the floor with her mum's hairbrushes and cooked mud cakes in the pots and pans in the garden.

After a long day at work, Letty boarded a mini taxi and went home to tend to her own children and family. She was never absent and never complained. Until a year ago.

Rose asked Letty if she was okay. Letty said she was fine. Later that same day, Rose discovered Letty prostrate on the kitchen floor with Chelsea, reading her a story from her Dr Seuss picture book.

'Letty. Letty. Can you hear me?' Rose said as she shook her shoulder. When there was no response, Rose dialled emergency services. They arrived half an hour later, by which time Letty was sitting up, sipping on a glass of water.

A week later, Letty returned, but she was not herself.

'So, when do you get the results from your medical tests?'

Rose asked.

'They are very busy, but the doctor says he hopes to hear this week.'

'That's good. Then we can get you well again.'

'Yes, madam. Thank you for your help.'

'Oh Letty, it's the least we can do. Until we know what is making you sick, we will continue with light duties until you recover.'

'That will be nice. I miss looking after Chelsea and want to teach her how to cook.' Letty gave a weak smile.

'Are you ready to eat, Letty?' *Ouma* said as she helped her off her stool. Her weight loss was becoming more noticeable by the day.

'You have been too kind, *Ouma*, and thank you for your work around the house,' Letty said.

'Don't you worry. We must watch out for each other. No one else is going to.' *Ouma* brushed her peppered hair to one side. Her slippers scuffed along as she put the kettle on to make everyone a cup of tea and persuade Letty to have a slice of anchovy toast.

'Okay ladies, I'll see you after work,' Rose said as she kissed the top of Chelsea's head — her face full of porridge.

'See you later, dear.' *Ouma* tucked a tissue into the pocket of her cardigan, fastened by a single button. 'We'll be fine. Won't we, Rory?'

'Yup. Let me have that shopping list,' I said.

'Don't you worry about that. It is long this week. The supermarket has great specials.' *Ouma* cleared the plates after holding Letty's shoulder. 'You rest up.'

'But *Ouma*...'

'Never mind that, Letty. You must rest to mend.' The old lady fussed.

'I'll see you soon.' Rose kissed me and grabbed her car keys, miming I must call her if I need to.

I gave her a thumbs up. 'See you at work.'

Themba roused himself and sat facing me with his elbows resting on his knees. 'A happy family life.'

'It was despite all that was happening in the country. We were happy in our bubble.'

212

We both looked at Lucky, who stirred but slumbered on.
'Sleep, my son. We are here.' Themba rubbed Lucky's back.
'Continue Mr Rory.'

I pulled into the driveway to find it blocked by vehicles I didn't
recognise. The dogs locked in the back garden wagged their
tails in greeting.

'Hey guys. Have you lot been naughty?' I patted each one
and went inside. 'Hello?' I called out when I heard voices in
the kitchen. 'It's just me. Please, guys, remember to lock these
doors. It's not safe otherwise.' I kicked off my shoes and put
my keys away.

The kitchen was quiet.

Rose emerged; her eyes were bloodshot.

'What's going on? Is everybody all right?' I asked, as I
reached for the 38 Special on my hip.

'It's Letty. She has heard from the clinic. They have
diagnosed her as HIV positive.'

My immediate reaction was of my family being exposed
to the virus; my brain took over, assuring myself that my fears
were unfounded. The heart seizing control.

'I'm so sorry.' After hugging Rose, I went into our bedroom
to change.

I sat awhile, not wanting to intrude on the gathering. *Ouma*
was organising everybody and everything. Rose held onto Letty
while she discussed the repercussions with the heath expert and
a local Catholic priest who offered counselling.

'Truth is Themba, I didn't want to get involved and cowered in
my bedroom and pretended it wasn't happening.'

'There is no dishonour in that. A natural reaction to things
we do not understand. You are the Chameleon after all, *jaha*.'
Themba dug out his snuffbox from under his shirt and inhaled
a pinch. 'Go on, my friend.'

Letty's decline was slow, but as the months passed, she lost
more and more weight. Cleaning the house became too much
for her and towards the end, she spent a couple of hours a day
just chatting with Chelsea and Rose.

One weekend Rose was watching Chelsea on the trampoline, while she sat next to *Ouma* on the outdoor furniture. I *braaied* a surf and turf of prawns and Texan steak to go with Rose's renowned sweet *pap* — maize meal with condensed milk. A fine blend of smoked, salty, and sweet on the palate.

'*Ouma*?' Rose said to her mother. 'It's time for Letty to stop working.'

'That is true. I don't think she's going to get better.'

I heard them talking, thankful I was behind a screen of smoke and flames.

'It is so sad.' Rose tried to hold back the tears. 'We will have to help her and the family even after she stops working. She needs the money. The government won't help.'

'Bastards.' *Ouma* screwed up her eyes. 'They only look after themselves with their big cars and overseas trips. The povo gets nothing.'

'How will we tell her?' Rose asked.

'She deserves the truth, dear. It is all she has left,' *Ouma* said through the pain.

'Monday?'

'Monday,' *Ouma* confirmed.

Mother and daughter held each other beneath the evening sky, the rhythmical squeak of Chelsea bouncing on the trampoline fused with the birds.

Letty's HIV developed into full-blown AIDS, and without the care and expensive medication, her prognosis was not good. Her family looked after her children and Rose asked me to deliver groceries to her house every week.

'A tough time,' Themba said.

'It was, but for the wrong reasons,' I replied.

'Why so, Mr Rory?' Themba asked.

'The trips to Letty's home in the township were much like the one you and Lucky have shared with me today.'

'I am listening, *jaha*. Let it out.'

I loaded the utility *bakkie* with the first week's groceries for Letty's family and headed for the black township of Vosloorus beyond the city limits. At the final traffic lights, before turning into Vosloorus, a window cleaner squirted a container of water and soap onto my windscreen and wiped it with a squeegee.

'Thanks boss,' he said as I put a two dollar coin into his open hand and drove off before the other street hawkers, pedalling illegal copies of games and DVD's, reached me.

The tarmac ended on entering the township, replaced by dirt roads. The houses no longer two hundred square metre homes on a hectare of land, attended by a gardener and domestic worker. Instead, they were two-room homes like the one you lived in at the bottom of the garden in Wankie. Very little had changed irrespective of who ran the country.

I drove on roads without pavements and the homes devoid of fences, separated by little more than a metre. Not a tree, a flower, or a blade of grass. Dust was everywhere. A cart pulled by a mange-ridden donkey collected items of interest along the streets. Conspicuous by my presence, I wound up the windows and locked the doors of my vehicle.

At Letty's home, her family waited outside and signalled for me to pullover.

'Hello, sir. Thank you so much,' an older man, who I presumed to be her father or uncle, said. He offered me a hand, which I shook and then he helped me with the boxes of groceries. 'We will leave them here. Letty sleeps.' He held a hand above his eyes for shade from the sun. The rest of the group sorted through the goods while others scanned the streets.

'I would invite you for a drink, but these are dangerous times,' the old man said.

'I understand. You will come and visit us when Letty is better?' I said.

'Thank you for what you are doing, sir.'

'My name is Rory, please. I will pass your thanks onto my wife, Rose. It is her wish.'

'Thank you both. Take care and travel safely.' He looked around with unease.

'Let us know how Letty gets on,' I said as I jumped in the pickup and swung back the way I came.

'What are you smiling at?' I asked Themba.

He held a hand to his lips and snickered. 'I mean no

disrespect, Mr Rory. Your feeling in Vosloorus is the way many of us feel in the white suburbs. All the time.'

It had never occurred to me.

'Do not hang your head, *jaha*. There is no shame in your ignorance.'

'Oh yes, there is. How could I have been so blind? So short-sighted?'

'Questions to change the world. Do not regret the past. Embrace it.'

I had nothing. Other than remorse, so continued with the story.

A month later, the old man I met in Vosloorus knocked on our door to tell us Letty had died from pneumonia because of AIDS. We continued to help with groceries. Until it was no longer wanted.

Could we have done more? Without the slightest of doubt.

Should we have done more? It is one of the few misgivings I have in life because we accepted a norm that allowed us a justification not to do so.

Temba lay in silence, his tears dripping to the ground.

Chapter Eighteen

Themba and I watched Lucky wake from his afternoon nap beneath the tree.

'Time for a stretch? Shall we stroll through the park to get rid of the cobwebs?' the old man said as he rubbed an eye.

Lucky smiled and clung to our trouser legs as we ambled over to the swings.

'Do you want to sit on the mat?' Themba asked.

'Yes, Uncle, I'm not strong. Can you tell us about more stories with *ugogo*?'

'Sure, my boy. It will take time for the *muti* the doctor gave you to work.' He cuddled his nephew. 'So, more of your grandmother, then?'

'*Yebo*, I miss my *ugogo*.'

We settled beneath the shade of the jacaranda tree amid the lavender blanket of sweet-smelling petals. I, too, loved to listen to Themba's tales as a child and understood how they benefited Lucky.

Themba cleared his throat. An unmistakable sign he was launching into one of his narrative extravaganzas.

'Are you ready, my family?'

'We sure are, *Malume*,' Lucky said.

The mine-dust tickled Lucky's nostrils. Buckets jangled in the wheelbarrows. Babies coughed in their beds. A car spluttered to life. The ten-year-old wiped the sleep from his eyes, then massaged the dents on his body to ease the pins and needles.

'I wanted to buy a comfy bed and relax for a full week,' Lucky interjected.

'That you did.' Themba resumed with the tale, as he rubbed his nephew's back.

Rats scurried over the rooftops. They leapt the inches between the shacks. A rancid smell of garbage and open sewers turned Lucky's stomach.

'Good morning, my boy.'

Lucky peeped from beneath the blanket and murmured, 'Morning, Gogo.'

'Breakfast is ready.' She warmed the previous night's dinner over a paraffin stove.

'Just one more minute, please?' Lucky asked.

'I missed my ugogo and ukhulu. Still do,' Lucky said.
   'I know, as do I. Now let me finish the tale,' Themba replied.

'Come, son,' his ugogo whispered, stroking his forehead. 'It is time to eat.'

Lucky slid out from under the musty blanket.

'Is there any milk?'

'Enough for your porridge.' She placed a bowl of sweetened maize-meal on a board.

'Eat. You have a long day ahead.'

'Thanks, Gogo.' He leant back against his grandmother, who groomed flecks of dry grass from his cropped hair.

Nearby, a cock crowed, accompanied by a squawk and the sounds of floundering.

'Somebody's having a feast tonight.' The old lady smacked her lips.

'Don't worry, I shall bring food home.' Lucky studied the lines on her weather-beaten face and how prominent her stoop had become of late.

'Will you wear your new shoes today?' she asked.

'No way they'll spoil.' Lucky reached for the canvas trainers hanging from a nail on the wall. 'Thanks, Gogo, they're the best birthday present ever.'

She bent over and returned his embrace.

'A kind-hearted woman, my sister. She was so pleased the two dollars well spent, even if it took her months to pay.' Themba stated the obvious to his modest audience in the gardens before proceeding with the narrative.

Lucky ate breakfast in the doorway as people went about their business. He gazed at the sun rising from behind the gold mine dumps, highlighting the blemishes of erosion.

'Friend.' A neighbour grumbled to him with half a wave.

'Hello.' Lucky greeted him.

The man didn't reply but continued at a downtrodden gait to his dilapidated shack.

Lucky tapped on the rusty steel and pallets that made up the walls of their shelter.

'*Ukhulu* was a great builder. They lived there for a long time, hey Uncle?'

Themba allowed Lucky to share the tale. 'Your grandfather was never afraid of work.'

'Why did he die before I could meet him?'

'That is another story, for a different day, my boy. Shall we continue with this one?'

'Okay.' His nephew lay back.

Lucky poured water from a plastic barrel into a chipped melamine bowl from the corner of the room and splashed his face.

'Be back in time to refill those containers.'

'Sure.' He agreed.

'Here, take bread for lunch,' Ugogo said.

He kissed his grandmother on the fingers and pushed the crusts towards her. 'Don't fret. I will get something there. Have them later with your tea.'

She waved to her grandson, who pranced full of self-importance.

Careful she didn't show her tears. She loved him as her own and rued the day the questions started.

Ugogo picked up a straw broom and swept the intrusive gold dust from the shelter, her arthritis tolerable once more.

Lucky waited at the gates of the municipal dump with his colleagues. Five minutes before the half-hour, a large pork-bellied man lumbered toward them and turned the key in the padlock.

'Morning boss.' The group called out.

'Welcome rodents.' Isaac wolfed an iced bun. 'How are my aliens today?' He reiterated in English.

A few stifled any notion of confronting him.

He held their next meal ticket.

Isaac worked at the municipality, in charge of a dumpsite where townsfolk brought their garbage. He thought of himself as part of the aspiring flock of entrepreneurs. Encouraged by the government.

He had discarded his overalls for chinos and wore the latest flowery shirts sported by the new order dignitaries. Gone were the days when Isaac got his hands dirty or broke into a sweat.

He was now a man of substance.

No-one ever checked up on him, they even paid his wages into his bank account. No mixing with the rank and file except at the annual wage negotiations. He was an ardent supporter of the union.

'Line-up so I can see you.' He barked as he swilled the last of his tea, wiping the dribble from his jowls. 'Come, abalimi — peasants in Xhosa. I don't have time to squander.'

He waved them into a ragged formation and stood in front of each, so no illicit person snuck in. He assigned the children to the adults. Each of whom oversaw a waste skip. Lucky worked with Enos, who urged vehicles to his bin, inspecting the contents and recycling what drew his fancy.

At the end of each day, Isaac took stock of the recouped items and recorded it in his pink notebook. The next day, he paid his team a cut of the spoils.

Five teams, working six days a week, explained his plush office in the old council shed. A three-litre Ford Cortina parked nearby, complete with fluffy dice and a dashboard of shag carpets, testament to his status.

Fridays, Lucky washed his car so he might team-up with Enos.

'Boy?' Enos tapped Lucky on the shoulder. 'Build umlilo and burn plenty of wood, for teatime.' He wiped sweat from his brow with his shirttails.

While Lucky prepared lunch, he checked out Isaac sitting in an armchair on the veranda. He presided over those before him, just as his colonial predecessors did. A station played the kwaito sounds of African house music on a transistor radio. A rickety fan blew.

'Hey, insect, fetch me another Coke.' The tyrant bellowed.

A girl rose from the throng of youths at his feet and hurried to the ice cooler. Her kneecaps threatening to trip her up in her haste she was so slender. Almost emaciated.

'Nanku.' Here you are, she offered in Xhosa, with its wonderful click of the consonant.

'You took your time.' He snatched the drink. 'Now get out of here and take them with you.' He pointed to the children playing amongst the scrap. 'None over the age of eight. Never mind, one day they will be strong enough to offload vehicles,' he said aloud.

The girl crossed the dump site with the other youngsters as instructed when a four-by-four truck hooted, swerved past and covered her in dirt. The driver swore, waving his cell phone out the window at her. She returned to the others and sat by herself, playing with the colourful braids on her head.

'Shame. What is wrong with people?' Lucky couldn't help himself interrupting his uncle's musing.

221

'That Isaac *Mvubu* deserved his name. He was a hippo. One day someone will put them in their place. Maybe it should be me.' Lucky pushed out his chest, scowling. We laughed at the image of Lucky standing up to the bully in the park's sunshine. Themba rubbed the top of his nephew's head and carried on.

Lucky threw tea leaves into the billycan and emptied his pockets of the loot liberated from the cleaned vehicles. He thumbed two copper coins and slipped them into his underpants, then whistled.

Enos acknowledged and sent the team on break.

After the last of the refuge workers returned to duty, Lucky squatted next to Enos, who peered at him from behind his cup. 'You are a good boy, a credit to our people.'

Lucky dropped his eyes. 'There is no need to thank me.'

'That is where you are wrong. It is important we recognise who we are and where we come from. Otherwise, how can we know where to go?'

'Where are we going?' Lucky asked.

'Home, to the land of our ancestors.'

'Okay,' Lucky said, not wanting the others to overhear. He had seen his share of intertribal squabbles. 'I must get back to work.'

Enos nodded and threw the dregs of his drink on the embers.

The dump closed at six o'clock, whereupon the supervisors paid their workers. Enos offered one dollar a day, enough for a loaf or a milk. Most of the coins Lucky gave to his grandmother.

Hungry and tired, he thanked Enos and prepared to leave, eager to make the last payment on his mother's memorial. He trotted home to complete his chores and collect the headstone. He thought of his father.

'I still do *Malume* Themba. Why did father go away? Is he alive? The mines killed *ukhulu wami*; did they kill him too, or

222

was it me, or this sickness?'

'I thought you had spotted me in the background when you were talking to Enos,' Themba distracted his nephew.

'Were you there?' Lucky looked deep into his uncle's eyes. 'I used to have dreams of you being at the dump,' he added.

'Do you think *Ugogo* would let you wander the streets alone?' Themba answered. The young lad lay back without saying a word, annoyed yet pleased with his family.

Themba pulled the frail youngster to him, not losing the flow of the story.

Lucky blinked away tears and blamed them on the thunderstorm coming in over the mine dumps. The cloak of acrid wood smoke shrouding the huts burnt Lucky's lungs. His eyes smarted as he picked his way through the warren of shanties.

'Hi, Gogo, how was your day?'

'Better that you are home.' They hugged, drawing strength from one another. 'Now fetch the water before it gets too dark.'

'Okay. When I get back, I'll have a surprise.'

'Shocks are not good for old women. Get a move on.' She hit his backside, raising a puff of dust.

Lucky loaded the twenty litre jugs into the wheelbarrow that doubled as their dining table. He skipped the frothy streams of sewage; thankful today the detergent masked the stench of human waste. Barefoot, he balanced the empties and wobbled towards the communal tap where he joined the unending queue.

After a brief wait, he turned to the girl behind him.

'Please take care of my things. I need to pick something up over there?' He pointed to the camp's only multi-shack. A ramshackle row of huts with the misspelt words **Funeral Dictator** *painted across them. Profiteers of the pandemic.*

On paying with the coins saved from working at the dump, Lucky found a secluded corner before unwrapping the tissue paper. On a piece of black marble, the letters showed.

Rest in Peace
Mamma Ndlovu.

Unable to read, he understood their meaning. He caressed the chiselled inscription and whispered, 'We are the elephant in our name, Ndlovu. Noble giants who never forget.' He clasped the stone to his chest and re-joined the water line.

'Thank you for keeping my place.' She reminded him of the girl, Thando, from the dump — undernourished and modest.

Lucky filled his bottles by the glow of the streetlight and the flash of headlights from the motorway, then pushed his barrow off home.

'What you did isn't wrong, but you must consider your future. Your mother wouldn't want you to spend money on her in such a way.'

'But Gogo...'

'I know, son, but those are my thoughts.' Her hand shook as she lit a candle stub.

He re-wrapped the shrine and tucked it under his pillow.

That night he cuddled the stone as a storm lashed the trees and threatened the crude walls of the hut. He slept to the rise of rainwater rushing through the ramshackle village.

The sound of coughing.

Always the coughing.

It reminded him of his mother.

The rain brought a fresh dawn.

Lucky sucked in the freshness, hurrying to work.

Cars honked, crows rattled and clicked, people chattered, revitalised after the dry months of winter.

'Morning.' He greeted Enos.

'It is a good morning. At least the air is clean.'

'Where's Isaac?'

Enos shrugged. 'Innocent is in charge today.'

'It will be a good day; He is a gentleman.' Lucky grinned.

The vehicles arrived earlier than usual and didn't stop until lunchtime, thanks to the rains.

Lucky lit the fire, then went to fetch bread from the office, where he found the other children.

'What's the excitement?'

'It's Thando's birthday.' They clapped.

'Happy birthday. How many years?' Lucky asked.

She raised seven fingers.

'Thando.' Lucky mouthed her Xhosa name. 'Love.' He translated. 'Hope you have a wonderful day.' He flashed her a smile.

'Join me?' Enos showed Innocent a place next to him at the fire as they watched the kids across the yard. Innocent patted his hands in thanks and shaped his impressive afro and chose a seat. Lucky got up and prepared another mug, all fingers, and thumbs, whilst gawking at the gold chains around Innocent's neck and wrists. His mock Ray Ban teardrop sunglasses hanging from his t-shirt collar: a rare occasion when the boss sat with the workers.

'Young man?' Innocent waved to the youngster. 'Get me another pack of cigarettes on the table, then leave us to smoke.' He crumpled the finished box he pulled from under his short sleeve.

Lucky rested beneath the trees where Isaac's car stood and observed the children fuss around the birthday girl.

'I choose a party with enough sweets and cake to make me sick,' said one, giggling.

'Pretty clothes,' another chipped in.

'Fizzy cool drinks?'

'Lots of dancing?'

'What's your dream, Thando?' The circle of kids listened.

Thando looked skyward and held her hands under her chin and said, 'A doll to love.'

The hooter sounded, signalling the start of work.

Thando's words haunted Lucky through the day.

At the end of the shift, Enos paid him his full wage of a dollar even though he left early and asked, 'What is it you seek?'

'No-one.' Lucky scanned the surroundings to avert eye contact.

'She has gone.'

'Who has gone?' Lucky blushed.

'Your little friend.'

'Thando?'

'Yebo, Thando. They must be back before three.'

'They? Back? Where?'

'The safe-house, where the orphans live.' Enos pointed to a red brick house across the road.

Lucky collected his parcel from the office and bid farewell to his colleagues.

'How do you know what I was thinking?' Lucky asked, tapping Themba's leg.

'You spent the day staring into the distance and daydreaming,' Themba answered with a teasing voice continuing, 'I've not seen you do that before or since, so it must be because of a girl.'

Lucky shook his head and shut his eyes and waved his uncle on with the story, a slight grin on his lips.

The trip to the cemetery took an hour, yet my nephew trotted the entire way. He clutched his package, getting heavier by the minute.

Lucky pushed through a hole in the fence to avoid the tedious walk to the entrance and scurried to his mum's place of rest.

A once white, ant-eaten cross marked the mound of his mother's grave. He sank to his knees and removed the winter debris and combed a pattern in the red earth with his fingers. He placed the headstone, sprinkling it with a handful of soil.

'What are you doing?'

Lucky spun around to find Thando with her pigtails tied with coloured beads and a posy of wildflowers. Her light brown face glowed with smooth skin and a slight smile.

'Is this your mother?'

He nodded.

'Did she die from the big sickness?'

'Yes, AIDS.'

Thando laid the flowers at his mother's feet. 'Should we sit?'

She took his hand and sat on a burnt tuft of grass. Green shoots reappearing after the ravages of the winter fires. Unable to trust himself to talk, he listened to her sing in an unfamiliar tongue.

Sweet tunes carried him to his place of warm remembrances before the AIDS pandemic.

A rumble of thunder brought Lucky back to reality. 'Time to go.'

'Come, I will walk with you,' *she brushed herself off.*

The two ambled in silence, comfortable in each other's company.

Before reaching the orphanage, a hawker sat in her rags for clothes on the street corner selling sweets, toys, and over-ripe fruit on upturned milk crates. Her face so covered in wrinkles Lucky could not tell if she was alive, let alone awake.

'Push the button. I will catch up with you just now,' *Lucky said to Thando, who ran up to the pedestrian crossing and pressed the green light.*

Lucky faced the seller, fumbling inside his pants.

He caught up with Thando and handed her a four-inch doll still in its box, 'happy birthday.'

He dropped her off at her gate and walked home with a bounce in his step.

'Ugogo and I can wait longer to buy that extra blanket,' *he spoke to the birds in the trees.*

'Can I get a drink from that thing?' Lucky asked from the comfort of his blanket in the park.

'What thing? That is a fountain. Of course, you can, son. Do you want help?' Themba replied.

'No thanks, *Malume*. I will try on my own. I feel better.' Lucky got to his feet and shuffled to the drink reservoir.

'I know why you told that story,' I said to Themba.

'You do?'

'It relates to Letty.'

'Yes, Mr Rory. It does. Illness, pain, suffering, and poverty have no boundaries.'

'You are a good man, Themba. I'm honoured to be your friend.'

'And I yours, Chameleon. And I yours.'

Lucky hobbled back onto the rug. 'Did you see me, Uncle?'

'I did. You made us proud, Lucky Ndlovu.'

Lucky gave him a look and there was no elephant phrase to follow.

'Do you want me to continue?'

'*Yebo, Malume*. This is such fun.'

After ugogo and Lucky Ndlovu ate that evening, he slipped out to see what the men were doing. He clasped his arms around his chest as if shivering at the images contorted in the firelight — on weekends; they reminisced about the days of plenty of rain and fulfilment. Of despair and ill health. Ghoulish eyes and hollowed cheeks. Alabaster teeth reflected in the new moon and heads bobbed in unison. In their grim expressions, I think Lucky saw his own heartache and loss. He pulled back into the recesses of the night shadows. A spiral of sparks spat and silenced the crowd. He loved to hear the tales of the elders.

'*Lucky? Lucky, what are you doing here?*' The deep-throated voice of his grandmother called. '*How many times must I tell you to stay away?*' The commotion reduced the fireside revellers to wails of laughter.

'*But Gogo...*'

'*Don't, but Gogo me. Leave the men in peace. They don't want children here.*'

'But tonight, is special, Gogo. Uncle has promised to talk of the old country.'

She stopped and hugged her grandson tighter than usual. 'Yes, my boy, your uncle is a fine man.'

'Do you see how respected I am?' Themba smirked at his audience, then resumed.

'So, can I listen?' Lucky's eyes settled on his grandmother.

Her face hardened as she glowered at the men. 'It is not a place for you. It's only romantic fools and drunks who dream of what was once.' She hustled the boy back to their lean-to.

Lucky stood at the entrance and peered into the night. 'I hoped he might mention my father,' Lucky said.

His grandmother scrubbed harder, despite the pain in her joints.

Lucky stood on tiptoes on top of a bucket so he could see the party in the distance. A constellation of fires flickered, highlighting similar social events. The mine-dump glowed from the motorway lights, filtered by the maze of dilapidated shacks.

Lucky glanced at the old lady, who was staring at him. Her head to one side, and her eyes were brimming. 'Go. You will not rest until you do. But stay out of sight. The men will kick your skinny arse if they catch you,' she said, flicking a tea towel at him and turned up the paraffin light, reaching for her dog-eared Bible before she indulged in her evening ritual.

'Thanks, Gogo.' He squeezed her neck and kissed her soft cheek. 'I won't shame you' He clenched his fingers into a claw. 'I'll be a leopard. No one shall know I am there.'

'Go before I change my mind.' Ugogo smiled broadly, a smile made bigger by the lack of teeth. 'Go, my child,' she said to the empty room.

Lucky crept as close as he dared to the bonfire and by the time he settled, a lone figure in the dimness greeted the men. 'Salibonane.' The group clapped their hands, as custom dictated, yet remained seated. To stand was a cultural insult, viewed as a challenge to the visitor.

'Good evening,' one said in English to impress his peers.

'Ngiyabonga,' I thanked them. 'I hope your reference to an old bull reflects my stature and not my tales.' I chortled and took a seat. I nodded to each; my wizened eyes locked with theirs. 'Please call me by my name.' I raised my head and straightened.

'Themba. The one my mother gave me.'

After the pleasantries, they offered me a fresh quart of beer. Life weary, I lifted a shaky hand. 'I will take in a cup, thank you.'

'Baba.' The man used the title, Father, as a mark of esteem.

'Lucky? Fetch a mug,' I called, knowing full well the little devil was hiding nearby.

Lucky scurried to the hut and searched in the zinc bath for one without a chip. The noise woke his granny, who snored with her head backwards in her deck chair, a book clasped to her chest. 'What's going on...?' she asked.

'A cup for the uncle.'

'Why didn't you ask?' She struggled to her feet. 'Take this with you. The night air has a bite to it, and your uncle is no spring chicken. Even if they call him old bull.'

Lucky ran back and gave his now adult cousin Sipho the mug and wrapped the blanket around my shoulders. I clasped his forearm. Lucky looked up into my watery eyes.

'You are kind to an old man, thank you.'

'That's okay, Gogo asked me to bring it to you.'

I rubbed my bristled chin. 'She is an angel.'

Lucky acknowledged the remark, sat beside me, and faced the group, who by now were feeling the effects of the alcohol.

'Will you stay to hear me talk?' I asked.

Lucky, unsure what to make of my question, sat in silence.

I rose and addressed the gathering. 'Are there any objections to this young man joining us?' I shot a glance at my son Sipho, who hid his protestation behind a fake cough.

'Come now, Baba. Let us begin ahead of the sun rising,' a neighbour said using the term of endearment. The others nodded and sipped their beer.

'A sip, to wet old lips.' I said, delighted at the prospect of a drink.

The rest sniggered and quipped about the luxuries of age.

I raised both arms for dramatic effect, cleared my throat and hummed in a baritone.

Lucky giggled into the softness of the mat. 'Here we go again,' he said, and we laughed, enjoying the warm weather, the company, and the KFC.

'Sipho is here in South Africa as well?' I asked.

'No, my friend. I know not where he is. I lost him many years ago,' Themba replied and offered nothing more before he continued.

I opened the indaba in a whisper, the crackle of the fire the only sound. Expectant faces watched. 'Thirty years have passed. It began earlier, around the time we felt the effects.' I studied the sombre expressions before me. 'We presume we know how the journey ends, but those who assume it is here in Umgodi Squatter Camp, Johannesburg, are mistaken.'

I paused for my words to sink in before I beckoned them once more. 'Listen.' I gazed into the darkness. 'Listen, my children,' I repeated. 'We must take hope from our past if we are to have a future.'

Lucky watched me transfix the audience. In this, he caught glimpses of his parents, aware of the sickness that claimed them. The gaunt skulls, eyes that wept, and the rattle of the cough. Regular callers to his nightmares. He snuggled closer to me. A sense of warmth and safety engulfed him as he listened to my voice.

'A time of plenty, when everyone worked, and a dollar lasted a

231

week. With cash left over to buy snuff and a drink.'

Sipho stood up and waved his beer from across the fire. 'You speak of pleasurable times, old man, when we fought for our freedom?' The crowd hushed. A few nodded, others shuffled their feet in the dust.

Lucky sat up at his cousin's provocation.

I tucked the boy under my arm, and to the relief of the small party, smiled at the heckler. 'You are right. It was a bitter fight and full of hardship. But do not judge my words until you hear them. Let me ask a question. Do you consider your country free today?' I waited for their answer, but nothing. 'We each have the vote. The Colonials have gone. Are things any better? Why are we squatters living here in the imijondolo — slums?'

I took another swig of my beer and put my head to one side.

'What is it, Old Bull?' someone asked, over the sirens and flashing blue lights. Lucky's cousin jumped up and placed a large drum over the fire before he dodged out of sight with the others.

'Duck.' Lucky pulled at my elbow.

'It is those who have done wrong who have reason to hide.' I gave the uneasy men hiding in the shadows a stare of defiance. The screech of brakes and gunfire persuaded me otherwise. 'Perhaps this is not the moment.'

The night held its collective breath and the muffled spit of the fire and the clicks of the hot tin drum broke the silence. More sirens, this time red lights.

Lucky peered from behind the rocks. Strange shadows out of the corner of his eye disappeared without a trace.

'Did you notice that?' Lucky shook my shoulder. 'Someone is sneaking through the shacks?'

'Your head plays tricks on you.' I answered.

A man removed the drum from the fire to mark an end to the tension. 'Another beer, madoda — gentlemen?'

I held up my hands. 'Thank you, but I'm tired.'

'I will walk you to your room.' Lucky offered and took my hand.

'Why praise you. Lisale kuhle.'

'Sleep well, Old Bull.' The rest chorused.

Discontent permeated the air and unease floated amongst the dust-filled atmosphere of the shantytown.

Themba looked down at his nephew asleep on the rug beneath the trees, a slight breeze caught his face. He laid back his head and closed his eyes in contentment.

Chapter Nineteen

By late afternoon, just as Themba and Lucky were waking from a short doze in the park's tranquillity, I suggested it was time to make a move.

'No Rory, please can we share one further story?' Lucky asked.

Themba raised his eyebrows at me. 'Of course, my son.'

'I thought we just did?'

'One more, Rory. One more.' Lucky put on a face.

'Okay then.' I winked at Themba.

The dawn stirrings of Umgodi (the Hole) Squatter Camp roused Lucky from a deep yet disturbed slumber. The previous day spent with me played in his mind.

He listened to the fuss of mothers waking their households and the convoy of laden wheelbarrows.

That ever-present cough.

Lucky eased open the door, careful not to disturb his grandmother. With a battered kettle in hand, he headed to last night's fire. He revived the embers, stretched, and yawned out aloud. The air tasted of the Blue Gum trees.

He mined the sleep from his eyes as he ran the cool golden dust through his toes. The lad dozed to the wild doves and stirred to the boiling water on the coals.

A mist of fresh brew steamed his face from the kettle as he filled the baked-bean tin he used as a mug.

'Gogo? Gogo? Here is your tea.' He shook her until she lifted her head. 'I will fetch water before the line is too long.'

She nodded, still groggy.

Lucky loaded the wheelbarrow and wobbled on his way. He negotiated the heavy erosion around the single pump, which serviced thousands of families.

'There is no-one here,' he muttered, filling the containers. 'Let me have a wash before anyone else arrives.' The water was softer than the bottled version as he splashed it over his face and torso. He cleaned his teeth with the beaten fibres of a twig sitting upon a boulder which gave him a view of the busy road.

Mini-bus taxis skidded and blew their horns to attract custom. Doors slid open and slammed shut as people clambered. Over-revved engines howled and puffed smoke. It was the commuter's only form of transportation; to work, the shops, or church. They hurtled travellers back and forth in their greed to squeeze in as many trips as possible.

Passengers stared out from the squalid windows of a battered VW Microbus as it swerved to a stop before him. Overloaded, the rust bucket crammed in a few more sardines. Then groaned away with its bald tyres slipping on the gravel kerb.

A taxi pulled up behind the wreck. It sported a trendy advertisement that suggested things go better when you drank their cola. He thought he caught sight of a figure watching him from amongst the shacks.

'That was a close one. I ducked out of the way and made matters worse because I couldn't find you for a while.' Themba laughed.

'That will teach you to follow me.' Lucky feigned anger.

'It was explaining to *ugogo* that I didn't know your whereabouts — that was scary.' Themba said, then resumed.

Later that day and with his chores completed; Lucky headed to my place.

A decrepit single room built of grey weathered crates stood higher up the mine-dump to one side from the rest of the hovels. The position implied the dweller was a social outcast with a psychological or physical affliction. The shanty town, thought I, Themba, the Old Bull, uncle to Lucky Ndlovu, fell within the two categories. It suited my purpose, and I played on the idea

235

for the peace it offered.

Lucky tapped on the garden gate, which held up the rusty chicken-wire fence at the front of his uncle's house. A vegetable patch of limp spinach grew in one corner.

'Uncle, are you awake?'

'Morning.' I emerged, rubbing my chest. 'What a wonderful day. Come in, come in, I overslept,' I lied. 'Make us a fire and let's have tea.'

'Did you sleep in your clothes again?' Lucky asked.

I looked down at what I was wearing and couldn't come up with a better excuse other than agree with my nephew. He mustn't know I was shadowing him wherever he went.

'I've brought pap from last night,' Lucky said, changing the subject somewhat suspicious by my behaviour.

'Hah, a king's feast. Warm it up next to the water.' I performed a rheumatic jig back into the house.

Lucky giggled. 'I have the best uncle.'

'Today we will have a fine debate. Not of tribal stories, but of need,' I said from in the room.

'Really?' Lucky prepared the fire, full of self-importance.

He uncovered my secret stash of kindling from between the fence and vegetable patch. The scarcity of firewood called for lengthy journeys away from the ballooning makeshift metropolis.

'Come in Lucky, take a seat.' The boy sat on the cowhide, his eyes unaccustomed to the interior.

I had decorated the house with sheets of newspaper and magazines. The earthen floor shone as if bee waxed. In one corner, a mattress displayed its springs. A stained pillow and speckled grey blanket lay folded at one end.

In the opposite corner, a primus stove sat on a beer crate, along with two enamel pots and a chipped teacup. A transistor radio with a wire coat hanger for an aerial crackled and faded whenever Lucky got too close.

'I have got you a treat.' I stuck my finger in the air. 'Now, where did I put it?' I came out of the gloom with a half-bottle of cola.

Lucky twisted the cap and drank the tepid sweetness without its fizz.

'Thank you.' He browsed the walls of my home. 'There is plenty of old stuff in here.'

'Tell me, my child.' I sat beside Lucky and prised open a well-worn tin of snuff. 'To what things do you refer?' I sniffed the powder which made me hack. 'Use more than your eyes,' I said to Lucky.

They smarted from the tobacco.

'A carving.' He pointed to a soapstone statue of a man smoking a calabash.

'Tablecloth.' A frayed crocheted cloth lay across the cardboard box of a table.

I closed my eyes in agreement.

Lucky scoured the room once more, making sure he had missed nothing when he came across a Quality Street tin.

'What's in the tin?' he asked.

'Bits and pieces, I hold dear.'

'Like what?'

I lifted the lid.

'Wow, Uncle. Who are those people?'

'This is your mother and father.'

Lucky took the black-and-white photo and held it to his heart.

'That is u-anti, my wife,' I said and did the same, then got to my feet and paused at the door. 'Memories, my son, are not objects of financial value. They are far more valuable.'

'That's better.' Lucky heard me return from washing my face in a bowel of water. 'Shall we take a walk?'

'Aren't you going to tell me?' Lucky asked.

'What about? Your grandparents?'

237

'No, the things on the wall?'

'No sun ever sets without its histories,' I whispered to my dear nephew, throwing an arm over his shoulders.

'Huh?' Lucky asked.

I gave the boy a gentle shake. 'Do not worry, I will explain. We shall not wander today for pleasure alone.'

We took a stroll through the slums that were our home.

Lucky waved to the kids who fooled around in a scrapped vehicles.

'Come Ndlovu, we are going to Durban.' They yelled from the shell of a bus. The chauffeur, hat over his eyes, hung his arm out the door.

'Not today. I have important business with my uncle.'

The driver gave Lucky a thumbs-up, dropped a pair of sunglasses from his head and drove off to an imaginary destination.

Further along, we stopped to chat with a group of women washing their clothes in the waters of a nearby stream. Its banks stripped of fauna by the heavy metals of the gold mines. It caked the water in scum from the waste created by the village, for there were no public services to deal with dirty water and waste.

'Let's rest here by Rosie's.' I wiped the perspiration from my trilby and sat in one of the plastic chairs.

Mamma Rosie's Shebeen. *A notorious drinking hole by night. By day she sold food, refusing to serve liquor until the evening.*

The blackboard menu read, pap and stew $3.00, sausage in a roll $1.00. Bunny chow $4.

'You have brought a friend with you?' Rosie appeared from behind the barbeque smoke.

'This is Lucky Ndlovu.'

She acknowledged the boy as she moved closer and said, 'what can I get you, old man?'

I could see that Lucky took an instant dislike as he studied her bloated face. Her piggy eyes and streaked hair reminded him of an anteater.

'Two glasses of icy water, please,' I ordered in a stately voice.

Rosie threw her tuck shop arms skyward and shrilled, 'last of the big spenders, hey?'

I didn't blink. 'If my money isn't good enough, we will find somewhere else to go.'

She stroked my shoulder and glanced at Lucky. 'Stay. It's not often we get royalty.' She disappeared into the tavern and returned with two cracked tumblers of water, chilled by a portable gas cooler.

I dug into my trouser pocket and fetched a handkerchief and gave Mamma Rosie a ten-cent piece.

'Kuyajabulisa,' I toasted, swallowing the contents in a gulp, and slamming the glass on the plastic table. 'Come, my little warrior, we are not welcome here.'

'But why?' Asked Lucky.

'There are those who see us as strange.'

'I don't see any abelungu — white people?'

'Colour is the least of our troubles. We will discuss the venture on our return. Now let's be on our way.' I said.

The harmony of choral singing attracted my nephew's attention to a clump of Blue Gums where he spotted worshippers. Each assembly wore different apparel, red cloaks, blue cloaks with white aprons and crosses embroidered across the front.

'What are they doing? Why do they dress so funny?' Lucky asked.

'They are the Pentecost's, Apostolic or Zionists, who believe in the Christian one-God worship but include the African ancestral spirits.'

Lucky swayed to the rhythm. 'Why are they always so happy, Uncle? What do they do?'

'A good question. Why do you ask?'

Lucky shrugged. 'They are never around except on Sundays.'

I shook my head in amazement at this young boy's mature grasp of the world. 'Shall we continue?'

We picked our way through the homes engulfed by the mine-dump. The sludge encroaching by the day.

'Duck.'

'Watch your step.'

'Careful the hole.' Lucky guided me as if I were an old man.

'Where to now?' He screwed his nose up at the lunchtime aromas of boiled cabbage and offal.

I looked around and stopped alongside the major road on the outskirts of the squatter camp.

'Look, Uncle,' Lucky pointed to the commotion near the taxi rank. 'Can we go there, please?'

I chose not to answer. I took the boy's hand and dodged the suicidal taxis until we reached the open-air commercial hub of the village.

Beneath shelters of poles and thatch, merchants plied their trade. Fruit, vegetable, sweets, cigarettes, and dry goods.

'Come, we must pass over the road,' I said, grabbing Lucky's arm.

'Why must we cross here?'

'To avoid that place.'

'What is going on there?' Lucky asked.

I stopped before answering, 'promise never to go there.'

Lucky looked up at me. 'Okay.' He had not seen me this serious. He watched as people across the street laughed and danced to the kwaito music.

I squeezed the ten-year-old's hand. 'Great from a distance, maybe. No good ever comes from such places. It is the curse of the poor and the weak.'

Lucky glanced over his shoulder at the shebeen, at the strange behaviour and ear-splitting din.

An old man, for perhaps that is what I am, and a young boy dodged the frenetic taxis, loaded trucks and luxury sedans oblivious of their surrounds.

'Where are we going? Ugogo said I mustn't cross this street.'

I ignored him and went on into the industrial park and said, 'I need you to remember what I show you today.'

'What do you mean?'

'Keep your questions until later. Then this will make sense.'

'Okay, Uncle.' Lucky skipped and held my hand.

Chimneys steamed and hissed. Sirens wailed, people shouted and whistled. Vehicles roared and hooted.

'Let's rest under that tree.' I stopped in a small park, an island retreat amid the industry.

Grateful for the shade, we rested on the grass with our backs up against the trunk.

Through the heat haze, Lucky watched a woman dressed in red and white trousers ring a bell, doing brisk business as workers bought from her frosty cart.

His mouth watered at the sight of the smoking ice lollies.

'We will get something closer to lunch,' I promised. How I would love to buy my nephew that ice-cream and everything he deserved.

Lucky amused himself and viewed the trade until I woke from a brief nap.

'How do you feel, Uncle?'

'I'm not asleep. Just wondering to myself,' I answered and sat upright.

'Old age does not announce itself,' Lucky finished the Zulu proverb, then hugged me. 'You are not old to me. It's time for ...' A loud hooter drowned out Lucky's voice. He clasped his ears and pulled a face.

'Is that the noise we hear every day?' he asked after it quietened.

I acknowledged. 'Twelve o'clock each day. This is what I want to show you.' I side-tracked my nephew to the labourers who spilt from the factories.

Lucky sidled up to me as I chuckled. 'Don't worry. They are only taking lunch.'

'Look at the different overalls the workers wear.'

I nodded and said, 'yes, but which colour is more dominant? The shade of their clothes or their skin?' I waited a moment for the information to sink in. 'Do not judge others by your own imperfections and shortcomings. See good at what you do and never stop dreaming.'

'Yes,' Lucky murmured under his breath, afraid of what the future held, considering the age of his ugogo and uncle.

'You are warning me of a life to come.' Lucky peered up at me, who nodded. 'To do what is right. No matter the cost.'

'Yes, Lucky Ndlovu. For you alone will live with every decision you make. But enough for one day, young man. Take this old man home,' I asked.

Lucky puffed out his chest, accepting the laurel from his elder.

A breeze picked up as the sun dipped, diverting Themba from his chronicles.

I hoisted the sleeping Lucky as Themba rolled up the rug and packed our things under his arms. He rested in the back seat with Lucky's head resting on his lap. We drove to the hospital in silence, lost in our thoughts.

Homeward bound, it was time for us to face the reality of where Lucky and Themba might live after hospitalisation.

'You are both welcome to stay on our property,' I said. 'We have a week to give it a lick of paint and refurbish it. There is both hot and cold water.'

Themba sat in the passenger seat, staring through the windscreen, but didn't answer.

'It is not a time for pride, Themba. It's the least I can do after what you have done for me and my parents.' I let it rest for a few kilometres, then tried again.

'You know, it makes sense,' I said in a faint voice.

Themba nodded. 'You are right, Mr Rory, but I do it for Lucky, not myself.'

'I understand. Thank you for your consideration.' We smiled at one another. Aware of what I did not say.

'Right home it is, then. We'll pick up your stuff from the town hall.'

'That sounds good. I will do chores to pay my way. I can paint, garden, even cook if you need,' Themba said.

'That you can, but Lucky will be our priority.'

'Thank you, my son. It fills my heart with both sorrow and joy.' Themba touched my wrist as I held the gear shift. 'Thank you, *jaha.*'

'It is I who should thank you.' We chuckled at the same words spoken but by the other decades earlier. A calmness filled the car. My stomach cramped and my head swam. Life was to serve another challenge. A familiar foreboding of life in Africa returned.

Chapter Twenty

We spent the week sprucing up the two-bedroom bedsit that years earlier had been the servant's quarters to a privileged minority based on ethnicity. Themba, the technician, I the gofer. We drove out to the hospital across the city every afternoon to make sure Lucky's recovery continued. Themba insisted he slept on-site with meals brought out to him and his nephew — comfortable in their own company. I joined them as often as commitments allowed. Weekends, we sat around a fire telling stories and swigging beer. Lucky progressed, but his mental anguish proved more complex.

Themba and I self-indulged at every opportunity. We spoke of world issues, of politics, human behaviour, ancestors, and legacies. There was nothing for which we didn't have an answer. I raised the subject of moving to safer climes in a first world environ.

'You do as you see fit, Mr Rory. Everyone makes their own decisions on what is good for the family. A man without a household is no-one.' Themba stared into the bottom of his bottle. 'It's not a simple choice, but we must make it. You have that experience. Where do you intend to go?'

'I am thinking of returning to the UK, although my heart is not in it.'

'What does the family say?'

'They are supportive, but not keen on the move.'

'Whom am I to judge you, my friend? For I have done the same. Zimbabwe to South Africa and Zambia to Rhodesia as a child. My decisions were not popular, but they were correct.'

'It will take time. So, let's not worry, hey?' I said to my old-time friend. 'Instead, what say you we light a bonfire and have a *braai*? I'll bring the meat and beer. You cook the *pap* and gravy?'

Themba's face lit. 'Do you have *sadza*, *pap*, or must I buy it?'

'I'll get just in case.'

'Shall we invite the family?' Themba asked.

'We'll celebrate Lucky's birthday and his return to good health.'

'*Nkosi sikelela* Lucky.' Themba became choked with tears and sang the South African national anthem, replacing the word Africa with Lucky.

'Beautiful, Themba. May the Gods bless, Lucky. Let us make it a party worthy of the moment.'

'Straight to God's ears, so it shall be. Enough of our small talk. We have important work to do, sir.' Themba adjusted his trilby and shuffled towards the garden gate. 'Where are those street sellers when you need them?' He waved his walking stick above his head Chaplin style.

The *braai* was a wonderful affair. A forty-four-gallon drum cut in half and mounted on steel legs sizzled an array of sausages, steaks, chops, chicken, sweetcorn, and *roosterkoek*. Homemade breads roasted over the fire. A three-legged, cast-iron pot known as a *potjie* boiled on the edges of the bonfire, with layer upon layer of cubed lamb, small carrots, baby potatoes and chopped onions. Themba safeguarded his recipe using turmeric, curry powder, sugar, milk, condiments, and lashings of red wine.

The sky higher than ever. The Milky Way flowed through the darkness, collecting lustrous stars. We sat on the Kikuyu grass sipping lager and Nederburg Riesling from Cape Town. A bottle of twenty-year-old KWV brandy stood in wait for the more *philosophical* debate later in the evening. Time stood still as we forgot our woes and enjoyed those in our company, told jokes and sang our favourite songs. All was pure, the light, the voices, the air, the animals, and the resolve.

This was my Africa at her finest when her people lived as one.

In the wee hours of the next morning, Themba and I sat in front of the dying embers, smoking cigars. The families had long since retreated.

'What will be your memories of South Africa?' Themba asked in a quiet voice.

'You and…'

'No, not that. I mean the country?' He scrutinised me.

I slumped my shoulders. 'There are many. I hoped it might be my home forever.'

Themba nodded and drew on his cigar. The glow of the tip lit up his expression. 'I'm listening.'

'I thought everyone would follow Madiba. That he could be the change Africa needed.' I rubbed my eyes with my palms. 'I shall never forget the 24 June 1995 at Ellis Park when I attended the rugby world cup final. Although the game was enjoyable. It was the day I fell in love with this country.'

'I'm told it was quite a day.' Themba savoured the brandy.

'It was more than that.' I raised my eyebrows.

'Tell me more.'

'The crowd was excited at the prospects of the Springboks in a final with the All Blacks, the South African's sang a rousing rendition of *Shosholoza*.'

'Ha, that old song. It came here from Rhodesia with the migrant miners,' Themba said.

'I didn't know that.'

'Sorry, Rory, go on, please.'

'The entire atmosphere changed when Nelson Mandela walked onto the field dressed in green and gold and waved to the crowd.' I caught my breath. 'Sixty thousand people of every ethnicity erupted, singing, and cheering his name — *Madiba. Madiba.*'

We sat in silence, contemplating the occasion and the events after that day.

'It was the birth of the Rainbow Nation. The win helped, but the enthusiasm, freedom and wellbeing spilt into the streets. Everybody, and I mean everybody, celebrated not just for winning the game but with the realisation of something special.'

'A chance?' Themba asked.

'To celebrate our differences as one. To show Africa that everyone's Africa was possible, that there was a better way and prove to the world we could stand on our own, together.'

Themba rubbed his knees to ease the stiffness from sitting for too long. 'Where do we find ourselves today?' He stood and raised his arms to the heavens, then bent forward and sang in a deep baritone, his feet and hands portraying the train's movement.

Shosholoza — Go forward

Kulezo ntaba — From those mountains

Stimela siphume South Africa — On this train from South Africa

Shosholoza — Go forward

Kulezo ntaba — You are running away.

Stimela siphume South Africa — On this train from South Africa

Wen' uyabaleka — We are running away.

Kulezo ntaba — From those mountains

Stimela siphume South Africa — On this train from South Africa

I remained silent; my heart broken knowing that I was losing my only friend. The dawn broke from behind the mine dumps and the scaffold silhouettes of the drill heads penetrated the horizon. Without another word, we hugged and called it a night.

Months later, because I hadn't seen Themba all day, I strolled over to their rooms at the end of the yard. The doors stood ajar, so I pushed them open. Both rooms were bare.

On the windowsill, a chameleon carved in soapstone sat on top of a folded piece of paper. Relieved there was no foul play, because home invasions continued to be endemic, I stared at the note while I caressed the smooth sculpture.

Please let them be okay.

I lifted the chameleon and unfolded the paper. Themba's familiar scrawl filled me with flashes of boarding school.

Salibonani my son.

I have taken Lucky back to his family in the north.

We found a place on the bus. It will drop us off before we reach the border.

From there, we shall walk the rest of the way.

My legs buckled, and I sank to my knees.

You and I must do what is right for our family.

I shall tell Lucky of our friendship.

By the time we arrive home, the Ndlovu's will forever speak your name.

My heart no longer feels pain, for it is beyond repair.

Before I rest with my ancestors,

I must do this for Lucky.

Uhumbe kuhle, my son,

Usale kuhle, Chameleon.

Never have I not had the courage. Until now.

Forgive me for not having the strength to say goodbye to you in person.

Otherwise, I could never leave.

I am Themba Dube and must live up to my name of Hope and the fearless zebra.

'*Lisala kahle baba.*'

I curled up on the floor and sobbed.

'Goodbye, My Father,' I cried aloud. The ten-year-old boy within me fought his way to the surface. I wept again for myself, for my household, my friends, my Africa, and the world until my face ached and my chest threatened to collapse in on itself. I turned and lay spreadeagled on the cool cement as I stared up at a spider building its web in a corner. Themba's gift stood on the windowsill — one eye on me, sprawled on the ground, the other stared into the distance — its mouth was open, ready to devour an insect.

I collected my thoughts and composed myself. It was time. When nothing keeps you or holds your heart, it's time to seek a place you call home. Where you are welcome and can live without fear and rage. Somewhere, the family will thrive and be free to choose what they wish. This is my second goodbye to Africa — vumani Afrika.

I needed to find a haven for my family and generations thereafter, so they had a choice in life. I took a speculative trip to New Zealand — *Aotearoa* — the *Land of the Long White Cloud*, about which I knew little. Reconnecting with my old acquaintance I knew of, but was not close friends with, from boarding school thirty years after leaving Plumtree. Such were the bonds that endured the test of time and distance.

The twenty-seven-hour flight from Johannesburg flew via Dubai and Sydney, before landing in Auckland. The City of Sails. A four-day turnaround to the other side of the world followed. Of regular online meetings with human resources, company directors, and psychological testing added to my fatigue. Joyful at a fresh start, yet mixed with despair at leaving my beloved Africa. Proud to help my family.

Customs and immigration were a jaw dropping surprise of professional etiquette, empathy and humour that roused my suspicions that something unique, beyond my understanding, was taking place. My old school friend met me as I emerged from the sliding doors and the hounds sniffing for illegal merchandise. He had not changed other than more weight and grey hair. We chatted about boarding school, who we were still in contact with, and the whereabouts of those we hadn't kept in touch with until the highway showed the Auckland skyline.

'Rory, are you okay, mate?' He nudged me, following my gaze. 'Amazing, hey?'

Although my mouth moved, I couldn't utter a word.

'It's okay, buddy, relax and enjoy,' he said as he wound down the windows and drove in the slow lane.

***

After a whirlwind of interviews, role plays, and analysis, I accepted the management position. The deal signed, sealed, and delivered, which included the bonus of a residence visa within two years. Rose and I cried together via Skype. This time with relief — it was beyond our wildest expectations and dreams. We stood a chance.

The next day, I looked around Auckland and boarded a ferry for a scenic trip across the harbour to Devonport. I climbed onto the top deck. The sky was blue, the ocean a deep green, and I had a fantastic chance to see the landscape. A seagull flying above banked to one side and headed in the opposite direction. I followed her flight and there in front of me was another view of the Auckland skyline. A sense of wellbeing from deep within engulfed me. I spent the day on the boat, back and forth across the Auckland harbour, planning how best to move the family.

I had the job. Now what?

I decided upon the Band-Aid technique. Short and sharp, but best in the long term. My thoughts turned to Themba and his bravery to travel without transport. His courage to face the unknown and his faith to seek pity on those he'd never met. Our journey, by comparison, was a doddle.

I purchased a cold drink, then leant against the port rails and paid homage to immigrants the world over, thankful that my journey had not been as hard as the millions searching for a place of normality and fairness. I thought of those who belittled others for seeking refuge in a safe country, branding them as illegal without comprehension of the fear they held for their life or their families. Queen Street was a diversity of people. There was no way to tell them apart.

It didn't matter.

My sense of wellbeing grew despite my efforts not to read too much into everything, but this time, it was different. My urge to return to Johannesburg and embrace my family increased with every step.

I arrived back in South Africa daunted by what lay ahead. December was a write off because of Christmas. It was a whirlwind of immigration applications, medical examinations, monetary compliance, and farewells.

We needed to complete our Christmas shopping and because we had grown tired of our usual consumer jaunts. I suggested we try the refurbished mall in Bedfordview, hoping it would be quieter than the rest. Rose agreed but she wasn't looking forward to the outing and instructed me to pack Chelsea's nappy bag while they got ready. We didn't plan to be out for long because her brother was coming over for a *braai* later in the afternoon.

Our daughter loves the malls, the decorations, the people, and the action — from her stroller. She waves at passers-by. On arrival, we noticed it was not busy, the renovations still incomplete. Regardless, we parked and ducked inside. Labourers were adding the finishing touches amid frustrated storekeepers. Above us, flashing billboards enticed patrons to the lavish cinemas. As a family, we wandered through the décor of marble, glass, chrome, and new lighting as we sipped on our sodas in the relative calm. We passed a jewellery boutique and when we found a new bookstore; we took a quick look. A crash outside the store startled us.

Was it something to do with the tradespeople? A sign falling off a wall or a shop window dropping.

People rushing past the bookstore followed smashing of glass. One of the panic-stricken couples ducked into the bookshop.

'Take Chelsea into the corner,' I said to Rose and pointed to a cubicle at the rear. 'Whatever happens, don't move unless you're told.' I pulled my daughter from her pram and went with Rose to the back of the store. They sat with the other customers, armed with revolvers, while I returned to the front of the store where I found a young Asian girl who was crying. Rose called out for me to bring her into the alcove where she was consoling the others. Rose's bravery under the circumstances was inspirational. I crept into the mall's main walkway, accompanied by others clutching firearms. The fear in the air was palpable, yet all my mind came up with was the scenes of Jeremy Irons playing a bank robber in *Die Hard*. I stopped at a nearby coffee shop to ask what was happening.

'A maniac is running around shooting,' a waiter said as he pointed to his mobile phone.

Another clatter shook the building. My heart leapt into my throat. My only thoughts were about my family.

Outside the jewellery store was a gunman cradling an AK-47 gun. I zigzagged back to my wife as gunshots went off, followed by the shattering of more glass. In the bookstore,

251

Rose was embracing Chelsea and the Asian woman. I tried to stay calm as I explained gunmen were robbing the jeweller's shop. I resisted the urge to make my family lie on the floor and cover them with my body.

'We should find a better place to hide,' someone said. 'Or an exit out of the centre.'

Chelsea sat stock-still, sensing the seriousness of the situation. The confusion outside lasted two to three minutes, but it felt like hours. We heard a commotion before we saw men chasing after the thieves. Then there was an eerie silence.

The Asian woman thanked us and told us she was a tourist who had only arrived in the country days earlier. She said she had heard about crime in South Africa, but she didn't realise it was this prolific. Rose assured her we had lived here most of our lives and had never been through the likes of this.

I offered the ladies a cup of strong coffee at the adjoining espresso bar to help calm their nerves and to make sure any danger had dissipated before we attempted to make our way home. The trembling hands of the waitress were apparent. Our tourist friend asked her if she had seen what had happened, but the sound of sirens and screeching tyres interrupted the conversation.

Police poured into the same entrance we had used ten minutes earlier and sealed off the jewellery shop with crime-scene tape and posted uniformed officers around it. In silence, we sipped our drinks and watched plain-clothed detectives doing their duties. An elderly man who was comforting his wife at the table next to ours looked at us with a wry grin and shrugged his shoulders. He told us the fleeing gunmen had knocked them aside in the car park and how four men armed with automatic rifles tried to smash the safety glass of the jewellery store without success. When they lost their nerve, they fled to a nearby taxi, firing into the air as they ran. A passing patrol car gave chase.

I ordered another round of coffee as we listened to the sequence of events. It helped, since there were no casualties, apart from the shaken-up staff in the boutique. We said our goodbyes once we had ensured the tourist was okay. She took a photo of us on her mobile and promised to keep it always.

At the *braai* that evening we relayed the saga to our family, who shook their heads in dismay before moving on to other subjects. They digested the ordeal better than the steaks on the fire. Normality returned in a blink. An indictment of our history when violence no longer shocked anyone. Something I refused to accept for my family. It was yet another sign that it was time. We were making the right decision at the right time. I never wanted to see my family facing danger again, in abject fear, then resuming normality as if it were a mere inconvenience.

After Christmas, I flew back to Auckland. Rose, my best friend, the mother of my children and my lifelong partner, endured wrapping up our life in Johannesburg. An arduous and guilt-racked venture requiring meticulous planning and selling the assets of a lifetime. There were tense meetings and tearful family farewells, as she said goodbye to pets and old friends while I settled in another country. Setting the foundations for future generations — a time of pressure and fear of the unknown — whether we were doing the right thing.

For me, it was a three-month stretch on the opposite side of the world, when not a single evening passed that I didn't sit in my rented room clutching my laptop or hugging a plush toy my daughter had given me for safe travels. Skype calls relieved the pain yet heightened the angst.

Another ten years passed before I resumed contact with my best friend, Alan, from Plumtree School. After a catch up of the last four decades on FaceTime, he asked a question.

'How is life in New Zealand?'

I shared the experience of living through the COVID-19 pandemic.

Not the uncertainty and scaremongering on the Internet or media click-bait headlines, but the reality where the people made the difference. We debated whether global HIV could have or should have been handled differently.

'You know, what I've seen over the last few months is miraculous,' I said.

'We hear about your prime minister and what the country is doing,' Alan interjected.

'*Ja, ouboet,* all I can do is tell you what I experienced.' I brushed my hand through my hair.

Alan sat back and lifted his mug of coffee. 'Go for it, dude.'

'Well, it's not specifics but an ethos,' I said and saw his confusion but held up my hand. 'The people have shown me how to be human. How to express myself and to consider others in doing so. I am at peace.'

'Wow, that's heavy, *boetie,*' Alan said. 'How many glasses of wine have you had?'

I lifted my glass of local Sauvignon Blanc. 'I've learnt that success isn't a measure, but an act of self-reflection, and that what we do with that contemplation shapes us into the person we become.'

'Now you sound like Buddha,' he said, and we laughed, enjoying each other's company once more. 'I get what you're saying, but the place isn't perfect.'

'Far from it, mate. That'd be boring.'

'You're still the same know-it-all from boarding school, Rorke Wilde.'

'Why don't you come and see?'

'Maybe I will. Are you offering somewhere to stay?'

'For sure, buddy.'

'Thanks, my friend. By the way, nice chameleon on your mantlepiece.' Alan pointed over my shoulder, then leant forward on the screen. '*Uhumbe kuhle,* old friend.'

The screen died, and our lives continued.

254

Epilogue

My name is Rorke Wilde. Most call me Rory. I am privileged to experience what many never will. That is both good and a cross to bear.

Themba and Lucky shall tell us more about their unique lives and exploits. I wait to hear their perspective of Africa, their trials and accomplishment in their own words.

I am home.

I live without trepidation.

I lie my head in serenity.

I am forever indebted to this gracious nation.

May my family never underrate the gift with which New Zealand enriches us. Thank you, *Land of the Long White Cloud,* people of the oceans, my Aotearoa.

E hoa ma ina te ora o te tangata.

This is my memoir.

My story.

Of a time as I saw it.

Rest in Peace, Themba Dube, you lived up to your name.

Themba — man of Hope.

Dube the Zebra — healer and mixer of colour.

My friend.

My mentor.

My guardian spirit.

Everything I think, say, or do is because of our camaraderie.

May your last days on earth have been all you wished.

You now roam the *vleis* and *kopjes* of Phelamanga.

The place of no lies. In our Africa, we so cherished.

I miss you every day and you continue to show up in my moments of fragility and joy.

I imprint your legacy on the full moon, so we will travel together wherever we pass. In solitude, I still talk with you, and for that, I am forever grateful.

Inyanga. The moon.

Size sibonane njalo. Until we meet again.

Kumele ngihambe khathesi. I must go now. Stay well. My father. My world.

Asimbonanga. We have not seen him.

Africa

No people have claim to her soil
Or beast exclusivity to her bounty
She is Eve to all humankind

Politics violates her virtue
Sickness and hunger her soldiers of fortune
Race and religion, pawns of expediency

Free from history's blame and guilt
Never forget your rightful place
Nor shy from your ancestry

Cower from nothing
Preserve this land that courses within
Praise your God without reserve

Warm your soul beneath African suns
Listen to the whisper of savannah winds
As Zambezi waters flow through your veins

Lightning dances across darkened skies
Thunderstorms beat to your heart
Rains soothe baked earth as tears of home fall

David Farrell

Guard against Africa's prejudiced
They build walls of doubt
Let no kith or kin hinder your return.

Africa is but a place
Africa is a dream

Not the end.

257

Acknowledgements

Thanks to my children Jody, Matthew, Toby, Michael and Chantelle, the house, and my heart is empty without you. To my daughter Amy, you are my world. I'm so proud of you.
This book possible because of you all and our special whanau (family).
To my muse Buddy. A Cocker Spaniel with the biggest heart and most loving soul I've ever come across. Thank you for being there, for listening to me babble when on our daily walks, for your unconditional love. This book is as much yours as it is mine.
A shout out to friends' past and present and to those no longer with us. You have shaped me into the person I am - that is your fault. Some I have known my whole life, others for half a century, some a few years, all of whom contributed to this piece of work.
Thank you.
To the powers that be and the souls who watch over my family, you are forever in my thoughts.
Special mention to Ouma, Gran Gran, Tanya, Shaneen, Ayu, Booby, Lala, Zana, Kitty and Morgana.
I am indebted to the Kingsley Publishers team for their patience and guidance.

Author Bio

David Farrell is a father of six who live around the world. From New Zealand and England to Portugal and Japan.

Born in Africa, his life experiences on three continents echo through his writing, in his favourite genres of historical fiction, coming of age sagas and non-fiction.

With an eye for detail, you can find him in the corner of a room or sat at a seat in the mall reading people. He has a fascination for human behaviours borne from 50 years of leadership.

David advocates for the Autistic community running an online group with over 20 000 members.

Find David on Social Media, he loves to connect with his fans!

Instagram : @farrelldavidm

He looks forward to reading your review of his latest book.

9 780620 993135